CURDLE CREEK

CURDLE CREEK

A NOVEL

YVONNE
BATTLE-FELTON

HENRY HOLT AND COMPANY   NEW YORK

Henry Holt and Company
Publishers since 1866
120 Broadway
New York, New York 10271
www.henryholt.com

Library of Congress Cataloging-in-Publication Data

Names: Battle-Felton, Yvonne, author.
Title: Curdle Creek : a novel / Yvonne Battle-Felton.
Description: First U.S. edition. | New York : Henry Holt and Company, 2024.
Identifiers: LCCN 2024023829 | ISBN 9781250362018 (hardcover) |
    ISBN 9781250362025 (ebook)
Subjects: LCGFT: Horror fiction. | Gothic fiction. | Novels.
Classification: LCC PS3602.A915 C87 2024 | DDC 813/.6—dc23/
    eng/20240529
LC record available at https://lccn.loc.gov/2024023829

Our books may be purchased in bulk for promotional, educational, or business
use. Please contact your local bookseller or the Macmillan Corporate and
Premium Sales Department at (800) 221–7945, extension 5442, or by e-mail at
MacmillanSpecialMarkets@macmillan.com.

First U.S. Edition 2024

Designed by Kelly S. Too

Printed in the United States of America

1 3 5 7 9 10 8 6 4 2

To Amira, Marat and Noah,
bringers of joy

CURDLE
CREEK

Home

It's three days before the Moving On and, just like the sun rises and sets whether you see it or not, the Moving On comes around year after year, same as the Warding Off, whether or not you believe in it. Traditions are like that, sure as a bronze church bell. We're all preparing for it in one way or the other. Even the ones who say there's no call for it, it's old-fashioned, we'll be damned. What does the Moving On care about their reservations now, umpteen years in?

Shadows flicker and dance along the walls like twin pall-bearers. Every so often my stomach drops. Must be all the excitement. Running of the Widows, the Calling, the Moving On, the Warding Off. All that coming and going. All that running. It'll be the busiest week in all Curdle Creek. I could die just thinking about it.

The living room is hot, a little too hot if you ask me but I'm not one to complain. Mae likes it that way. And, Mae's company. Besides, an unwelcoming host is maybe not the *worst* thing you could be here but there's no sense in getting on Mae's bad side. Not on the night before the names are called.

Folks say the Calling is down to luck. Folks whose names get called don't have much of it. If you believe that, you'll believe just about anything. Not that I think Mae would have anything to do with my name being called this year. She would do it if she had to, we'd all do it, but who would listen to her, a widow with a chorus of dead husbands as wide as the Creek is long? Mae's name don't have any more luck to it than mine does—at least not until the Running of the Widows. A good run could change everything.

"Do you have your eye on anyone special this year?" Mae asks. She's standing in front of the mirror, staring at me over her shoulder while her slender fingers lace up her girdle, pushing parts into places I'm not sure they're meant to be.

I lean back into my soft leather chair, tilt my head to the side, lick my lips and roll my eyes slightly. Having my eye on somebody's got nothing to do with marriage. The first time's for love, the second's for luck. The third one . . . well, if you live long enough to have a third one, the third one's for life. So they say. Everybody knows that. "Mmmm," I say.

"Try again," she says, "you look like you're drooling. No one likes a desperate widow. You'll scare off all the good ones before it's even time and you'll be single for another year."

It's just like Mae to blame me for my predicament. Sooner or later we all run out of luck. The Running of the Widows is like a second chance at it—says so in the book.

"How is it seductive when you do it, and not becoming when it's me?"

"Practice, dear," she says sounding just like Mother Opal. "*An unpeeled fruit is sure to waste.*"

I roll my eyes for real this time. "Book I, *The Law of Attraction*," we say together. We laugh and, since we're alone, we do it out loud. It feels good too. I haven't had much reason for laughter since the children left, and then my Moses, first the Calling then the Moving On not twelve months after. Mae's bent over, holding her sides, and even from here I hear the pop followed by what sounds like a hot pan full of popcorn kernels but isn't. Mounds of stretched brown flesh burst through the polyester girdle, leaving it pockmarked and wide open.

She doesn't have to ask, I slide my tray of varnish, nail files and ice to the side, slip my feet into my slippers, careful not to mess the polish, and start the operation of pulling and prodding things back into place. "You sure you don't want to try a bigger one?" I ask.

I don't mean it to sound mean but Mae flinches anyway. Everyone loves a supple bride but loathes a supple widow. "We can't all afford to pray to the gravity gods and hope for the best."

I nod. I'm wearing two corsets, one for luck and another because I don't believe I have any. But if this body looks natural to her, who am I to say otherwise? "Please don't quote my mother," I say. I touch my hand to her shoulder.

Mae flinches once more. "Your hands are freezing! Have you been playing in the cemetery again?"

"Are they cold enough?" I've been dipping my hands in and out of ice all evening. Cold hands yield good luck. It's an old widows' tale but, if nothing else, anyone who lives long enough to be an old widow knows a thing or two about luck.

"If they were any colder you'd be lying up next to Moses."

"Down. I'd be lying down next to Moses, may the ancestors watch over his soul."

If there is one, there ain't no way my Moses made it all the way to Heaven. Not with all his carrying on in life. All that begging. *Spare me! Spare me! Take her instead!* Shameful. We make the sign of the cross to ward off my dead husband. I'd light another candle but with the sitting room full of them one more might cause a fire. We're meant to be praying to the Mother of Fertility like every other single sister but instead we're getting ready for the Running of the Widows like any widow with good sense would be. Better than throwing salt over your shoulder, jumping six times before crossing a bridge or spitting in the well, latching on to another family is an almost foolproof way to—not exactly beat the system, but the bigger the family, the better the luck. Or the better the chances your name won't be called in the morning. Not that Moving On's not a privilege and all.

"You know *cold hands mean a cold heart*," Mae says.

She's always quoting one book or the other, trying to out-holy me. It's not a competition but I throw in Book IV to shake her up. "*Desire is for the young, matrimony for the ready*," I say. She giggles.

Once we're dressed, I take the rollers out of my hair. It's twisty just as I like it, with coils of gray blended with dark brown. Age looks good on me. I pucker up, slide on dark red lipstick. Mae's dark plum looks good against her skin. I tell her and she blows me a kiss across the room.

We set the table for four. One place for each of our dead husbands. I fix them both generous portions, plates piled high with macaroni and cheese, juicy slices of beef, plump shrimp, fat potatoes dripping with soured cream and fresh-churned butter.

"Isn't that too much starch?" Mae asks. As if dead people count calories.

"I think it'll be just fine," I say. "I'd imagine they burned off a lot when they passed—from the running."

I might have been a bit *overzealous* when it was time to ward off my Moses but it was nothing as undignified as Mae's whooping and hollering chasing poor Clifton's soul away. I could hardly bear to watch, although of course I had to. Nobody in Curdle Creek misses the Warding Off, and what sort of best friend isn't at her friend's ceremony? One that's courting trouble, I can tell you that. Missing a ceremony as important as the Warding Off is just plain unneighborly. It's a good way to get yourself shunned. Being shunned is one step from being nominated, and being nominated is just as good as one foot hovering over the grave. Well, as being Moved On.

It's been three years since Moses departed. Wasn't Mae right there by my side helping his spirit to Move On? Then, year after year, right there performing the ceremony to keep him from coming back? So of course, when Mae asked to join me tonight, since there was something *unnatural* about waiting for a dead husband you hoped wouldn't come to come,

I said yes. Truth be told, once the Council stopped checking that Moses wasn't hanging around haunting my bed at night, I stopped worrying about him coming back. I didn't tell anybody though. There's nothing worse than an ungrateful widow.

We mostly eat in silence, listening out for *whooooos* and moans. Mae jumps when the bell tolls six. That's not even the time when Clifton Moved On, but we all have something that reminds us. Mine's the barn owls' eyes bright and wide like Moses's, deep voices singing *I love youuuu, youuuu* the way he would have done if he'd ever said such a thing. The beef is too bloody, pink slides around the plate, and I can't help but think the fork looks like a tiny pitchfork hunting it down. Still, it's tasty, and I pop it in my mouth as if it's my last meal. In a way it is: in two days' time I'll be a new woman, or at least a new bride again. I hope this next one has better luck than Moses, though. Imagine, your name being called on your wedding anniversary. As if bad luck runs in the family, I haven't been invited to a wedding since. If Mae and I hadn't married the same year, she might not have invited me to hers either.

"A toast," I say. I raise the jam jar full of mint julep and pretend to clink it against Mae's raised glass. "*May the dead find comfort in their graves.* Book XIII."

"To the Moved On."

We leave the plates around the table and settle down in the sitting room to gossip about wedding nights and first and last times. At forty-five, we're lucky to have second chances. We have the Moving On to thank. A good Moving On yields a robust harvest. Twenty years of plenty means there've been more births than usual. The Running of the Widows, the Calling, the Moving On, the Warding Off—it's all a small price to pay for the safety of the town. It could be worse.

"Imagine being alone forever," Mae says.

She's settled into Moses's chair, feet up on the coffee table like he used to do. The chair creaks and stops, creaks and stops the same way it did when Moses was sitting there. Only, he'd stop to listen for footsteps. As if one of the children would be fool enough to sneak back here after so long.

Mae's still talking about the departed like they're still here, reminiscing about the time Moses fell off the ladder trying to fix the roof. "You should be grateful the old fool didn't die that very day."

"Mysterious ways," I say. Thankfully, it was the Moving On that took him.

With one leg tucked under the other, her toes peeking out to wiggle when she rocks back, Mae looks like the chair was made just for her. We could grow old together. Best friends rocking back and forth, back and forth, sharing secrets like we did when we didn't know any better.

My mouth is suddenly dry. My hands are shaking. What if the old folks are wrong and the Moved On can come back? Wouldn't take long before the whole town was overflowing with Moved On husbands, wives, sisters and brothers. Comeback schoolmarms, pastors and neighbors popping up in the middle of services, living rooms, gatherings. It'd be enough to drive us all to the Creek. I'd like to think they'd come back thankful. Once they'd seen the memorials, their names etched in the town stone, their leather-bound Life Books shelved in the library, the bustling town with its new stop sign and paved road, they'd be grateful to have played their part in Curdle Creek history. *Not one soul left behind*, we like to say. They'd be forgiven their ungraceful departing. The howling, name-calling, second-guessing and all. Until their names were called again.

According to Book XXVI, the Warding Off keeps souls from returning to Curdle Creek. As if anyone with good sense would come back here. Of course, there's worse places to end up than here. But if the dead suddenly do come back, it means the Warding Off don't work. Ain't nothing worse than Warding Off someone you loved. All that screaming. I hate to think what would replace it. But if they could come back, and Moses among them? There's a drumming in my ears. My throat is dry and I can't hardly breathe. Moses back after all this time. He wouldn't come alone. The threats, the accusations, the lies and all that screaming would come right back with him. And the spite. Ain't no way he'd come back without a heart full of spite. It wouldn't be love that brought him back to me, it would be the Running of the Widows. You can't be a widow if the body comes back—no matter how it left, Moving On or otherwise. I'd be disqualified. It would be just like Moses to find a way to ruin this for me too.

I take a deep breath and say Ordinance 27.9 in my head. *The ground beneath my feet is steady, steady as the handheld bell, when it's my time, may I be ready, and seek no solace in a well.* It's Mother Opal's favorite. As soon as I think about it, I feel my breathing sort of right itself. My hand is steady again. The old folks are right. If the Moved On could make their way back to the Creek they'd be forgetful. Wouldn't know the rules so they couldn't hardly be expected to live by them. They'd be misremembering rituals and reasons why and that it's better not to ask questions in the first place. They'd cause chaos. There would be too many names in the Calling, too many grievances to dig up, too much gossip to sift through. Upsetting everything just because. Wouldn't even need a body to do it. Wouldn't have one to do it in if that was the case. Lord knows their old bodies wouldn't be worth nothing. It'd be like putting on a wool sweater that's been hanging in an unlined closet. Full of moths and holes. They'd have to slip into someone else's body, if such a thing was possible.

Maybe not Moses, but it would be good to see my brother again. Remus was always good to me. He was my favorite. He's been gone twenty years. I'd like to tell him I miss him. I can't hardly think of Remus without seeing him huddled near the brick wall of the Old Post Office. Shivering. Mouthing some sort of prayer. *Don't do it, don't do it, don't do it.* Till it was running together. *Dontdoitdontdoitdontdoit.* Didn't work either way. Seems like the sticky sound of the *thwack*, rock against skin, surprised us both. Him most of all though.

There's a thud and the creaking stops. Mae purses her lips. I don't know how long she's been waiting on me to serve her. It's rude. More than that, it's unbecoming. I reach for the teapot but she beats me to it, slender brown hands picking up Moses's favorite cup, holding it close enough to the teapot to clink china against china and rattle the lid. I don't complain. Of course I don't. It'd be something she'd have to hold against me and Lord knows I don't need no one else holding nothing against me. Moses done enough of that for a lifetime. I offer my own cup, the homemade one that's thick on one side, thin on the other, lined with a chipped gold strip of paint that flakes when I touch it. The handle's long since broken off and I hold it by the middle so Mae can fill it with sassafras tea. It scalds my lips, burns my tongue. My mouth fills with bitterness.

"You like it?" Mae asks. "I grew it myself."

It's suddenly hot. Sweat drips down my neck. I feel it pooling beneath my armpits. There are two ways to answer a question like that. Offending my closest and dearest friend wouldn't be worth it. Just shy of the Moving On, there wouldn't be time enough for her to forgive me so she'd have to hold the grudge. By now, most people already know who they're nominating and who they aren't. But it's never too late for someone to change their mind. I've seen it happen too many times. People get comfortable just before. They start smiling when they should be frowning, frowning when they should be smiling. Getting ahead of themselves, thinking they're bound to make it through this Moving On just as surely as they made it through the last one. Not me. I've seen too many Moving On Eve nomination changes to last my entire life. I can almost hear Mother Opal calling my name at the Calling. *Osira Alexandra Turner*, she'd say. I wouldn't mean to but I'd yell out, I know I would. If it came down to it, I wouldn't be no more ready than anyone else—believer or not.

"It's all right, you can tell me. I know you don't like sassafras." She's back to rocking, talking in between sips and creaks. "I only bought it cuz Clifton didn't like it either. I've got bags and bags of the stuff drying out at home. I've been giving it away every chance I get. Every time someone knocks on the door I give whoever it is a bag of leaves to take with them. I donated a whole tin of it to the church. Tried to drop some off at Carter's Everything Store. You know what they told me?"

I lean forward. Wait, to be polite. Carter's don't accept nothing they can't sell.

"That old lady said no. When I tried to tell her the store says they sell everything, she said 'everything but that.' Well, you know who I'm nominating this year."

I hop up to look outside. The trees are thinning this time of year. The wind rustles the few leaves left. The street is bare. The doors of the Old Post Office have been locked for years, the windows shuttered. The few houses in the cul-de-sac are mostly dark with families already settled in for the night. Other than the occasional hooting owl, screaming fox or arguing neighbor, it's a quiet street surrounded by modest houses with neighbors who should know how to keep themselves to themselves. Still, folks got a way of being where you don't expect them to be. I take a final look before drawing the living room curtains shut.

"You know you aren't supposed to tell who you're nominating. It's a secret."

Mae rolls her eyes clear to the ceiling. "You've seen how high them prices are these days? Ain't no secret who's getting the most nominations this year."

If it was anybody else but Mae, I'd tell. I'd have to. Book XIII is filled with ordinances about influencing nominations. Every Curdle Creeker gets one nomination, regardless of age. That don't explain how last year there were a thousand votes and ain't but two hundred people living here. But mostly, the system works. It has to.

My heart's beating loud so I almost don't hear her when she says, "Remember when we were kids and we'd run up to the sign to see if the numbers changed?"

"It was better than reading the *Curdle Creek Gazette*. More reliable too."

"Except it never said names."

"Except that one time when they ran the 'Predictions' section."

"Those predictions stirred up too much trouble." Mae fans herself with a slice of lemon cake, sending crumbs here and there when she laughs. "It took the Council and the Mothers weeks to get the retractions printed."

"Didn't matter one bit. The only name they got wrong was the editor's. Don't expect she predicted that, though I don't know how she missed it. Even I saw that one coming."

"Well, there's no way they're changing that sign. It would cost a fortune to list all those names. Besides, if it's good enough for the Founders, it's good enough for us."

I add another lump of sugar to my now-tepid tea. I take a sip, swill it in my mouth like brandy before gulping it down. Tea leaves swirl in the bottom of the cup. It's bad luck to leave them there. I put the cup to my lips, slide my tongue around the bottom. When I'm sure I've gotten leaves, sugar, grit and all, I put the empty cup between us, an offering. Mae's too polite to check while I'm watching, so I cut a polite sliver of cake and chew as slow as a new bride. She peers into the bottom of my cup to check that I drank it all. Nods like she's adding to a checklist in her head. I would have missed it if I weren't watching her from the corner of my eye.

"I like the sign just fine. Says all it's got to say. Even with the fancy counter. *Curdle Creek, one in, one out.* It tells you all you need to know."

There ain't a sign wide enough to hold all the names of the Moved On. Folks been Moving On since the Founding in the 1800s. Probably even before that. It would be far wiser just to add the names of the Gone. The few who had stolen away from Curdle Creek before being Moved On. Isidore Stenton, Elijah Cross, Ezekiel Yates, my brother Romulus, my own children Jasmine, Cheyenne and Little Moses. All slipped into the night leaving hardly a ripple, just like Well Walkers. Ungrateful. No, there ain't no need to be reminded of that every time I walk to town.

"I hear some places don't even have Moving Ons," I add. "No Warding Off either."

I wait for Mae to ask me how I know. With only the one radio station, TV channel and newspaper, anything I know about anyplace else, Mae knows too. Unless someone told me. And the only people who would tell me anything if they could are my children. Lord only knows the world they're living in. If they're living at all.

"Know what they got instead?"

It can't be nothing good. Wars, lynching, murders, riots, fires. I can still see the photographs from the *Curdle Creek Gazette* "Around the World" edition. Police dogs, wide-open mouths, rows of sharp teeth straining against leashes pulled tight. Then, dogs running, leaping in the air, leashes dangling.

Blood. Brown arms and legs every which way and all those children. Babies really. Dead, every one of them. The world ain't hardly a safe place to be. I've seen the pictures. Heard the rumors. We all have. Curdle Creek couldn't survive without the Moving On. The harvest counts on it. The water relies on it. Even the land. Heck, the weather's probably tied into it one way or the other. A place with no Moving On is courting problems.

A chill runs down my spine. There's a draft seeping down the chimney. Nothing another log on the woodstove won't cure.

"Chaos, and you can take that to the mill and grind it." Mae tucks Moses's throw around her legs.

"To the Moving On," we say at the same time.

We're suddenly quiet. Both thinking of the ones who slipped out of town, walked right across the town line and never came back. I don't say it, but when I'm doing the Warding Off, I'm doing it for them. I'm not worried about the dead coming back to Curdle Creek, but if the living ever do, we're all in trouble.

Mother's

It's two a.m. when Mae leaves. I snuff out the candles, snap off the excess wax to save the shavings to mix with juice for next season's Halloween candies. What child doesn't love a wax-juicy? The house is dark. The boiler hums, the floors squeak, the windows rattle. I picture Moses trying to force himself back home, riding on the breeze to slip under loose floorboards. He could, if I hadn't had the whole house reinforced right after the Mourning Period. No widow should ever have to Move On the same husband more than once. If he did make it back to Curdle Creek talking about *it's your fault the children didn't stay, you helped them*, I'd send the damned fool right back where he came from.

It's both of our faults. We lay in this very bed making babies like multiplying was the only math we knew. If it had been up to me, I would have left with them. Or, if I'd had any sense, bundled them up in the middle of the night and left just like the non-believer Mother says I am.

With the candles wrapped and put away, the dishes washed and blinds drawn, I have a few hours to be myself before I turn into someone's wife or daughter. It's a small price to pay to throw their lot in with mine.

I lie on my Jasmine's floor. The carpet is thick and tickles my cheek. My daughter's big canopy bed, trunks full of homemade clothes, thick store-bought curtains, ordinance posters, diaries and schoolbooks are long gone. Even her collection of records by the Curdle Creek Band and her rare collection by the Curdle Creek Wonders—a teen band that didn't even last through their first Moving On—are stored away in the archives. Her room is emptied. I could be anywhere. Although the Sisters stripped each of the children's rooms as soon as the Council confirmed they'd absconded, the room still smells like the jasmine perfume my daughter loved to wear. Especially here on the carpet that even after all that scrubbing still carries leftover dabs and drops of crushed jasmine petals and oils. It smells sweet, innocent, just like my Jasmine. Eighteen and already somewhere mothering her little brother and sister. *May the ancestors send you breezes that lead you far away from this place,* I pray. I cross myself and just in case, I make the sign of the bell to seal it tight.

* * *

THE sun rises the same as usual and, just for spite, it's bright and full. There's no sense rushing it. Everything in its proper time. First, the Running of the Widows, then the Calling, the Moving On almost smack-dab in the middle of a too-full week, and finally the Warding Off. All that and, in my head, today will always be about Moving On.

My leg's cramping but I won't get up and walk it out. Instead, I settle into it, roll with the pain trickling up and down my leg. My stomach tightens and loosens, tightens again. The window's still closed but there's a sudden hot breeze in the room. My skin is flushed. I'm sweating all over. My scalp prickles with it. The sudden moisture makes my skin itch.

I deserve to be uncomfortable. Wasn't I lying in this very spot three years ago when the Messenger knocked on the door? Didn't I already know it was time when Moses's gargled voice made its way up the stairs, screech first? Of course I knew his name had been called. We were all at the Calling. I just didn't know they'd come to collect him so soon. How little time there was to prepare. How hard it would be to know what to say when the time came. I got up, rolled up the quilt, closed the bedroom door, tightened my robe, and went down the stairs to comfort him, slumped over, knees already on the floor. I had already made peace with the news. Of course there'd be a price for the children. First my seat on the Council, then Moses, then my job as a teacher. *The Lord giveth, and the Lord taketh away.* One thing for each child. But like Moses said, it's a whole lot easier to make peace with Moving On when you're not the one doing it.

I check the clock anyway. It's six o'clock. The Messengers will just be starting their rounds. The mail comes this time every morning but nobody really wants to see them. They could drive to deliver the mail, throw their costumes and sacks in the back seat—it'd be easier on all of us. But instead they walk, no matter how long it takes, as if folks prefer the sound of their slow-footed heels clicking down cobblestones, delivering bad news door-to-door. Sometimes it takes hours for them to make their way. The longer it takes, the better the news, though, so no one, including me, wants to hear from them first thing.

I put my bedding away, close the door, and settle by the woodstove with a cup of coffee. I have the kettle on for the Messenger, a cup on the sideboard, a plate of biscuits with jam and butter in case the Messenger is hungry after a long day's work. I keep the lights off and unplug all the electricals; it's bad luck otherwise. I am sitting with my back to the window and facing northeast, chanting, "I'm open and ready to receive good news, I'm open and—" when there's a knock on the door.

It could be the newspaper kid expecting a tip for throwing my paper on the porch, like it's not her job to do just that. Of course I'll tip her anyway. The last thing I need is her complaining to a parent and that parent complaining to the wrong sister, brother or Heaven forbid Charter Mother. There won't be enough *I'm sorry*s to protect me. Not this close to the festivities. So I fish out some coins from the jar, open the door with a smile and a welcome at the ready.

The Messenger's on the porch, hand raised about to knock again, head already shaking as I swing open the door. With the pursed lips, midnight-black wig pinned up in a stiff bouffant, mustard-seed dress with matching cinch, gloves and clutch, I know the message is from Mother before she even says a word. Leave it to Mother to send a Messenger instead of ringing the party line. Mother likes the drama of it all. The

Messengers have been delivering news ever since the Curdle Creek Theatre was shut down. That's forty years of delivering bad news. All those actors out of work gave Mother an idea. The Old Post Office was closed and the theater became the New Post Office/Theatrics Society. The actors became mail carriers, delivering news in character. They've gotten good at it. Even won awards.

I step back, unsteady, but of course the Messenger comes inside when I invite her to. It's rude not to invite the Messenger in and if nothing else I'm always polite. She saunters down the hall, too-high heels clacking on the wood floor. Before long she's in the living room. It's a short walk but, since Mother's corsets make her unnaturally thin around the middle, the Messenger's struggling to breathe. My heart's not beating so I can hear her panting. She must have rushed straight here.

My hands are shaking but I take the envelope from the Messenger's fingers. It's customary to settle the slip before the reading of the message. It wouldn't be fair to let bad news sour a good performance. I sign the receipt and add a generous tip, stuff the slip back into the envelope and seal it.

The Messenger sits down in my chair just the way Mother would. She takes the letter from the clutch and places it on the table between us. She moves deliberately. She doesn't settle into the chair; she perches, hovering over it. *That's just how Mother sits*, I want to say, but of course she already knows. It's a small town and Mother's on the Council. Everybody knows the Charter Mothers.

What does she want? Maybe it's news about the children. Maybe she's heard where they are, that they're fine and they want to come home. Or an apology for blaming me for the leaving. Or a— My heart's beating fast again and my fingers ache. I can't crack them, not now. Not with the Messenger looking more and more like Mother by the minute. *If you wouldn't do it in front of the person, don't do it in front of the Messenger,* they say. Not that the Messenger will judge you for it. Messengers will tell the person about it, though. Unless you pay them not to—which is against the rules. Or, you nominate them for the Moving On—which isn't. Anyway, I already know who I'm nominating and I don't have no change to spare.

I fold my hands in my lap and wait for the reading to begin. The Messenger puts my cup to her lips. "May I?" she asks.

She's thoroughly in character now. I couldn't stop her if I wanted to. "Of course." The words come out on their own. "I'll get you the biscuits." As if I can't stop myself, I cut one in the middle, slather it with butter and jam for her.

The Messenger clears her throat. I drag over the ottoman; she raises her feet, settles back. Ten minutes pass with only the loud beating of my heart, occasional rattling of the wind, and her steady wheezing. Before long, it gets kind of comforting. It can't be bad news. If it were, Mother would have directed the Messenger to start before now. Mother hasn't been here herself since the children left and that was only to check they'd really gone. As if I'd have hidden them in the cellar so they would miss the Moving On just to spite her. The only reason it wasn't reported right away was because Mother hadn't believed they'd gone. *No grandchild of mine would disgrace my name! They have a debt to pay to this town and by blood or by dollar, they'll pay it.* It was frightful. I was half worried she would find them under a bed or in a closet somewhere even though I'd already looked myself. I knew just as sure as I'm breathing that they must have been long gone by the time Moses sent for the Messenger. They're dead. I just know it. If they weren't, they'd find a way to get word to me. Not through a Messenger or the party line operator who'd just go straight to the Council. But they'd find some way if there was one. And the first thing I'd want to know after being sure they're all living is whether leaving was worth all they gave up to do it.

"Oh-sighhhh-raaa!" she suddenly screeches. The Messenger's voice is high trilled. My name trips over her tongue in that awkward accent Mother uses to make *Osira* sound like a sin and a curse all at once, and, just like when she calls my name, I jump.

"Ma'am?"

"What in Heaven's name are you doing home at this ghastly hour? You should be out exercising, running laps, preparing for the Running of the Widows like your competition! You don't see Mae Miller sitting around eating bonbons and scones, having extra sugars in tea, and doing whatever it is you do with the shades drawn! And open those curtains this instant!"

The Messenger waits while I tie the curtains back and straighten the bow. Since I'm already up, I pour myself a cup of tea with two cubes of sugar though I would usually take four. I half curtsy and lower myself onto the settee, back straight, knees bent, toes pointed inward. I take the form of shame, careful not to look too comfortable, so she can continue.

"It's almost as if you want me to be shamed forever. As if

you have no plans for upholding your duty to replenish the town after *your* children robbed us. If that's the case, tell me now and I will change my nomination for the Moving On, because a child of mine who would not do whatever she could to save the family's name is of better service to the town if she is Moved On expeditiously." The Messenger gets up, gathers her clutch, straightens the wig. "I'll expect you at the house right away. Since you don't have a family of your *own* to take care of, you'll come take care of your sisters and the house."

The room goes dark. For a second I can see me back in my old room, painted blush pink, ordinances framed on the wall like trophies surrounded by awards for reciting the most books, praising loudest, ringing the most bells at a time. I don't fit in that house any more than I'd fit my full-sized body into my old single bed. *Why not?* Mother would say. *You are single.*

"Oh-sighhhh-raaa!" the Messenger squeals again. "You have one minute to get back to this house. Do not make me tell you again. Your father is at a meeting with the Deacons and I'll be having company for supper later. I'm in preparation for mourning. I just know your daddy's name will be called this year. We need to prepare. Before you ask, yes, Brother Jacobs will be by later. And, before you leave we'll talk about who you're nominating this year. And who you're not."

It's as if she read my mind. Of course I'm nominating Brother Jacobs. He and Mother are carrying on like she's not a married woman, as if Daddy doesn't have a vote in the Moving On. Like they're first-time beaux, holding hands in public, whispering in each other's ear, plotting. Mainly, it's like they don't even care who sees them or who they tell about it. I have this sinking feeling because I know why. Each year, Mother predicts that Daddy will be Moved On. Every slight—real or imagined—leads to her having premonitions of his name being called at the Calling. One year she'll be right.

* * *

BEFORE I go to Mother's I shut the windows against more bad news and check that my Moving On bag is where I left it. Like most Curdle Creekers, I keep a bag packed just in case my name's the one called. A good dress, a sewing kit, clean underthings, ointments, coffee grinds for the bags under my eyes, comfortable shoes, a slip, hair supplies, and a spare bell for the waiting. You never know how you'll feel the morning of and who wants to waste time packing when you might not have that long anyway? Mother Opal's right. *A packed bag is a life saved.* It wouldn't be fair on anyone to have to pick out what clothes to lay me out in.

My heart's still beating loudly when I make my way back downstairs. Mother lives across the street. If she was watching when the Messenger left, she'll be wondering what kept me. *Please don't let her be sitting by the window, please don't let her be sitting by the window, please don't let . . .* I'd pray out loud so the elders could hear me but Mother can read lips and she'll know I'm talking about her. Although I know there's nothing coming, I look to the right, then the left, then the right again. No one drives up Pleasant Mills Road unless there's a good reason to. Otherwise, people park down on Main and walk up the road to show proper respect to the neighbors, who will already be out front, hands half-raised, expecting a hello from whoever's passing by. I make my legs move faster than my head wants them to, in case she is watching and isn't already dressed in her mourning gown ready to receive the visitors who will be coming as soon as the mourning bell tolls. I stick to the pathway so as not to crush the grass, tiptoe up the three stone steps, take a deep breath when I reach the landing, and slowly swing open the screen door so that it doesn't squeak.

I press my fingertips on the front door and push. It opens and I slip inside. The windows are covered in thick black curtains so that the sunlight fights to get into the house. It makes everything look black and white. Like we're inside one of those sepia prints Jeremiah's so fond of snapping. I'm holding my breath. Still, the silver mourning tree quivers, the black bells tinkle. I've let in a draft.

"What grief-stealer is this sneaking around my house?"

I swallow the air I've been holding. "Mariah, where is Mother?" I ask. I stand still, eyes watering, throat burning as my younger sister waits at the top of the stairs, hands on hips, leaning on one foot then the other so that she's rocking like the pendulum of a clock. She stares for a full minute not blinking. How can she do that? It's like she doesn't need to blink. Like she's not really a girl but some sort of doll. A thirty-year-old haunted one. And here comes her sidekick, Rumor. Knocking on twenty-eight, she'd be a bargain doll, any joy used up before you even unwrapped it. Of course, she stares down at me too. They block the way. My breath dislodges in a little gasp that sets off a fit of coughs. I could die right here and they'd still be up there grinning. I'm blinking back tears. This sets the two of them off to giggling. Rumor winks.

"She's here," Mariah calls.

Mother practically glides up behind the girls as if she's been waiting just behind the corner. She rests a hand on each of their heads. They both lean into her. She *hmmms* down at them. "Go finish getting ready."

They are already dressed. Matching twirly gray dresses, Mary Janes buckled and shined, hair half-cornrowed, half-out the way all the little girls are wearing it. They skip down the hall to their room as though they aren't way too old for childish games.

Mother settles herself down in the parlor to receive me. I sit across from her in the guest chair, clasp her hands in mine. She already has the touch of the widow. Her hands are ice-cold, still clammy. It's just like Mother to have already started the rituals.

"I'm so sorry," I say. I bow my head.

"It's not your fault."

I squeeze her hands. Make the mistake of smiling.

"It's not like you didn't remarry to spite me, is it?"

My fingers tingle where she's pressed her fingers into my skin. Starting at the knuckle and working my way up, I rub warmth into one finger, then the next—

"Stop that!" she says before I get to the third one. "This is the year. I just know it. I've been preparing all morning."

With her black dress, manicured nails and hair freshly dyed, Mother looks like a model perched in her chair, feet, already slippered, planted firmly on the floor. Her face is made up in

Illusion of Grief Number 5. All the widows wear it. The pharmacist can't keep the stuff on the shelves. It's gotten to the point he keeps it locked up. We're friends though. He gives me my one allotted compact once a month in the store and swings by one night a month with a special delivery that I don't even tell Mae about. Mother would be appalled.

Daddy's with the Deacons preparing for the Moving On. This is the busiest time of year and Daddy has so much to do that we hardly see him for days. It would be just like him to miss his own Moving On. It's the Deacons' job to manage the ushering out of the departing. Without them it would be uncivilized chaos with all that hooting and hollering and the whole town running through the streets like there's a sale at Carter's. The Deacons are in charge of choosing the Caller, clearing debris from the Moving On route, keeping the nominations orderly, and organizing the cleaning up. The Council is in charge of the rules. Making sure we abide by the agreed-upon ones and replacing the less popular ones like burning at the stake. Everyone's responsible for gathering their own rocks—or sticks. And Mother Opal is responsible for all of it and all of us too. Anywhere else she'd be the mayor. Here she's the Head Charter Mother, the most powerful person in Curdle Creek. The closest thing to her is my own mother. Been that way since they were kids.

It's bad luck to court Moving On the way Mother does. No one would dare tell her that. She's bound to be right one day. But Daddy didn't do anything wrong. He hasn't offended anyone. Hasn't spoken out of turn. Hasn't even had much to say about Mr. Jacobs stopping by for "ordinance study." Daddy's got nothing to be afraid of. Mother's just superstitious. When we were growing up, she used to say *Bad things come in threes*. Back then, she meant my brothers and me. One day, I won't be here for her pre-mourning party. I could hire an eldest, someone to take my place and help around the house. They'd be like an extension, a substitute me. They could fold up in my small bed, hold Mother's hands at night, be her mourning partner. If only there were such a thing: someone I could buy for a year or two then put back on a shelf. But even if there were, even if everyone else was doing it, I'd never live it down. Mother would take care of that. Besides, I could hardly live with myself. I need to do this right for Daddy so he doesn't worry about the girls, Mother, me. So he knows when it really is his time he can count on me. Then his soul can rest. Mostly, though, so he doesn't come back haunted and restless.

"I'll stay here for as long as you'd like," I say.

"You've done enough already." I feel my heart stop. "Just you being here is all the blessing I can handle." My heart starts again. Mother is a Charter Mother. Before long, the other Charter Mothers will be here mourning in unison, putting out food, receiving visitors as if Daddy was their husband too. I kiss the air above her cheeks—*close enough to hear the peck but not too close to leave a speck*—so I don't brush off her rouge. I go find the girls.

As if the whole house has forgotten how to mourn, there are balloons left to fill. I lay them across the floor between the girls and me. Rumor's job is to stretch them. They are brittle from months of waiting. She rubs them, teasing life back into them so that Mariah and I can fill them with breath. We work in silence, stretching, blowing, tying until half-full black balloons cover the floor. They spill out into the hall like a carpet. While the girls scatter them around the mourning tree, I string up the streamers. We clear the table for the trays of food that will arrive when the mourners do. When we finally finish, the girls and I take our places behind Mother. We don't have long to wait before the mourning begins.

The bell strikes thirteen. The mourners arrive with the thirteenth gong like they do every year. Daddy is much loved. The mourners arrive in cycles: one enters, one leaves; another one enters, another one leaves. They come in with a kind word, a plate of warm food, and their favorite memory. The Charter Mothers take the food. I take the gifts. The girls give out the balloons. It's efficient. By the time the whole town has said their goodbyes, there are at least a hundred presents beneath the tree. Daddy touched a lot of lives. Each year, Mother stacks the gifts, still sealed, in the attic. If Daddy's name really was called, we'd open them after the Warding Off and join the town in thanks the day after. The whole town would be grateful, and lucky us, giving and giving till there's no one else to give up. I swallow the bitter words before they settle in my heart. If I'm not careful, Mother's superstitions will become my own.

I can't wait for Mother Opal to arrive. She's usually here by now, reminding folks to prepare their own hearts and homes just in case someone else's name is called. She won't flat out say Daddy's name *won't* be called—no one can say that, what with the nominations not even done and the Calling still to come—but it's comforting. She must be tied up with one of the other families or settling a disagreement between neighbors. It's not like she could cut a visit—especially not a scheduled one—short. Not that she has to worry about being nominated for the Moving On. First she would be cast out of the Council, then stripped of her role as Head Charter Mother, then the worrying could begin. It hasn't been done before but folks are always looking for a reason to change something or other. Grudges have a way of carrying on here, like nobody can let a grievance go. If Mother Opal doesn't settle it for them, folks will nominate one another out of spite. And when they run out of people to nominate they'll blame her. Mother Opal will get here when she can. This whole town runs on her time. Who would blame her if she slipped out to be with her dearest friend? *It won't do to show favorites*. I can hear her saying it, mouth full of snuff, tucking it beneath her tongue to make room for the words. Everyone would blame her. Every single soul, living or not.

I'm still watching the door when the final bell rings. It's Glory, the grand bronze bell with hand-carved flowers and the names of the Moved On etched inside. The bell's perched down by the Town Hall so it can be heard *from the Creek to the peak and everywhere in between*. The mourning has ended. There's one balloon left. Still no Mother Opal. The Charter Mothers account for each dish and weigh up each gift. "So-and-so brought such and such," one says, and then the scratching of pen on paper while another makes a note of how grateful the giver was. Gift times food equals grief. Some of them wonder out loud if they should wait for Mother Opal. Others say she's forgotten and her absentmindedness about something this important at a time like this is a sign. "A sign of what?" Rumor asks. *Division*, I think, but I keep it to myself. No sense worrying the girl just because I can't shake this feeling that something's wrong.

"It's nothing, sweet pea. Mother Opal didn't forget us. She's just got a lot to do this time of year." Of course she does. She can't be everywhere at once.

When the Mothers leave, they pack up all the grief with them. They take down the streamers, dismantle and fold up the tree, stack the gifts in the corner. Still its shadow is everywhere. In Daddy's favorite chair, under his side of the couch, on his special mug. The whole house is heavy with Daddy's memory. I pinch myself. He isn't even gone yet. Mother locks herself away in her room to finish freshening up. I go to my old bedroom, which is done up now in teal. I make the sign of the bell, run to the kitchen and take a spoonful of castor oil to clear my head. I chase it down with another one: *One for the body, one for the mind*, Mother Opal always says. I make it to the bathroom before the purge, knowing that when I come out I'll feel lighter and whatever's gotten into me will be long gone. *There's no place for treacherous thoughts in a civil mind*, the saying goes.

I get dressed. Stretch my calves. Say a prayer: "Dear mothers, fathers, spirits of my ancestors living and otherwise, please let this be my last year on God's green earth as a widow." I say my mantra: "I am strong, loyal and true. I will enter the Running a widow and leave a bride." It's the same mantra I said last year, and the year before when I was a new and tender widow, certain I would be swooped up like the prize Curdle Creeker I am. If I'm not careful, next year I'll be running against Mother. I can't help it, I laugh out loud. A Charter Mother running like the rest of us? Even if that was a thing, I'm certain she'd cheat.

The door is closed still, and I whisper, heart racing, "To all spirits, good and bad, if you're listening, please take me far away from this place. And please, let my father leave with me." I wrap my index fingers around each other, a promise, the sign of the cross and the bell. Surely both will seal this plea.

The Running of the Widows

It's nearly dawn. It's colder than a coffin at a wake and the race is about to begin. This year there are six of us running. Six widowed, and four potential suitors waiting at the altar. There's no way one of them won't end up mine this time. I'm in my best running gown. Though the two first-time widows opted for white ones with long trains, mine is hen's-egg cream with a full skirt and an altered hem so the gown doesn't *sweep the floor* when I move. Instead of taffeta and lace, I opted for cotton so I can hitch my dress up when I need to and not get weighted down with extra fabric. Mae's dress is gingham with a cinched waist and hand-sewn buttons down the back. One hundred buttons in all. All those months working on it together and soon as she gets in runner's position she rips the seam clear up to her calf.

The judge deducts two points right then and there just as I told her he would. It's just like her to test the rules. She's my dearest friend but Mother might be right: Mae will be the

death of me. Like the rest of the widows, Florence is in position, head down, one foot on the chalk start line, the other
behind her. Florence is more an acquaintance than a friend.
Still, I wish Florence the same amount of luck as I wish Mae.
Not enough to beat me but enough to come in tied at second.

"Luck, Mae. Luck, Florence." It's so cold that my words
are little puffs of air between us.

"See y'all at the altar," Mae says.

"Save your breath for after the Running. You're both gonna
need it." Florence is a Messenger. She can't keep nothing to
herself.

I focus on the numbers sewn on the backs of the thick vests
they make us wear on top of our running clothes. Mae's number 28, Florence is number 25. Mine is 18. Same as the house
numbers we live in. The official walks through the line ticking
off items on a checklist. Final checks made, Mother Opal stands
at the starting line, arms raised high above her head while the
judge gets into position. It's customary for an official to say a
few words to inspire the widows before we set off. This year it's
Mother Opal's turn. She looks beautiful with her deep brown
skin glimmering and complementing her plum Glory dress and
matching gloves. Her hair is fresh pressed and curled beneath
a feathered hat fit for the church service she'll lead after the
weddings.

"We are gathered here in honor of a long-standing tradition of granting second and in some cases *third* chances."

She stares at me when she says it so I know the "third"
is meant for me. After the mourning, Mother sent word for
Mother Opal to *come by when the mood struck her*. I set up

watching from behind my front room curtains to get a good view of the knocking. Of course Mother would hear the door from wherever she was in the house but because she's stubborn sometimes, Mother would keep Mother Opal waiting to prove a point. She might be Mother Opal to everyone else but to Mother, she'll always be the same little Opal she grew up with. The reminding wouldn't last long. They're like sisters. Mother would check that nobody was looking before tapping Mother Opal on the shoulder, pressing forehead to forehead in a warm show of forgiveness.

The knock never did come. Still, I just know from the way Mother Opal looks at me with her mouth in a perfect line of not smiling, not frowning, that she knows this year is my year.

"The Running of the Widows is an opportunity to increase your luck and fulfill your obligations to the town at once. *The more you sow, the more you reap, the more we grow as Curdle Creek!* Your loved one has Moved On. It is now up to you to race toward a new life. To beginnings!"

"To beginnings!" the racers cheer.

The rest of the town is at the church setting up to receive us. The eligible brides won't know who they'll end up with until we come crashing through the door. What a gift to be on the receiving end. Moses would have been too. If the children hadn't left, everything would have stayed as it was meant to be and when I Moved On, my Moses would have been able to wed without running. Instead, here I am racing against my best friend and there's no telling which groom I'll end up with: Jeremiah, the good doctor, Brother Lee, or Langston.

Jeremiah's my other best friend. I'd never tell him, but if I could choose anyone, it'd be him.

The sky is rose-colored. Just above the hill the sun starts to peek through. We run at dawn. I repeat Mother's inspirational words. *Run for your life to have luck. Run for your life to have luck. Run for your life—*

"To the altar!" Mother Opal yells.

We take off running faster than a lost outsider. Not that outsiders make it to Curdle Creek. We're set far from other cities and towns so they can keep their trouble for themselves. But if anyone did find their way down the unmarked, unpaved road that leads to the center of town, they'd better be running just like I am now. I keep my head up, eyes looking straight ahead, arms pumping, and, whatever happens, I make my legs keep moving. In a pack, we sprint down Main Street past the Bank of Curdle Creek, the Old Post Office and the new one too. We're foot-to-foot until the library, where Eustice stumbles over nothing much at all. She's tottering, arms out to catch herself when her sister Eunice crashes into her, pushing her down. Eunice jumps clear over her and carries on. We all do. Unlike Eunice, none of us looks back. Eunice is waving to her sister when she runs into Carter's billboard for handmade leather running slippers that are "good for the soul and the sole."

With two out of the race that leaves me, Florence, Mae and Gertrude. We run past Pickled's Haberdashery and Gran's Guesthouse. Gertrude gets a burst of speed and shoots by me, kicking up dirt and gravel as she goes. I don't wipe it off. Ain't nothing graceful about the Running. There's no sense slowing down to try to look cute doing it. She can go on ahead. She's turning the corner at the mill when it happens. Poor Gert leaps over when she should have gone around the slick mud at the bottom of the swell. By the time the three of us catch up, she's bent over crying about how her leg is twisted and calling for one of us to help her up out of the ditch. Like we'd fall for that trick.

It's just Florence, Mae and me. I'm out of breath but there's this voice in my head saying *Don't you dare slow down* and it sounds just like Mother.

"You better run like you want another chance!"

I look up and see Florence grinning as she passes me. She's so good at putting on other people's voices, props or not, that for a minute she looks like Mother would if she were dressed in two parts of a three-piece dress, tattered veil blowing in the wind. I can't let her beat me. My right thigh starts to burn and soon the other one does too. We're passing the schoolhouse, Florence in the front, followed by me, and Mae huff-puffing behind me. She's got the cutest little wheeze. My side's cramping and one of my ankles doesn't feel as sure as it did when we started. I slow down a little when we reach Luckey's Hardware store and Royal Emporium Roller Skating, which is part-time rink, part-time barn. Its windows are still boarded up. Has been ever since the fire. Cheyenne, Jasmine, Little Moses and poor departed Little Liza caused a ruckus for weeks when the Council decided the rink was causing idleness and shut it down. Those kids raced up and down

Main skating into shops, zipping through produce, bumping into folks, and making nuisances of themselves even though there's an ordinance against it. I warned them not to mess with the sign but darned if they didn't do it anyway. Painted dark red zeros all over it. All four of their names were called. Four babies gone. Well, three gone and one Moved On. I wonder if she still loves to skate.

I'm thinking about getting myself a pair of skates when I don't so much as *see* her pass but feel her doing it. Mae's caught up to me and in less than two seconds I'm looking at her back. In front of us, less than a yard away, is the church all lit up with candles in every window, the door wide open. Florence is about to cross the threshold. I should be next. I reach out, not to cheat, but to sort of slow Mae down, and my hand gets caught in the fabric around her collar. Mae's head jerks back and before I can catch myself, we're both falling backward. I can tell it's hard for her to breathe, what with her choking. I mean to let go but there's yelling and scrabbling behind me and here come Eunice, Eustice and Gertrude wrestling one another to get out in front. Gertrude's swinging a branch, trying to hit the sisters. Eunice and Eustice get her in the middle and try to squeeze her in some sort of sisters sandwich. The Running of the Widows changes people.

It don't change Mae though. She slaps me across the face, her fingers crashing against my lips. "This just ain't your year," she says.

She scrabbles up, slips off her shoes, and takes off running. That banshee just busted my lip. Everyone knows you ain't

supposed to aim for the head, especially not the face. It's right
there in Book XVI, Volume 2, Section 18. After all that practice. Weeks of strength, endurance and etiquette training and
as soon as we get the chance the rules are tossed in the wind
like an afterthought bouquet. Now I'm squatting in the dirt,
ribs sore, lungs hurting, out of breath, lip busted open and
bleeding, knees skinned, hands raw, a stone's throw from the
church door. Lucky me, I'm close enough to see Mae about to
go right through it.

I can't spend another year like this. I just can't.

I grab a stone. Swift, I raise my arm level, aim, throw. The
stone is bigger than it's supposed to be so I try to make sure it's
smoother than it has to be. We're friends, after all. No sense
in breaking regulations. Mae tilts her head, ducks. The stone
thuds against the doorway as Mae slips inside the church. I
get up. My body's screaming *Stay down, stay down* but Mother
will kill me if I don't finish this race. Besides, there's still two
more to go. Mae and Florence will have picked the best suitors and I'll be stuck with Langston or Brother Lee, the oldest
of the old-timers. I suppose I can't complain. Anyone who's
lived through as many Moving Ons as Brother Lee has must
have an abundance of good luck. Still, if I can't have Jeremiah,
I would prefer Langston if it came down to it.

Just as I make it to the steps of the church, here's Gertrude
trying to knock me down again. I pop her square in the back
of the head where the bullseye would be if I'd painted one.
She falls forward, first on her knees, then to her face. She's a
tangle of legs and bones, a small patch of blood and missing
hair. A bald spot she'll hate me for until she dies. I hop over

her quick before she can reach out to grab hold like I would do if I were her. Her fingers graze my ankle, a nail slices skin. I falter but I'm nearly at the top of the steps and the scrape might burn but it's not enough to keep me from reaching the door, blouse ripped, skirt hiked up halfway to bejesus, mouth hanging open, just in time to see Eunice and Eustice push me out of the way, take the steps two at a time, skid across the threshold, then hobble, both of them one shoe on, one off, down the aisle.

The church cheers. All four suitors are claimed. Mother turns to the doorway like she just knew I'd be there. She looks past me, must see Gertrude a heaving, sniffling mess behind me. She nods, sharp. I may as well be last. I'm the disappoint-ment of my generation. I'll be her cross to bear but only for as long as I live or until my name is called. Whichever comes first.

I settle my skirt, straighten my twists, breathe in and out, stare forward. I can't do anything about my lip except suck on it and I can't do that here. Mother would die. If I couldn't have the good grace to come first, the least I can do is stand here looking like I fought for it. The first year I lost, I sat down as close as I could to Daddy. Just wanted to be near him and his smell of menthol and lye soap. Last year, Mother for-bade it. Made me and my bad luck sit way in the back of the church in the Penitents' box. I'd wait outside if it was allowed.

Mae stands before the altar. Mother Opal mouths the blessing so only she and Mae hear it. She's radiant. Mae is too but Mother Opal just glows. She could be the one get-ting married, in her thick red velvet wedding robes with gold tassels, gold-heeled shoes adorned with bells that strap to her slender ankles, and thick spiral bracelets winding around her long brown arms like kisses. Her hands cup Mae's face. It's tender and unexpected. Mother Opal never shows favoritism. Mae is so lucky. Mother Opal is offering her forgiveness and bestowing her with a full womb.

Mae waits to say her piece. There's a chance she won't know the words. I know them by heart. All the widows should. We've been practicing it for months to get the words right when the time came. It would be awful to cross the threshold, make it to the altar, and forget the words. It's the sort of thing that gets you disqualified.

Mae's smiling. She'd never be lost for words. Mother Opal must be at my favorite part: *With these words I cleanse your family's name, for those before and those to come, I set them free, one by one.* Now she's asking Mae to swear before church and tomb, ancestors and not-yet-borns, on the souls of the Moved On and the Moving On—the ones whose names will be called tomorrow and who will give their lives for a good harvest, peace and prosperity, etcetera, etcetera, amen, amen, amen.

With the words said, Mother Opal hands Mae a slip of paper. The note is handwritten, thin-looped and long-lined, and on it will be the name of Mae's next husband. Of course, it's the doctor. Mae Elizabeth Miller will have a husband of her own. Till death do them part. That's not a rule, just the way it is. The rest of them will get whoever's left. Leftover luck. And I will get nothing.

I always imagined I would win. I read the Books section by glorious section. Trained in all sorts of weather, dug trenches through waist-high snow, scaled ladders in the baking sun, waited for hours in autumn rain, ran everywhere I went as often as I could, practiced holding my breath for minutes at a time, polished the tower bell. Even prayed. More than once. Florence and Mae hadn't trained half as hard. Almost like they didn't want to be saved. Or didn't care half as much. No one expected them to win so if they did, it'd be something close to a miracle. Everyone reckoned it'd be me, and if they didn't, they should've. A widow three years in a row is unheard-of in Curdle Creek. Mother's been talking about it since the last Running. The one that sent Gladys Jones tumbling, virgin-white dress—even though she wasn't—raised, baring her chubby little legs for the whole town to see, down the moss-covered hill into the cold, red-colored Creek. She wouldn't have fallen nearly as hard or as long if she hadn't tried to race me for the door. I'd been a two-year widow by then. It was my turn. If she'd slowed down a little, it wouldn't have been so bad for her. But no, some folks are just selfish and I had built a trap. Nothing elaborate. Leaves covering a spring, child's play. Not good enough to win, though.

I just want to go home, lie out flat on Jasmine's floor and do nothing for a little while. I don't even want to read one of the Books, especially not Book XXIII on the virtues of being a widow. Again. But no matter how I feel, tomorrow it'll be time for the Calling. Then, once the names of the Moved On are called and verified by Mother Opal, I'll come home to bake the pies. Mother is known for her plump pies bursting with fresh fruits and mulled wine, her generous sprinkling of cinnamon, and extra pinch of love. More than one soon-to-be-departed stayed a little longer to get a taste of Mother's thank-you-for-your-sacrifice pies. The family of the Moving On always said knowing Mother was coming with an apple, blueberry or sweet potato pie still warm from the oven almost made the loss bearable. If only they knew. Mother hasn't bothered to bake one of her pies in years. Not since her luck ran out. Since then, it's been me picking near-to-rotten apples, squeezing out their fresh juice, peeling them like skin, then chopping, mixing, sprinkling. If they taste anything after the gin, rum, whiskey, wine, half bottle of whatever's left in the cupboard from the year before, it isn't thanks. The pie will make the news easier to take, though. Poor Moses's Moving On certainly would have been worse without my extra-special gin cherry pie waiting for me when I got back.

Now, Mae's standing next to her new husband, the good doctor. He's just right. Fullish head of hair, cold hands, good job, jolly laugh ... dead wife. Mae doesn't even have to wait for her to be Moved On. She was Moved On two years ago, bless her soul. Her name was called the same year as Mae's mother's. Of course, Mae's father remarried right away. He's a Deacon. The doctor saved himself, settled into mourning and it suited him. But all that mourning isn't healthy so of course the Mothers declared an end to his mourning period. This year he gets another wife. According to the Council, his family has proved themselves year after year, what with birthing all the babies, tending to the dying, settling the souls, declaring the dead. The vote was unanimous. He made the list of suitors without the need for provisos and lobbying.

The good doctor's steadily grinning, shaking hands with all the other brides and grooms. He's not bad to look at and he has a good grip. He's a solid handshaker. Always been one of the best ringers. Mae's mother used to say, *A man with a good bell-ringing arm is a keeper.* Mae's new mother says that too. She's a lot like Mae's mother. Told Mae to call her ma'am and everything. If she hadn't won this time, Mae would probably have kept on staying with her second mother until one of them Moved On.

She could have stayed with us. Mother would have been glad to have her. She'd fill out the paperwork before she even needed to. Probably volunteer to take her in. She would want it to be official. An extra mouth to feed is no trouble at all when you ain't the one cooking and when doing the town a favor means they owe you one in return. Not to mention the extra luck that having Mae would bring. If each house has the same number of chances as the next one that someone's name will be called, then by rights, more mouths means fewer chances your own name will be called. Mae would bring us luck even if she didn't have much of her own.

The service is starting and I'm still standing here wishing my daddy would leave his place next to Mother and the girls, hold me by the hand, lead me out of the church and take me home. But Daddy wouldn't do it. Wouldn't stand up to Mother and wouldn't take me home neither. If anything at all, he'd take me fishing down at the Creek like he used to do. I could have gone my whole life without knowing anything good could come out of that water. But the size of them bluefish makes my mouth water just thinking about them. And even better than frying up fresh fish right there on the bank was sitting next to my daddy listening to his tall tales about people who could slip into wells and travel anywhere they had a mind to go. Even outside of Curdle Creek. Not that there's much worth seeing outside of Curdle Creek. Lynchings, massacres, plagues. I've seen the headlines. The world beyond Curdle Creek ain't nothing but bad news.

Nobody ever comes back to Curdle Creek. Not even Well Walkers. Daddy used to say we come from a long line of them. They'd pop in and out of towns and come and go as they pleased. But something about Curdle Creek put an end to that. Not that Well Walking is true, but, just in case it is, there's an ordinance against it.

I'm not saying I'd want to leave. Curdle Creek ain't no better nor no worse than anywhere else. *Pop.* Oh, God, no. *Pop, pop.* It feels so—*pop, pop*—good and I shouldn't be *pop, pop, pop* doing this but *pop, pop*, if it wasn't for Mae *pop, pop, pop, pop, pop* it would all be *pop, pop, pop* mine. I crack my knuckles one at a time. I just can't help myself. I look up. Mother's lips are moving. She's across the church hall but if words had wings they'd be floating in front of my face, hissing, hot breath whispering, *Stop embarrassing me!* I bow my head. I hold my breath to still my hands.

The church fills with organ music. Reverend Father pounds on the keys, pumps the pedals, squeals in that off-key voice Mother swears will lead to his name being called sooner rather than later. The hymn "O, Thank Thee for Protecting We" shakes the rafters. Thank God it's a short one. The last Reverend Father could carry a tune and the rhythm at the same time. He made the four verses sound like a symphony might. His name got called as soon as the tithes went missing. The hymn hasn't been the same since. It's a shame too. He was Moved On and then the money was found. A miscalculation. Mother Opal said mathematics had nothing to do with fate and that the schoolchildren would keep studying that, baking, engineering, and anything else the town needed until the town didn't need it anymore. The hymn's not meant to last this long. He's *ooohhhhh*ing and *Lord have mercy*ing something fierce. Four weddings in one Running is a blessing.

I've been holding my breath since forever. It shouldn't have taken more than ten Mississippis for him to finish. But no, Reverend Father's repeated the chorus two extra times and I'm near sixty Mississippis and my eyesight's starting to blur and the congregation's waiting for someone to answer Mother Opal's invitation, "Should anyone present know of any reason that this couple should not be joined in holy matrimony, speak now or forever hold your peace."

Even the candles are starting to go out. The church is hot. The first-rowers work their fans like the only thing wrong with this moment is the heat. They look as if they'll wait all day if they have to. What difference does it make to them? Service won't be over until it's over. The betrothed will be wed, the Moving On will be Moved On, the sun will set today just as it will tomorrow. Behind them, the second-rowers, the row reserved for community leaders, Mothers, and elders who got to church too late to sit in the front row, move in time to the choir. The choir isn't helping any. They've been holding that same note, a low hum that rumbles like thunder or a disappointed preacher, just waiting on someone to speak up. My eyes are welling up. The church itself is shaking like it caught the Holy Ghost. Lines dance and squiggle up from beneath the floor like heat. There's two of everything. Two preachers, two choirs, two Mother Opals, two Mothers, two Daddys. Two mes. Both single.

Tiny pinpricks sting my legs. Do I have a reason why Jeremiah shouldn't get married? I shift the wad of mint chewing gum I'm not supposed to have beneath my tongue. It's sucking up whatever spit's left in my mouth. I swallow it. It's brittle and dry. Instead of making my mouth "kissing fresh" it will probably kill me. Get stuck right in the middle of my throat. *That's just what you get, Osira!* I can almost hear Rumor's singsong voice dancing right over my grave.

They're not really expecting anyone to object but the asking is part of the ritual and so is the waiting. Curdle Creek runs on rituals. One year, before I was born, the town skipped the Warding Off. Called it off "for no good reason," according to Mother. That year, hundreds of last-chancers swarmed the town, if you could call it that. They dragged into Curdle Creek coughing, heaving, dripping with fever. Mother Opal recognized it right away—didn't even need Book IX. Plague. It was late and unplanned but the town rallied together, belatedly honored the Warding Off.

Babies with fat legs dangling off parents' laps, old people with eyes straining, heads lolling, folks in their starched celebration clothes, my family: the girls and Mother decked out in Moving On mauve, *the perfect autumn color for mournings and weddings*, Daddy in pressed dress shirt, trousers, and running shoes—they all stare straight ahead. They seem to be leaning forward, breaths held. The least I can do is play my part. I stand straight, tilt my head. It's Pose 76: thankful but thoughtful. It's a privilege to sacrifice for the town. If I can't be a bride, I'll be a mourning widow. I'm a beautiful mourner, according to Jeremiah. When Mae makes us practice the mourning after, I'm always the first one picked to mourn. Jeremiah says it's because of my *soulful eyes and spontaneous wailing*. If he only knew how long it takes to practice spontaneous wailing.

There's no reason Jeremiah shouldn't get his bride except for the fact that I love him. It's wrong, I know it is. If I'm meant to have someone, the Council will send him to me. What if I just took what I want this one time? The hairs on the back of my neck stand up first. Tiny pinches travel along my arms, legs, back, face. My skin tingles all over. Stings. I look up and Daddy's smiling at me like I'm the right me at the right time and it's okay that I'm not up there about to have our sins washed away. *There's always a second chance for people who do right*, he says. Please, Lord, let that be true. Daddy deserves a second chance too. It's not his fault he married Mother, that Romulus ran off, that Turners don't carry nothing but bad luck.

Blasphemy. It sends chills through my body. If it's meant to be, it will be. "Forgive me, ancestors, for I have—" I'm whispering but someone shushes me anyway. Mae is practically glowing, holding out her hand to the good doctor. He takes it. The choir sings. The whole church seems to shake. Mother Opal waves her hands above their heads, proclaims them a union. Mr. and Mrs. Mae take their seats in the family pew to wait for the rest of the couples to join them.

Now it's Jeremiah's turn. He's marrying Florence from across the Creek. They look besotted with one another. Happy.

After the ceremonies the organ will play "The March of the Widow." It's an upbeat jazz number designed to make your feet move faster than they are otherwise inclined. Gertrude and I will make our way down the aisle to have counsel with Mother Opal. Just like last year, she will tell me I must try harder to "fulfill my obligations." That if I'm not careful I will look ungrateful, and ungratefulness is a sure way to get nominated to be Moved On. I will repent.

Jeremiah does not look as though he is just "fulfilling his obligations." He looks relieved but also happy. Like, maybe he didn't love me much at all. Not that he ever said he did. Nobody in Curdle Creek says that. But, didn't he show it when he was sidling up to me even before his dear wife was Moved On properly? He was sitting there eating my pies, talking about how good they would taste if we ate them together. And how nice it was to have my company in his time of mourning. When he started whispering in my ear about leaving Curdle Creek it was me, not Florence, reminding him how lucky we are to be living here. How much better it is to live here than to die somewhere else. Of what would happen if the Council found out he was even talking about it. If Mother Opal found out Jeremiah had thoughts of leaving, he'd lose everything. Any favor he gained by wedding Florence would be squandered before you could say *I do*. He'd have nothing. No wife. No extra luck. No blessings but me.

Mother Opal issues the invitation. I object. I do. I'm practically running, feet tripping over each other toward the altar. Mariah giggles. Never too far behind, Rumor starts in. Before long they're both near squealing. I picture Mother, dignified, gliding down the aisle, dainty and lovely. What would she say? She'd say something practical, remind me I don't have too many more runs left before the town chooses someone for me, my name is called, or both. "Stop this foolishness!" I whisper. I sound so much like Mother that I frighten myself. It works. I slow my walk, my breath, stop swinging my arms. Still, not two steps later and I'm at the altar. It seems bigger and wider up close.

Mother Opal is standing huddled close to Jeremiah and Florence. "Are you sure?" she asks. "There is no rule against it, but none *for* it either."

Like twins, Florence and Jeremiah nod. Just look at the two of them, already in cahoots against me. I open my mouth to tell all of the many reasons that this man and this woman should not be joined together in holy matrimony. Mother Opal hushes me with her warm hand pressed against my lips. She turns to the congregation.

"In an act of generosity, Florence and Jeremiah have given Osira one of their blessings." The congregation applauds. "I have decided the form of the blessing is to be a new role in service of Curdle Creek."

Except for the click of heels against the wood floor that I recognize as Mother's shoes, the congregation is silent. Mother stands, resting her gloved hands on the pew before her. Even from here, I can see her fingers curled into fists. Her voice is calm, almost sweet. "I would respectfully remind you, Mother Opal, that Osira has a role already. As my eldest living child, her role is to return to my home and be counted as one of us."

"But she is not your oldest *living* child, is she?"

Is she saying Romulus is alive?

Mother Opal directs a long, pointed fingernail at Mother. "And I don't think I need to remind you of all people of my role, or yours either."

All eyes are on Mother now. "No, Opal."

No one calls Mother Opal by her name. I don't care how long they've known each other, no one does it. Not to her face, not behind her back, not in the church surrounded by the full Council and all of these witnesses. I think I've stopped breathing. This must be what death is like. I'm too hot and too cold at the same time. It's a cacophony of sounds. Feet shuffling, voices whispering, birds squalling, Mother, still standing, staring.

"You will not deny me," Mother says.

I love my job at the library. I get to read all of the Council-approved books before anyone else does and sometimes I even see the banned books before they're pulped at the mill. It's not the same as when I was teaching. There's nothing quite like teaching children spelling, ordinances and rituals, but of course, when my children ran off, I couldn't be trusted to mind other people's children. I could hardly expect more than to be allowed to keep our family house with the garden and a plot in the back. The Council providing me with a new job after stripping me of my own was a gentle kindness.

"I think you'll find that a role in service of the town is a role in service to us all." Mother Opal pinches my lips together as if I'm the one speaking out. "You are not being denied. You will surely gain as much as anyone else has a right to."

My eyes are watering. My lips are tingling. I'm whimpering and I can't help myself.

"Book XXIII says a thrice-widow belongs to her kin," Mother says.

Mother Opal twists my lips a final time and lets go. "And Book XIII says a resident of Curdle Creek belongs to us all. She draws for a new role. If you'd like to object, you can do so officially." Mother Opal pauses, narrows her eyes. "After the Moving On."

The girls pull on Mother's arms, begging her, "Please sit down, please, please sit back down." Daddy leaps up, raises his hands and his voice in apology. His voice is beautiful. No one can sing apologies the way he does. He holds the final note so long that folks start applauding.

Mother isn't watching him. She's watching Mother Opal. Mother Opal's watching her too. Soon, everyone stands up to join Daddy's song. They're all singing Mother Opal's praises. Well, everyone but Mother.

* * *

A Deacon prepares the barrel and I prepare for my new life. I close my eyes. You're meant to make a wish. To close your eyes and think of the sort of person you want to grow old with or the difference you want to make to the town. Your contributions. I make mine. *Please keep my children far away from this place.*

I reach in. It's like bobbing for apples. The bundles of paper, origami shapes with embroidered roles if you're lucky, blank if you're not, all feel the same. By weight and texture, each one is just as likely as the next one to be something I'd want to do. If there were such a thing, it's as though the Saint of

Widows is guiding my hand, leading me to the slip of paper with my future on it. My hand brushes against one, making my palm itch. It feels like it's *the one*. I dig a sliver of a nail in it, not enough to be accused of ripping it open, just enough to hold on tight, and rub the tip of my finger along it. Do I feel the word "Mother"? The rest of the Mothers are voted in, but surely being a Mother is of service to the town. I can be a Mother too. Make decisions, guard the rules, measure the thanks. Or is that curve too round, too close to an O to be anything but "accountant"? I like numbers just as much as the next person, but I'd rather not be in charge of counting the dead.

No, there's no way it's "accountant." I would know it if it was. This paper feels right. So, I hold on to it, slip it into my other hand and keep feeling around for another one, just in case. It isn't really cheating. It's insurance. Like carrying a spare set of keys to Mother's house so the girls don't get locked out, even though the door's always unlocked because no one would break into anyone's house in Curdle Creek.

The inside is darker than I remember it being. Maybe I'm deeper down than I planned. One foot grazing the bottom of the hardwood floor, the other dangling in the air.

"Osira." It's soft, hushed as a reverend in a brothel. Low as a muffled amen. Still, my name echoes. Who was that? My hand tingles like it's touched something hot. But I've just scraped the bottom of the barrel. Scraping don't sound like names and something said my name. It's a whisper but it's in my head so that might not count. I'm still shaking, though. I sure hope nobody out there can hear my teeth rattling, my breath catching. My eyes are closed. I don't need to open them to see the rows of papers folded into themselves, grinning like teeth waiting to taste a bit of skin. Maybe it was the shifting of papers, the shuffling *whoosh, whoosh* as I part them.

Other than my own breathing, I keep time by marking the muffled beat of the bass guitar. If I'm too quick, they'll say I'm arrogant. Too cocky to deserve anything other than what I get. Too long, and I'm indecisive. Too unreliable to deserve this third chance. Mae and I timed it. Three minutes, thirty-nine seconds is respectable. Not too fast, not too slow. I'm counting beats. I'm at 4/16ths when I feel it. A warm light on my skin. There's something warm close to my face. *Don't look, don't look.* Wouldn't it be just like the devil to be waiting in the bottom of a barrel right there in the middle of the church? Just hunched down low waiting to pull one of the devoted in there and take them to some sin-haven of a city beyond the Creek? The thought of a barrel-sized devil tickles me. The sound of my giggles echoing back to me slaps me like a cold washrag. There's nothing funny about a forty-five-year-old woman wriggling in the bottom of a barrel, fishing for a piece of paper for the job that could change her life.

Please let me see a miracle. Mother said that one year all the men said they'd seen Seamus Creek, the town's first and only Charter Father. Seen him right there in the bottom of the barrel, sipping whiskey and smoking that long pipe. They claimed he said they needed to right a wrong, that they'd been called to put an end to the Moving On. The women said they saw poor Seamus's wife, Mother Creek. She was dressed in a long black gown, hair pinned up, plain faced, barefoot. She told them the Moving On was right and proper and that some years more than one name should be called to balance the year before. There was a lot of talk about who had seen right. That year, the Caller saw each and every one of those men's names. That seemed to settle it.

I open my eyes and curl the paper against my cheek. It's the right one. I can feel it. It has to be. My body stops shaking. I can see it now. I'll be a Charter Mother just like Mother— only kinder. I'll make new vows to the town, sign the Curdle Creek Charter, have my name chiseled in the archives. I'll accept my blessings. My past will be expunged. Then the kiss. Cheek, cheek, and finally lips. Sealed. There will be cheering, congratulations, presents. Then, arms linked, waving hands, strolling home through the city with Mother, Daddy and the girls following behind like a procession in time with the ring-ing of the bells. It will be a good way to end a day like today. With our good name restored, there won't be a need for me to move in with Mother for her to practice her yearly mourning, for me to worry that I'll be Moved On. No hunting of souls, chasing down the living. Of course, we'd do it anyway.

I say a prayer for good luck, then push out of the barrel, settle my clothes, and then, practically whistling the Wedding March, I turn to the altar. The wedded couples wait with Mother Opal ready to receive me and my good fortune.

"Congratulations," Mae says without moving her lips. She's such a good friend, always happy for me when happi-ness is called for.

I rub the paper between my fingers, nod slightly. There's nothing better than a new start.

The choir leader jerks her head at me like *You had your turn, hush now.*

The organist plays the Fresh Start March, which is just like the wedding one. Everyone turns to watch me glide back down the aisle. I left-right-left slow to the altar just like we practiced in the preparation for surprise classes I took down at the Hall. Daddy's grinning at me. Mother's head is bowed, lips silently moving. The girls wriggle like impatient little joy-sucking leeches. The tune picks up. I walk faster to keep in time. The church is full; even the non-believers are here today. Who am I to judge? I nod and smile at everyone. The carpet feels lush beneath my feet. The candles are bright, there's a slight breeze, the babies have stopped whining. I hadn't noticed it before, but the March really is lovely. When I'm a Mother, I'll make a proclamation to play it more often. The rhythm is sort of catchy, and I'm *dum, dum, dum-dumm*ing along with the organ, snapping my fingers as I walk. Look at me, changing my fortune, and I didn't have to get married to do it.

I'm nearly at the altar, one foot on the bottom step, when a Mother-in-Waiting steps in front of me with her hand out. Does she want change? I didn't bring my wallet so I don't even have the customary two bills to slip into the collection plate. Her hand is empty, fingers wiggling. "The paper," she mouths in a pretend whisper that even the back row can hear. I'm about to kneel in thanks. She unfolds the paper carefully as if it's Exhibit A in a trial and shakes her head. She lifts it above her head, turning from one side of the building to the next so everyone can see the picture of the bale of hay. The music stops. Mother moans. The woman waves me away.

A farmer.

Mother Opal is on the top step, back turned like she can't stand to look at me. Mae and the good doctor stand beside her now, heads bowed. I step forward to push past the would-be Mother. "It's wrong! I'm supposed to be a Mother! I just want to be a Mother!"

Two hands grip my arms tight, pulling me down the aisle in reverse.

Mother clamps her fingers across my mouth.

"You should have thought about that before your children left," Mother Opal says.

Daddy tightens his grip. The girls follow behind, shaking their heads like *Poor Osira, what else could we expect?*

The Eve of the Calling

The walk home feels longer even though we didn't stop in the Five and Dime like we usually do after a service. The girls take turns getting on my nerves.

"A farmer. That's just like nominating your own self for the Moving On," Rumor says.

"Everybody knows you can't grow nothing," Mariah joins in. "Roses, pumpkins, sunflower seeds—everything you turn your hand to just shrivels up and dies."

"I've grown y'all, so you must be right. Everything I touch ends up rotten."

"She's just jealous because we're getting forever husbands and hers was only ever gonna be temporary."

"It serves her right. If she'd spent half as much time teaching those children of hers the laws of Curdle Creek, they'd still be here."

Mariah likes to sound like a know-it-all but she doesn't know nothing. My girls won just as many ribbons for reciting ordinances as anyone else around here. It was knowing all them rules that made them leave as it was.

"How are you going to feed the whole town and you can't even keep a plant growing?"

Ain't nothing wrong with tilling the ground. It's honest work. Especially when the harvest is abundant after a bountiful Moving On. But a farmer has to feed the town whether it's a year of plenty or not. Nobody ever says it's all right if we don't have enough grain, we didn't Move On as many people as we ought to have. No, first they say there's not enough wheat. Then they say there's not enough meat. Before you know it, you're nominated for the Moving On.

It's not Mother Opal's fault. I'm the one that plucked it. But, a farmer of all things. The girls are right, I'm as good as Moved On.

Rumor's been begging to hold the refolded slip of paper ever since the usher pressed it into my hand before opening the door, pushing us out, and locking it behind us. Rumor's hand starts to tremble in mine. "You really are going to be Moved On, aren't you? Promise you won't mess this up."

"I'll study farming. The library's full of books on everything from sowing to growing. You'll see."

"Poor Osira," the girls sing together in high-pitched voices. "Poor, poor Moving On Osira."

"Last year," says Mariah, "Bethany Anne's father Moved On and she didn't come in to read the forgivings for two days. Everyone fussed over her when she got back. Her eyes were all puffy, skin dry as a gourd. All that sniffling. One of the Sisters came in and told her to stop it right then and there. Said she was old enough to know how things worked around here and besides, she'd voted for her father just like everyone else did. It wasn't anyone's fault but her own that he had enough votes to be Moved On."

"So don't you go crying about how it's not fair, Osira Turner," Rumor says. "Don't you dare do it."

I really want to push her, with her matching dress and purse, smart shoes and white gloves, blessed life and luck-filled future, down in the middle of the street. But then Mother will launch into another rage about how I've disgraced the entire family and nothing good will come from this, and why, Lord, has she been burdened with such an albatross around her neck? It hasn't been a minute since Daddy got her settled down from her last tirade. It took him whispering in her ear, kissing her full on the mouth in broad daylight right in front of anyone who'd care to see. Mother's cheeks went brighter than Caught Me Red-Handed blush. Before long they were both giggling, swinging their arms, holding hands and walking slow, telling us to run up ahead so they could have some privacy.

"Last one to the house has to wash the dishes," I call out. I'm already running.

Rumor can't stand to lose anything so she takes off as fast as her legs will let her. Mariah's calling after her about being a little hooligan but she's just saying that because Mother's there.

"Go on, join them," Mother murmurs.

It's as though she's set a wild horse free. Mariah comes huffing, arms swinging, hair flying. I'd let her win if it didn't mean her talking about it for the next three winters. I don't let loose until she's right behind me, then I do it. I take off. It's like I'm flying. My arms and legs must be a blur because I see the street sign, the row of houses, everything all at once. It's why I'm the first one to see the line of Deacons, Brother Jacobs among them, lined up against the gate. Why I stop, one hand on my knee, the other holding my chest, trying to catch my breath and not pass out. The Deacons always stop by to pick up Daddy before they go fishing, smoking, Moving On, Warding Off. They're usually good for a laugh, a warm smile. Today's different. There are no jokes. No smiles. No looking me in the eye.

I watch Mother and Daddy still loving up on each other even as they near the house. I know they've seen the men by the way it takes them half as long as it should to reach the walkway.

"My brothers," Daddy says. "To what do I owe the pleasure of your esteemed company?" He smiles wide like this is just another day.

The men start *Brother Osiris*ing right away. It's *Brother* this and *Brother* that. Everyone has a word of gratitude. They're thankful for his sacrifice to the town. Thankful to have worked with him. There's advice and goodwill flowing. If I had a glass, I'd be drunk off of Curdle Creek kindness. They are up to something. I know it. *Did one of you nominate my daddy for the Moving On?* I'd ask, but it's against the ordinances to do that. My stomach is flipping like it did before they called my babies to be Moved On. For the right words at the right time, a Curdle Creeker would call their own mother's name, no matter what names were nominated. And above all, the Callers are Curdle Creekers. The true believer kind.

I pinch myself to clear my head. These men are like uncles to me. When Romulus ran off, they were the loudest ones convincing the town that Mother and Daddy were as heartbroken as the rest of the town and hadn't had a hand in it. They couldn't vouch for Moses and me but that wasn't personal. They were right there packing and stacking boxes for Moses's sending-off so I wouldn't have to do it. These men are family. Sure, one of them is plotting to be Mother's next husband, but that doesn't mean they're up to no good.

The men are here to take Daddy fishing. They say they're going to play a quick game of cards, then watch an edited version of *Curdle Creek Then and Now*, Daddy's favorite film. Nothing's wrong, they say. Can't they do something nice without it being suspicious? Mr. Jacobs asks, like that's not what makes it suspicious. After the film they will go to Spruce, Daddy's favorite barbecue/bakery for Daddy's favorites. There's nothing wrong, they say, but the priest will say a few words. The Council will send a letter that some poor child will read out loud as Daddy eats. The letter of deeds is enough to take away your appetite so why it would be recited between the scraping of forks, the swallowing of tender meat, the cracking of rinds—depending on what everyone had ordered—is a mystery. I don't want to know what mine says. I have no intention of listening to it being stumbled over, misremembered, mispronounced as a teary-eyed child stutters through my good and bad deeds. I'd like to live my whole life with my deeds unread, thank you very much.

Daddy's about to leave with the Deacons. Everything's fine, he says. Why does it feel like goodbye? Because I can't keep my feelings off of my face, I head around to the back of the house. The grass is fresh cut, sweet. Clippings scatter as I walk. The least the Jones boy could do is clean up after he cuts the lawn. How hard is it to remember? Trim the bushes, mow the grass, burn everything you cut, scatter or bury it on barren land. Most people interpret that to mean behind the Grammercy Guesthouse since nothing good grows from there anymore. Only that boy interprets it to mean leaving it right here. I don't mean to, but I pull a branch off one of Mother's rosebushes. It feels mean and spiteful to do it but it's in my hand and I'm bending, then snapping it off. Before long, the only thing I hear is the swish of my stick cutting through the air while I pretend-beat each and every one of the Deacons. I'm working on Uncle Dread when I feel someone behind me.

I didn't even hear him walk up. That's what folks say about Daddy during the Moving On too. One minute they're all alone and the next, Daddy's there. Even before he became a Deacon he had a reputation of being *hard to get*. Couldn't no one sneak up on him then or now. It's not so much that he's faster than those being Moved On, it's that he's quieter and more patient. When he has a mind to chase someone down, he aims to catch them. He's a blessing to the town. As long as you ain't the one being Moved On. I smell him now too. His pipe's always full of cherry wood, cherry leaves, cherry stems, cherry seeds. He said it's sweet like Mother. I wish he hadn't told me that.

He's standing there grinning so I know just what he's thinking before he even says it.

"Don't you dare tell your mother I'm smoking. She always says it will be the death of me." He puffs a round circle that would look like a misshapen ball any other time but now looks a bit like a broken wedding band. He chuckles. "You know how she hates to be wrong."

He leans against the fence, standing far from Mother's rosebush so she'll know he wasn't the one tampering with it. I lower my arm, my head too. There's a whole family of ants just wanting to climb onto the branch. It hasn't even hit the ground good. The soil's dry. If the ground's drying up, the crops will be too. A bit of water, some fresh manure, a bountiful Moving On, and the harvest and I could survive this year.

"Do you think Mother's right about your name being called?"

"I don't see how I'd know it, since we ain't had the Calling yet."

"The Deacons being here don't feel off to you?" I can't face him.

"Deacons have been Moved On since the beginning. None of them got a special send-off. I'm not special, Osira. The system works because there's a system. No use in doubting it. The Deacons and me are just having ourselves a little gathering before the festivities get started."

Daddy puffs slow. Like he has a lifetime of puffing left. A bubble of smoke seems to stream out of his mouth.

He's right. Deacons have been Moved On from time to

time. But none of them had been married to a Charter Mother. I poke holes in the ground to catch the rain when it comes.

"Have you ever been outside Curdle Creek?"

Daddy bends down, rests his hands on his thighs. "Why would I do that?"

I've always traced our bad luck back to Romulus leaving, choosing himself over the family. Then, it was my children. Like the family's cursed. The whole town felt the same way. Isn't that why we keep paying the same debt year after year since they've been gone? Daddy's a believer; Mother is too. Both of them are as devout as twice-starched dress shirts. Still, he has to be a little suspicious.

"Maybe the Deacons know something they ought not to know." I whisper it and step back in case lightning has good hearing and aim.

Instead of running to the phone, calling the Council to arrange a special meeting or turning me in, Daddy looks like he's thinking it over. His head is tilted to the side. He's rubbing his chin.

"I suppose that's not entirely impossible," he says. "Everyone gets to cast one nomination. If they asked folks who they were nominating and who they weren't, they'd have a sort of tally of the most likely names to be dropped into the well. But they'd have no way to know which name the Caller would draw. There ain't no way they could know that, is there?"

Unless someone got to the Caller first, I think. Slipped them a piece of paper with a name scribbled on it. Or, if they threw in extra slips with the name of the person they wanted Moved On, that would sure shift the odds, but not as much as if *all* the papers had the same name on them. Then, there'd be no way the Caller could pick anyone else.

"No, I don't suppose there is," I say.

"I don't have to see what's beyond Curdle Creek to know I don't want no part of it. Everything I've ever wanted is right here." Daddy points at the house, the garden, me. "My family's here, and where my family's at is home. That's where I belong."

"What if we're the only place left with the Moving On?"

I'm not looking at him but I know Daddy's shaking his head. I imagine his scar crinkling like it's winking. It isn't actually a scar, it's a birthmark. Mother says it's from the midwife rushing a baby set on coming in his own sweet time. But Daddy says he was anxious to see the world and pushed out so fast that he almost slipped out of the midwife's hands, one of her slender nails catching him as he wiggled free. Dropping a baby. Right here in Curdle Creek. That midwife apologized for two days straight and her name was still called the next year just as sure as if she'd called it herself.

"The Moving On keeps us safe. What do other places have? Killings, that's what. Danger at every turn. No outrunning it. Hiding from it. Ignoring it. Could happen at any time too. Maybe they don't have a Moving On but there are whole towns living just a whistle away from being burned to the ground. No, thank you. I'll take my chances right here in an all-Black town tucked in the middle of nowhere. When my name is called it will be because it's my time." He looks up at the sky like God has something to do with it. "Now doesn't seem to be the time to be questioning if the system works or not. *It may not work the way we want it to, but it works the way we need it to.*"

Suddenly even Daddy's quoting scripture. There's a thousand ordinances I could quote back at him but they don't sit right in my mouth. "Do you think one of them would nominate you?"

"Who?"

I nod toward the men. Sure, we're family but not blood-related. Curdle Creek has a strict population policy. One in, one out. What difference does it make which one it is? "It could be any of them, really. Uncle Dread, Brother Oslo." I turn to face Daddy. "Mr. Jacobs."

"Osira Alexandra Turner!" Daddy's hot-whispering too. He empties his pipe, scattering tobacco in the dirt. Then he wipes the pipe with a handkerchief and hands them both to me. I wrap the pipe, still warm, in the handkerchief and tuck them both in my pocket. I'm still staring at the grass, flat beneath his feet. "That man has been nothing but good to this family. You must see how he takes care of your mother. He's a comfort to her. I'd like to think when it does come time for such goodbyes, he'd be right there taking care of my family. I'd do the same for him if it came to it." Daddy shrugs his shoulders. "If it ain't this year, it'll be the next. Sooner or later it'll be my year. I'd like a man like Mr. Jacobs to be there when it happens."

I don't need to remind him that a whole lot can happen in a year. People die all the time. With a bit of luck—a plague, fire, or some sort of accident—we won't even need to call names. Just do the Warding Off to protect the town from the spirits. I can almost hear the hooting and hollering, the chants from the townsfolk with their pre–Warding Off shenanigans. Besides, in a year, Mr. Jacobs won't even be here. Not if my nominating him has anything to do with it.

I picture Daddy running through the streets, hot torches sizzling and popping, shadows taunting and practically taking shape as the town closes in. "Will you be scared, when it's your time?"

Daddy straightens up. Takes a step back. I didn't mean to offend him. I drop to my knees to apologize.

"No, no," he says. He grabs my arm tight, yanks me to my feet, still shaking his head. "You didn't do anything wrong in asking." The Town Hall bell rings. "You remember when you were a little girl, and we'd talk about Well Walkers down by the Creek?"

I would hate for him to Move On thinking he'd raised a non-believer. "Of course I do, but they ain't real and if they were, what they'd be doing would be wrong. When it's my time, I'll go like I'm called to."

A breeze blows, carrying the smell of fresh cow dung, exhaust, and sweet cut grass. Flies fat with all the time in the world buzz and settle one after the other near Daddy's feet. He pats me on the back like I'm one of the girls.

"I thought you might say that. But if you change your mind, if you ever need to, see if you don't find what you need when you need it. Don't tell your mother. She has enough to think about right now."

She sure does. Why else would she be sewing mourning clothes before the Calling? Running around flirting with

Mr. Jacobs like she didn't already have a husband and Mr. Jacobs hadn't already had three wives.

A woodpecker knocks three times on a nearby tree. It pauses, then knocks and knocks and knocks as if somebody's home and it's found them. Imagine knocking on somebody's door knowing all along, even when they invite you in, that you're there for dinner and dinner is them. It's unbearably hot. The sort of day you'd run down to the Creek *Do Not Swim* signs be damned and just jump right in. You'd have to do it eyes closed. Otherwise, you can't help but think about the last time you were there, the time you chased someone in and held your breath waiting for them to come up for air.

Daddy hugs me quick before anyone can see it. No one in Curdle Creek hugs. People say it's bad luck for the hugger, or for the one getting hugged, but usually for both. It's awkward being so close to him; his arms, normally strong, feel soft. His skin is warm sunshine and hot cocoa with whipped cream. Delicious. Too quick, he lets go. His eyes cloud over. His jaw straightens. "When the time's right, promise me you'll leave this place."

"Don't talk like that. You know as soon as I set one foot across that line they'd call Mother's name, the girls' too. They'd be carrying my sin their whole lives and wouldn't even get to carry it long." Quick as it got hot, it gets cold. I'm shivering, teeth chattering, fingers getting numb. The sun's still shining; the flies are still there lined up like a little band, ripe for the squashing. Daddy doesn't seem to feel it, this sometimes hot, sometimes cold air. It could be the Time. My body turning against me, turning its back on the young me to make room for the older one, pushing her out of the way, settling into young skin and bringing old wounds and new feelings with it. Maybe that's why what was good enough last year doesn't seem to fit anymore. I take a deep breath. It'll pass.

"Your mother will remarry as soon as I'm gone."

I want to say that's not true but the lie gets caught in my throat.

"That's how it's been, that's how it's supposed to be. She's a Charter Mother. She'll need someone to carry on if you don't."

I step away from him so the lightning doesn't get me too but the sky's still clear, not a cloud in sight. "There ain't nothing wrong with being a farmer, Daddy. I can learn how to irrigate and fumigate, how to plant and when to do it. I'll make you proud."

My legs are so cold that my knees knock. I rub them together. The *frssk frssk* of stockings only makes me colder. My feet are two slabs of ice. I picture them chipping. Neatly trimmed toes everywhere. Through chattering teeth, I give Daddy words of wisdom to soothe his poor wayward soul. "*Mercy is as mercy does; the past's more true than mercy was.*" It's Book XIII but I suspect he doesn't need me to remind him.

"Osiris," Dread calls, "it's time."

I can't stop shaking. I can't think of a single ordinance to stop this or a good reason not to. *It's always been this way* doesn't seem to fit when it's my daddy.

As if they didn't say anything worthy of disagreement, Daddy nods.

The Brothers are thin smiles, downcast eyes and murmurs.

As if they have their own way of talking, they shift for Daddy to make his way to the front of the group. He shakes hands with Mr. Jacobs. Pats his back like he's happy to see him. Then he tips his head to Mother, the girls and me. We wave good-bye like we would any other time. The Deacons march into the distance, taking Daddy along with them.

Mother bundles the girls up, leads them into the house.

"Should I come over?"

"Go home, Osira. You've done enough for one day," Mother says.

I really don't want to be alone. Not tonight. I lower my head, raise my palms in atonement. "Can I please stay with you all? I just need my family. Y'all are all I have—"

There's a click as Mother closes the front door behind her. Then the *whistle, click, grind* sound of the lock sliding into place. I walk across the street to my own home. I can feel the neighbors watching me from their luck-filled houses.

At home, I put on the kettle, set out two teacups. Daddy will want to visit when he's finished with the men. I make a quick batch of butter biscuits. While I wait, I prepare the house. A clean house yields good luck. The night before the Calling, Curdle Creekers clean their houses from roof to cellar. There's no better time than the Moving On to get rid of stuff you don't use anymore. I place a lit candle in all the windows for good luck, sweep the house free of cobwebs and bad news, sprinkle salt across thresholds and polish all of the bells in the house. There's so much to do to get ready. I wash the linen, pack away autumn clothes, air out the house, vacuum. I'm so busy cleaning and recleaning I almost miss the sound of the men shuffling back to Mother's to drop Daddy off. His shoulders are slumped. He doesn't stop over to talk like he usually does. Instead, he tips his hat in my general direction. He tries the doorknob. Before I can run out to tell him why it's locked in the first place, the door opens. Daddy steps inside but before it's closed, there's a muffled scream. The door clicks shut. The lights in Mother's house go out one at a time.

I'll finish my chores in the morning. I blow out my candles and go to bed. In the morning, the Calling will come whether I'm ready for it or not.

The Calling

The whole town is done up. There are streamers everywhere. There'd be confetti too if it hadn't clogged up the drains one year. We're all grouped up by family. Kin next to kin. Last year and the year before, I stood next to Moses's family. Now that three years have passed I'm standing with Mother, Daddy and the girls again. I was almost late, what with rehanging the curtains this morning. Daddy's sharp knock at the door nearly made me fall off the ladder. That's bad luck. But it's even worse luck to be late to the Calling. I had to take my rollers out as I ran out the door and would have forgotten to take off my apron if it wasn't for the girls snickering.

Mother ignores me for most of the way. We join the procession of families to the well for the Calling. It's almost like a picnic with the laughing and joking, kids carrying on, running in and out of clumps of people. This part is always cheerful. Stragglers rush to catch up and, because we are all one big community, we slow down so no one has to turn up last or late.

It would be awful to go to the Calling alone. Jeremiah and his wife and Mae and the good doctor join in with their respective new families in tow. Mae makes a lovely stepmother, doting on the little boy like he's her own. Curdle Creek is home. These are my people and I'm where I belong. Of course I am. No one with any good sense would even joke about leaving Curdle Creek. Whatever we need is right here, and anything we don't have, we don't need. Out-of-towners come running from miles around to get here. They're usually running away from disease intent on killing them or mobs intent on killing them. Dead is dead. We're their last chance. The only place standing in the way between whatever's chasing them and dead. Curdle Creek is *a haven*. Last-chancers call us angels—they're always making that mistake.

Strolling arm in arm, some of us are humming; some folks are even singing down Main Street. Just past the Town Hall we turn the corner off of Main Street onto the road that leads to Miller's Barn. The Calling's always been at Miller's. It sort of makes it more official. The Millers are one of the last founding families. Soon, we'll be at the well. The bell, Old Glory, strikes the Opening Call. That bell has been through more tribulations than anything in Curdle Creek. When the Great Depression hit the rest of the world, it didn't touch Curdle Creek. But that didn't stop folks from speculating on melting her down. She's still got a crack rippling through her from where the blacksmith tried to break her wide open like a walnut. She carries every scuff from a careless cleaner, holds every gong of past bell ringers. If bells could talk, Glory would spill all our secrets.

We pass by the bell chamber and there's a hush; even the children, the older ones gathering stones along the way, settle into it. We walk the last few feet in a sort of reverence, some folks thinking about supper, some about babies yet to come, others about someone they miss. I suspect we're all hoping not to be Moved On this year.

Across the street, the ushers clear away any debris and remnants from last night's wind so as not to distract from the Calling. The stage is set up, covered in bunting. We all know who the Caller is. One year, it was poor, sweet Remus. Romulus never did recover from it. Started questioning everything. Proposing ordinances to end ordinances. Crying at the well. Wailing. His name was called the very next year. He wasn't around to hear it though. This year the Caller is a girl. She's small and shaking. The wind stirs up, whipping her braids around her head, poor thing. The well will do that to you. If she lives that long, it will be a few hours before she can breathe without the fresh air burning. Before her eyes adjust to the sun.

I hear that when they come up, Callers don't recognize none of us. They say we all look like shadows creeping around on stilts. Our voices frighten them. In just a few hours, they grow accustomed to the echoes, the absence. Or maybe they get to thinking about how just last night they were tucked in their own bed hardly worried about the next day. Hoping not to see any of their family's names and then hoping a little that they do. Not a parent or child but an uncle, a second cousin, someone distant. After the mourning, they'd be a celebrity for 365 days. Everyone knows somebody who's been Moved On, but when it isn't you it is a little exciting. I don't suspect it would be any different for a Caller, especially if you didn't know you'd be in the well. You'd wake up, brush your teeth, eat if you had a stomach for it. Your parents would probably be gone before dawn, out telling tales, reminiscing like they always do the night before. You'd get a message to come down to the well in the morning. You'd wonder if it was a general message, another practice—but you'd know. Your stomach would drop. Your hands would shake. Your legs would wobble. You would know that come morning you'd be lifted up in the air, folded inside a bucket that seemed to be just your size. Maybe you'd wonder how long they knew it would be you. Maybe you'd hesitate, make them ask you twice to climb in or wait until they scooped you up, weightless. They'd remind you that it was just for a few hours. Hardly worth all that fuss. That all you needed to do was to pick through the hundreds of scraps of paper and pull up the one that *felt* right. Not worry about the name it bore. When it was all said and done and you had the right paper, you'd know it was the right one by your instincts. You should trust those. Don't bother trying to read the name for yourself. It's too dark down there and it's bad luck even if it wasn't. When they pull you up, you'd read the name. If you gathered more than one scrap of paper, even if it stuck to your hem, your hair, clung to your skin, it's included and gets considered too. You'd call all the names loud and clear so everyone could hear you on the first try. The name would spread like pox from one to the next until Mother Opal repeated the Calling to make it official.

Surely you'd ask about the lid. If they could please, please leave it open for you so you could see the sun or breathe some air. They'd say no. Unless they lied. It would be worse if they lied—if you went down an inch or two, believing, only to hear the lid rumble and slide into place. It would break your heart. You'd panic because the training does not prepare you for this, or for the smell. It smells like death. It has to, because, otherwise, it won't work. With light, it won't work. With fresh air, it won't work. The Books say so. So even if they lied, you knew it when you heard it. Maybe that's why the voices hurt when they pull you back up.

After the well gives you a name and you pull on the rope at noon—you'll know it's noon because even if you've pulled on the rope all morning, begging for them to pull you up, they won't pull you up until noon—you'll lean over to whisper the name. It's always a whisper the first time. The fresh air takes your breath away. Only Mother Opal will hear you. *Speak louder*, she'll say, and you'll cough, spit the name out like phlegm, wipe your mouth, say the name clear. You'll collapse, dirty and shaken. You won't see the Messengers, light satchels packed, backs already burdened with the weight of the news. You'll be lowered again. *Three times more, just to be sure.* By the time you've delivered the third name—if there is one— you'll be relieved to be lowered that final time, because otherwise, even from the town square, when the news has been delivered, you'd hear the wailing. The wailing always comes after Mother Opal makes the announcements. From the well, though, you will only hear muffled voices and silence. If loved ones come to spit in the well, to throw words or curses upon your head, the marshals standing guard will protect you. You will not hear the doubts questioning your honesty, the neighbors calling you names.

Later, when the wailing ends, when the Moving On have been led through town for the last time, and you have grown used to the lack of air and light, they will pull you up again. After the Moving On have been led through town, those remaining—not the family, never the family—will thank you for your wisdom, wish you a life full of luck, abundance, and years. The Sisters will lead you home.

In the morning, you'll jump. Even though we'll all be tired, spent from the Warding Off, there will be a service for you. A few words, a short prayer, a quick Warding Off, the Creek.

*   *   *

MOTHER Opal opens the ceremony with the Original Speech of the Calling. She invokes the ancestors to watch over the proceedings, to guide over us with fairness and justice. She talks about the lost places. Cities, towns, whole countries rife with war, poverty, sickness. Places so filled with spite, hate and ignorance that it bubbles, festers and overflows, contagious, spreading from one body to the next, generation to generation like a birthmark. She talks about slavery, of course, and the long toil, the centuries-long wait for freedom. The waiting feeling like a curse, another chain. The promise of it skittering and haunting. She reminds us that the Founding Fathers and Mothers did not wait to be set free. Did not hope for it. Pray for it even. They fought for it. Paid for it with blood. This land we stand on, this place we call home is the only place where a

Black man or woman can be free. Can have hope. Can have much of anything. Curdle Creek is a blessing. If not a cure for the festering, it's a relief from it, a respite. A refuge. It's as true now as it was when the ancestors declared it a hundred years ago. As necessary too.

She invites us to turn to one another. To peer into the face of our neighbor, no matter the shade of brown, and declare that person kin. To promise them safety. We're all feeling it, the tenderness of that promise. The frailty of it even here. Especially now.

By the time she finishes, the mood is somber. There's a chill in the air that's got nothing to do with the October breeze. Everyone in Curdle Creek is eligible to vote, just as we're all eligible to be nominated to be Moved On. The Deacons hand all of us, except the ones who can't read or write, one slip of paper. One coal pencil. Just like the ancestors would have used. Children, and anyone who can't write for themselves, whisper their nomination to a Deacon to jot it down for them. All of us gathered have a responsibility to vote based on our own experiences. Secondhand slights should not be considered. It's a serious moment that calls for reflection and reverence. As always, the children finish first. They are sent to gather more stones while the adults consider our selections more carefully. We have fifteen minutes to deliberate until the bell signals the end of the waiting.

The clock strikes ten. It's time to vote. By the time it gets to me, the voting box is stuffed with scraps of paper. Our whole future relies on four-by-four folded squares. I fold mine the same as everyone else's, flat, flat, over, under, tuck, tuck, seam,

seam. If it sticks out in the slightest, there's a good chance the Caller will take a special notice of it and call that name instead of another. I wish Mr. Jacobs all the luck that he deserves and stuff my vote in the box. I pass it to the left and watch Mother place her vote, then the girls. Then the box is off to another family. It takes a long time for the box to make its rounds under the watch of the Deacons. The Deacons vote before handing the box over to Mother Opal. In her hands, the battered box looks brand-new.

The box is practically bursting.

"I can feel that this year is going to be a good year for Curdle Creek!" she says. "It will be a year of plenty and a year of peace. But first, the Calling."

The lid of the well is slid across. In the well, the Caller moans even though it's only been an hour or two of dark and damp. The box is put in the bucket; the bucket is lowered. Yanked back up before she has time to scramble inside. The well is sealed again. The moaning stops.

We wait with picnic baskets and lunch boxes. Cucumber sandwiches, dollops of potato salad in good porcelain bowls, battered pork cutlets, slices of strawberry shortcake and carafes full of sweet tea make their way around the waiting crowd. I don't have an appetite for none of it. Even though it's too late to be nominated this year, I don't turn my nose up at it either. I nibble and swallow what feels like dry hunks of wood and I smile doing it.

Daddy joins us with a mug of coffee for Mother. It's sweet and sugary the way she likes it but she doesn't so much as sip it. I don't suspect she has any more of an appetite than the rest of us. Mother Opal moves through the crowd, fanning herself with her pink, embroidered special occasions fan. It's not hot but she's sweating. It's not like her to be burdened by the weather. We have plenty to share so I pour her a glass of tea and make my way to her.

"Mother Opal, can I get you anything?"

Her smile drinks me in from head to toe. "Don't you look lovely? You make quite the becoming farmer. And look at you, just reading my mind. I would just love an ice-cold glass of tea." She puts the glass to her lips, then pauses. "This tea wasn't made by your mother by any chance, was it?"

"Yes, Mother Opal, it was. Mother makes the best tea in all Curdle Creek."

"So she does." And Mother Opal turns the glass upside down, sloshing the fresh tea and a slice of lemon onto the ground. It feels like everyone has stopped talking, eating, and worrying just to watch Mother Opal do it. I just know Mother knows.

* * *

WHEN the bell rings again, it's noon. The Caller is pulled up. The well's crank is rusty so it catches every so often, sending her back down an inch or two before making up ground. Finally, the bucket reaches the mouth of the well. It takes two Deacons to help her out of the bucket but there she is, bedraggled as if she's been down there a whole month. The well will do that to a person: age you.

She uncurls her fist and holds up the first piece of paper. Reads the name.

"Sister Mildred."

Mother Opal repeats the name. It isn't really a surprise. Mildred stopped paying tithes when her firstborn was called a year and a half ago. Like he wasn't nearing fifty-five. The Mothers saw it coming; Sisters tried to warn her. But each time the collection plate passed her way, she turned her nose up, pursed her lips, held her bag tight to her chest, and refused to even hand it to the next person in line. Made a big show of it. She's stubborn like that.

Despite screaming and hollering, the Caller is lowered again. When she is brought up for the second time, her face is streaked with tears. Her braids are unraveled. Her dress is torn. Her voice is coarse. "Brother Isiah."

Mother Opal makes it official. Brother Isiah sort of got caught up in Sister Mildred's protest, saying if the good Sister could be called *and wasn't she just filled up with grief already?* it proved that whatever kept Curdle Creek going *was rotting—curdled to the core* and, like neighboring towns the world over, we should *let loose the old ways*. Of course the Caller saw Brother Isiah's name too.

Still, my heart is beating so loud I'd think Mother could hear me. She's standing stiff watching them lower the begging Caller down for a third time.

When the Caller is brought up for the third time, she is bent over. Broken. Her shoulders shake. Her tiny chest heaves. The Deacons check that there are no loose papers stuck to her. They lift her off the ground so we can see her feet: bare. Nothing stuck to them either. She opens the final piece of paper. Whispers the name. Mother Opal leans closer. Urges her to speak louder but she can't. The words will not come out again. The message is between the Caller and Mother Opal. We turn to Mother Opal to relay it.

"This will indeed be a year of prosperity for us all. The final name is Osiris Turner."

There is no mirth, no malice when she calls Daddy's name. But it feels like a cut. The crowd breaks out in congratulations and thanks. Folks are relieved. No need for them to worry. Mother Opal has already turned her back to the crowd. She's on to the business of scheduling the Moving On. Due to the inclement weather, she says, it will take place this evening and be followed the next day, as always, by the Warding Off.

I have to see the Caller. To hear my Daddy's name from her mouth. It's my right. It says it in the Books. But it's bad luck for the family to question the Caller. Though it doesn't seem like my luck or hers can get any worse, of course it can. Still, my feet move closer to her and I don't stop them. Everyone wants to touch her, to rub her skin for luck. They press close around her. They are grateful that theirs wasn't the name that fate, spirits, luck or sulfur-laced hallucinations led her to pick. They praise her, lay empty blessings at her feet. Her shoulders sink with the weight of their thanks. They chant her name, "Beth, Beth, Beth." I'm nearly there, close enough to face her. I just want to know why. What did Daddy do to make anyone nominate him? How did she pick the one scrap of paper with his name on it? Was it only one? Did she really say Osiris? Could it be me she meant to call?

My mouth moves before I make it through the crowd. She's two feet away from me. I step out to block her way. She looks up, slow, eyes unfocused, dazed. She looks through me. I'm pushed back by hands reaching for strands of her hair, scraps from her clothes, slivers of skin. The Sisters press forward, parting the crowd like stalks of corn. The Caller is lowered back into the well for the final time, for her own safety. An usher rings the bell. That's how we all know when to start. From pockets, wide skirts, hats, backpacks, air, they all pull out their bells. Some are metal, others are made of wood. Everyone has one. For one full minute, they cling and clack, rattle and ping, clang and tinkle. They look rotten, the whole lot of them. The men in their sweat-stained shirts. Women in dresses creased and plastered against skin. Children dirt-faced. Even Mother, the girls, Daddy. They stand still, except for their arms, staring forward like soldiers into the eyes of the person across from them. Each tries to out-shake the other. The damned bells ring and ring. My hand itches to but I won't pull mine out. What do I have to be thankful for?

The bells echo. They pound in my head. Louder and louder. The minute passes. Everyone faces me. No one speaks to me. I turn to leave. I have to get home. As if they can hear my thoughts, they close in on me. Their heads bob in time like they all have the same thought in it. *Get her.* They're mouthing some sort of wordless chant to a tune that I don't know. The air around me is a squeeze-box so tight I just want to get out. Their skin, breath, sweat, nails, teeth, words are everywhere I want to be.

I'm panting, trying to catch my breath, to have something to hold on to. I know it just feels like their fingers are playing piano on my skin, running up and down my spine. Really, they won't touch me until someone sounds the signal. At least, that was the rule when we were kids playing Outsider on the playground. At school, the game ends when the bell rings. Sort of. It's the bell that says playtime is over so of course the game ends then. But this isn't school. These are perfumed, powdered, sweaty bodies, stale-coffee breathed, whiskey-skinned. Their stench turns my stomach. They're too close. Someone clangs a bell in my ear. It's sharp. My nerves rattle in high C. A woman grabs my arm, shoves a tin bell in my hand. Her strong fingers clasp my wrist. She shakes and shakes. My whole hand might pop off but of course the bell rings. On the other side of me, a man with bony fingers cups my face, forces it forward. Folks line up across from me. They stare. If I look at one of them, they will forgive me. I close my eyes. The bell keeps ringing.

It should be one of them. One of these lying, sinning, luck-grabbing banshees that had something to do with Daddy's name being called when it wasn't even his turn. It should be any one of them. Mother Rogers is always grinning about something—why not her? We could all use a rest from her under-her-breath gossip. If that's too spiteful for comfort, what about Brother Simpson? I don't see why not. He's always touching and feeling on folks. A close-talker, leaner-in like him could be called and who would complain? I sure wouldn't. If not him, what about one of *them*? One of the triplets wouldn't be missed. Everyone says they all look alike. What difference would one less make?

I sound like one of them: infected. Ready to throw in my lot with theirs just like a second-chancer. Even worse, I sound

like a non-believer. One of those lost souls thinking the old
ways don't fit this *new world*. Desperate for change soon as
their names are called. To be fair, they call for changes before
that, but out of politeness we pretend not to hear, so out of
politeness they call even louder. The louder they call, the more
certain it is that the Caller will see their name when the time
comes. It's like fate. There's no room for a non-believer. Not in
Curdle Creek, and, to hear the last-chancers and the Council
tell it, not anywhere else in the whole world either. I don't
care. I'd rather be anywhere else than here.

But the melody is so lovely, so freeing. It's like honey pouring in wounds I didn't know I had. Like there, that hurt when
I breathe, and there behind my heart, and there, there, there.
It's like balm settling like skin on water. I'm where I belong.
We're all ringing in time. It's the rhythm of Curdle Creek.
It moves everything. I just needed to be reminded. Now, my
heart beats in time. My breathing falls in line. We're all doing
it, *breathe in, breathe out, breathe in, breathe*. It wasn't a mis-
take. The well decided. The Caller called his name. Mother
Opal confirmed the announcement. Daddy's Moving On.

The ringing is louder. The woman drops my wrist. My
whole body shakes. My hand convulses around the bell. I can't
set it loose. This must be the Hallelujah. I've played Catching
the Spirit before but I couldn't have known that the truth
would feel so right, so pure. My daddy is sacrificing for the
town, for the whole world even. Could anything be so beautiful, so painfully sweet? They must all see it now, my holiness.
I feel it bubbling, the blessing moving through me. I must
anoint them, my flock, the first witnesses.

The words feel old inside my mouth. I can't stop them. *"One by one before it's done. Two by two until it's through. Three by three just wait and see! More and more will grace death's door!"* My body heaves, unburdened. It—because I would have never done anything like this—wails and sobs. I'm overcome. The ancestors have given me a message. The Moving On must stop tonight. Who would have imagined? Me, the bearer of salvation. Mae will be so jealous. I can almost see her now, writhing on the ground, moaning. It would be just like her to foam at the mouth if she could. Not even a Mother yet and I'm chosen by the ancestors. Folks closest to me lean in, watching my mouth, trying to catch the words before they fall. They will write my name in Book I for anointings. My name will never be called. Mother and the girls will have years of pass-me-down luck. Jasmine, Cheyenne, and Little Moses can come back home, Romulus too. Daddy won't be Moved On after all. I'll be a saint. There's no ordinance about it, but that's just because Curdle Creek hasn't had a saint before now.

I look around to tell Mother Opal. I see her slipping through the crowd, Mother's close behind her. "Mother Opal! Mother!" I call. They both slow for a moment; Mother looks over her shoulder. Neither stops. Mother Opal is walking faster; now she's running. So is Mother. Daddy gathers the girls, the crowd disperses. Everyone leaves to prepare for the Moving On.

Reason

It can't be more than five minutes later and I'm standing in front of Reason feeling like I'm about to throw up. My legs and stomach are seized *tight as a widow's knickers.*

Mother Opal's is one of the only houses left in Curdle Creek with its own name. Reason. Like everything we do is for her and this house. A pink and white Victorian house shouldn't make your heart stop but it does. Just looking at it makes my mouth dry up. Nobody should have a house this grand, not even the Head Charter Mother. Whoever heard of a house with three floors, four if you count the cellar, five with the attic, a bathroom on each one, a kitchen, and a whole other house beneath it, all for one person? She could run up one set of stairs and slide down another. Between the passageways behind the cupboard, the hidden crawl space beneath the cellar, the back room in the attic, a person could disappear. Never be seen again. Eight bedrooms. No children. No living husband. What does one person do with all this house? I know what I'd do. I'd open the whole thing up to any last-chancer who made it past the Curdle Creek sign. Anyone running from a pack of wolves, dogs or men could have a safe place to stay the night. As long as they didn't come bearing plague again.

I steady my breathing, run up the steps and bang on the front door. It's not really the front door, it's the door to the front porch. Nobody touches Mother Opal's actual front door. They don't usually need to. She says she knows who's out front before they even know they're on the way there. She sees things. Nothing much goes on in Curdle Creek that Mother Opal doesn't know about. It wasn't more than two months ago that everyone except Mother Opal had one of them tinkling, off-key bells to announce company. As soon as Mother Opal said she could see why some people needed them, since *not everyone had the gift of common sense*, the Charter Mothers started not needing them either.

Mother's always trying to out-mother Mother Opal. If I had a nickel for every time she had me sneak out back and snake around to the front of the house to peek at who was on the porch so she could call out *So-and-so, I knew you were coming!* I'd have a handful of nickels to throw at one of the sunporch windows to get Mother Opal's attention right now. I wouldn't even need to break the glass; just a sharp knock would bring her running. I don't have a nickel and I wouldn't dare throw it if I did. There's no telling how long the apology would take and I don't have that much time. There I'd be mid-apology and the phone would ring. Everyone would pick it up, of course, even though it would be for Mother Opal and they'd know it by the high-pitched beeps the line makes when the call's for her. They're nosy though so they'd pick up too. Someone—probably not one of the Deacons, they'd be too ashamed; the wife of one most likely, someone who couldn't wait to get in a good word with Mother Opal and against Mother—would be telling her that I've had a message before I could tell her myself and wasn't it a coincidence that the ancestors chose me to end the Moving On the year my father's name was called? How could I be trusted? By the time she got off the phone, there would be no use in apologizing about the window or anything else. My whole family would be damned, and Mother would blame me and that window.

I wait to hear her shuffling footsteps, a creaking door, a whining floorboard. I know she's in there. Mother too. I followed them even though I couldn't hardly keep up with them. I listen for the sounds of a full house. Teakettle whistling, oven door opening and closing, a friendly *Come in!* Instead, there are birds singing. Bees buzzing. Even with my ear pressed to a window, I can't hear anything inside. Soon, one of her nosy neighbors will come out, asking me what happened to my good sense? The knocking doesn't do much of anything except echo in my ears. I expect the wood to splinter. The door to shatter. It doesn't. If anything, that old mahogany door swallows up all the sound. If Mother Opal really is just like everybody else, the door isn't locked. I could walk right in.

I scan the neighbors' windows. Even though everyone's busy having an early supper to ward off hunger, I'm sure someone's peering back. I look to the house across the street. The curtain flutters. I can't stop myself: I'm cracking my knuckles.

I'm nervous. Just this once can't hurt. The pops are satisfying, like extra puffs of air. My hands still shake. I close my eyes, hold my breath to twist the knob. Of course it's locked. I'd keep my door locked too if I was in charge of deciding who lived and who didn't. I almost hear her correcting me: *I don't decide. I declare. Fate does the deciding; the Caller calls the name. I amplify their voice.* Mother Opal considers herself the bearer of the news, not the maker of it. Still, if I was her, I wouldn't trust a soul in Curdle Creek, living or dead.

I knock again. Wait a few minutes. My foot's tapping. I don't have much more time. I'm going to have to do it. I press my knuckles against the closest window. It's cool against my skin. Clear as ice. Imagine how much they would have cost. The town paid for them, *Least they could do for all she's done for them.* Mother Opal's is the only house with a full porch made of windows. No wonder she can see the future. She can just sit on the front porch and watch the whole town if she wants to. Today, the blinds are closed tight. Not an ounce of daylight can squeeze its way in without Mother Opal's permission.

I rap on the window hard. It seems like the whole thing rattles. I can't afford to pay for broken glass. I'll try around back.

At the back of the house I run my fingers along the iron fence the way I used to do when I was a kid. I'm a grown woman and the fence is still taller than I am. It's high enough to make you think twice before trying to jump over it, but not too high to keep someone out who has a mind to it. What would it look like if I tried to jump over it still dressed from the Calling, lipstick probably smeared across my face, nails chipped, curls heavy with sweat? Years ago, I'd sail over it like I was ten, fresh from ordinance recital practice, impatient to show off what I'd learned. Now, I'll probably only make it halfway over. I'll be stuck with one leg on this side, the other dangling in the garden, skirt hitched up, snagged on one of those gilded iron leaves poking out the top of the fence until someone, probably Mother, comes along to rescue me. The thought alone makes me cold. Mother would kill me.

I walk around the house. The side gate is always unlatched anyway. Today, it's wide open, swinging. I close it behind me. It'd be rude not to. I don't bother going up the back steps and knocking on the door. If she didn't answer the front door, she won't answer the back one. She must get tired of daughters, sons, mothers, fathers, sisters, tired of all of that begging her to find another way, choose another neighbor, spare them that much longer. Just selfish.

There's a breeze whipping up. I know that's not why I'm shivering, though. Everyone in Curdle Creek knows, if your name is called, more often than not family had something to do with it. You might be paying for something they did or something they didn't do years before you were even born. Family. I sure wish I were an only child.

I stroll past the rosebushes, one for each of Mother Opal's dead husbands, across the cobbled path, and head for the cellar door. I wait for a minute, half expecting her to call down from the kitchen porch, inviting me in like I'm just here for tea and a biscuit or two. I smell it first: rain. I love the way it fills the air. I imagine it's going to put out the fires for miles around, scatter people like secrets. Maybe, if it rains hard enough, the

Moving On will be canceled. The earth will swell with water, the crops will burst with seeds, the animals will breed. The town will flourish. The Moving On could be skipped, set aside for at least another year.

It would take a flood for that to happen. I need a sign. I'm leaning against the door waiting for one. When it comes, it comes as hot rain. The drops are full and thick, full of spite. Each splash seems to make its own puddle. It's pouring. The sky is cracked wide open. Rain falls and falls and falls. My clothes stick to my body, making me look bloated and misshapen. I feel heavy. If it keeps raining like this, the Creek might overflow, flood the whole town, and me and my clothes would sink. It's the lightning that makes up my mind for me, and the thunder. The whole world, or at least the whole yard, fills with thunder and I jump. The boom roars longer than it should, rattling across the sky. I push against the door; it's bloating and damp and doesn't want to open. I push it with both hands. There's a sharp crack. I'm in.

I'm holding my breath. I've never been inside Mother Opal's house uninvited. It feels different without a welcome. It's darker in the house than it is out of it but I close the door behind me anyway. There are worse things to be scared of than the dark. "Mother Opal?" I call. I whisper but I may as well be shouting. I shouldn't be here. But if they hadn't chosen Daddy, if she hadn't let them, I wouldn't have to be. If she's upstairs, she won't be able to hear me call anyway, but I don't want to pop out of her kitchen unannounced. If I move a few boxes and chairs along the way, maybe that will let her know I'm in the cellar and heading up. That way she'll have time to get decent if she isn't already. She wouldn't know it was me, though, would she? Well, if she can really see the future she will. But, if she can't, I could stop her heart or something if I scare her.

I'll call her when I get to the top of the cupboard stairs. I know the cellar enough to feel my way around. I don't need to light a candle. When we were kids, me and Mae would play down here while our mothers met above. When we were older, we had lessons in the front room. Piano, reading, Warding Off. Then, when we were older still, the ordinances.

There are stacks of boxes lined up everywhere. Most of them are Mother Opal's dead husbands'. *Stuff they couldn't take with them though they tried*, according to her. Boxes of clothes, shoes, coats. I don't see why she couldn't keep them upstairs for the next one but she said most new men don't want to wear old clothes. So each time a husband Moved On that Father Opal's clothes came down here. It's a museum for departed men.

I'm just through the '50s aisle. That Father Opal didn't last long. They weren't married two years when it was his time to Move On. Mother Opal has to be the unluckiest woman in all of Curdle Creek. All of her husbands get called sooner or later. I walk through Memory Lane: the row of couches, bureaus, tables, chests and lamps Mother Opal or past Mothers didn't have space for. I'm at the door to the stairs. With my fingertips I feel my way up the stone walls. At the top of the stairs, I press my fingers against the tip of one panel and the bottom of the other. Like witchcraft, they slide open just enough for me to slip through. Mother Opal keeps this cupboard filled with cleaning supplies. *If you want to hide something*, Mother Opal always says, *hide it behind a mop.*

I'm inside the cupboard, keeping company with overused things. A straw-haired broom and corn-husk mop guard the door in a giant cross. I would knock but she's liable to think it's one of her dead husbands come to complain about being called, or the ghost of some departed Mother wanting her Council seat back. It could be a burglar but I don't think that would scare her as much as a visit from the grave would. It would mean the Warding Off didn't stick. Whatever makes its way back after being Warded Off the first time is up to no good. Damp, pine, bleach and fresh air. I try not to breathe. The gap beneath the door is like a mouth breathing in air and breathing out sound. Mother Opal always said she could tell the weather just from standing in front of the cupboard door. Turns out you can hear it from in here too. I wonder if she knows that.

"Why would it be his time now? I told you I would do it when the time was right." From where I'm standing, it sounds like Mother. I can tell she's angry because she's doing that pretend whisper. The one that sounds like hot, spitty words and deep breaths. If it were anyone else but me, they'd say her eyes were glowing, smoke streaming from her mouth, her fingertips on fire. They would say it behind her back the way they do when they say she's some sort of evil spirit. Like it's her fault her first husband Moved On before his time. She's not a spirit. She's just Mother. Somehow she's caught Mother Opal's bad luck.

"His name was called," Mother Opal says. I can tell from her voice that she doesn't have her teeth in. Her words are sticky and slow, like she wasn't expecting company, or not expecting to be caught by company. This is an emergency but, as Mother Opal would say, *An emergency ain't an emergency for all of us.* Maybe because they were friends, Mother's pain is Mother Opal's too. It wouldn't have been right to have Mother waiting on the steps while she fixed her hair, popped in her teeth, put on her grief hat. "We put the Caller in the well same as we do for every Moving On. No one knows who's been nominated or what name's on the paper before it's called." She's using Mother's *there-there* tone.

"How do we know it was his name? Nobody heard it but you."

"That doesn't make it less real."

"Says who?"

"It was good enough last year when it was Jude's time. And the year before that, when it was . . ." She pauses. A chair scraping the floor, the pucker of the icebox lid, cracking of ice, breathing. Then the pop of a cap, the *ahhhh* of the fizz, the swallowing of words. That year was Jeremiah's father. Things haven't been the same at his house since. No lights on, even though the whole town has electricity. No running water, no nothing. His mother says she don't want nothing more to do with *this backward town and its hard-earned evil.* If they can't grow or make it, she doesn't want it. I'm not supposed to go over there anymore. No one is. The Council decreed her officially shunned and the shunning does not include popping over for biscuits no matter how good they are or her homemade punch no matter how much rum she puts in it. Since I lost Moses, though, Mother Adelaide and I have a lot to talk about, even if I do have to slip in like a ghost in the middle of the night to do it.

My heart is racing. It's *boom, boom, boom*ing in my head, making me dizzy. I close my eyes and mouth soothing words to calm my spirit. *My mind is steady, life complete, trust the land beneath your feet.* If Mother finds out I'm here, she'll burst from the shame of it. Her own daughter breaking into people's homes, slithering and slipping through their houses just to eavesdrop would be bad enough. Claiming to have a message from the ancestors would be too much for her to bear. Mother might disown me. Erase me right from the family book like she did Romulus. Mother Opal could hardly intervene twice. I'll be erased, disremembered. It'll be almost as bad as the shunning that will surely come with it.

I'll get to keep the house. Even if the land's the town's, Moses and I built it, so by rights it's still mine. But what good will it do, with the whole town pretending I don't exist? They'll mark my mail *Return to Sender*, not that it will be anything but bills. Nobody writes to the erased. I'll have to shop after hours to avoid the embarrassment of being served last no matter who arrives after me or, even worse, have to go to the *only* entrance around back like Mother Adelaide, as if my money is no longer good enough even to spend.

No, if Mother knew I was here, she'd have opened the door by now, flung it open with an *Aha!* worthy of a classic Curdle Creek detective film. Mother Opal must know I'm here. She must be wondering why I'm waiting like a thief.

"Let me see the box!" The tone of Mother's voice snaps me back to the cupboard. It's so sharp that I almost jump. No one but Mother Opal sees the box, Mother knows that. All that history, years of names, dates and notes. It would be dangerous for anyone other than Mother Opal to have it. Someone with less sense than her would start looking for patterns where none existed. It says so in Book II.

"In my house—" Mother Opal begins.

Crackkkkkkk. The sound of a hand against skin silences her. Even my heart stops. If my mother hit Mother Opal, surely she'll die right now. Lightning will strike them both. It might hit me too by accident. *Please don't strike me down, please don't strike me down, please don't.* I don't say the words out loud but God and the ancestors can hear me. I know, cuz I'm still standing. There's shuffling and tussling and sobbing. They speak in grunts and moans, finishing each other's sentences, answering each other's silences. It's like hearing two sisters fighting and making up. I shouldn't be here. By rights, I should be running to gather the Council together. But if I do that, Mother will be gone just as sure as Daddy. I'll be a forty-five-year-old orphan. There would be no waiting for the Moving On. A special ceremony would be called. Mother would be Moved On by sunset, with the first blow dealt by the offended Charter Mother. Even then, with the debt paid, the criminal's family could be sure to inherit at least a generation of bad luck. Mother's just damned our whole family. Now we're double cursed. Maybe triple.

There's no one for me to tell. It's not like Mother Opal needs me to tell her what Mother's done, and Mother would be the second in line to be told. There's no sense in getting involved. Nothing good can come of it. Mother will fix this herself. She'll make it up to Mother Opal, do right by Curdle Creek and the family.

I slip out the way I came, travel backward through the cellar. I close the gate. I take the long way home. Someone else can tell Mother Opal about my blessings. Mother will intervene for Daddy. Mother Opal will recall the Calling. *Just because it ain't never been done before, don't mean it can't be undone now.* Besides, there may be a way to fix everything before they even need to know. "Spirits of Curdle Creek," I say. I can't stand on my tiptoes in the middle of the street so I whisper in case somebody's watching. "Spirits of Curdle Creek, please make everything all right." I don't say what *all right* means. Who am I to interpret for spirits who know better than I do? There I go, sounding just like Mother Opal again.

The Sign

I'm wandering around town and all I see is ghosts. I walk from Reason, by the library, down Main Street past the Town Hall, Grammercy and Carter's. I slow down and force myself to breathe slow. No sense hyperventilating so early in the evening. I slow down even more at Fleming's. There's no music coming from inside the shop. Its shutters are closed. All the shops are. Everything's shut tight until after the Warding Off. It wouldn't be fair for folks to have to miss it on account of needing to work, and it just wouldn't be proper to have folks running through town disturbing customers. Business can wait until after the Warding Off.

Still, I'm at Fleming's Keys and Keys Music Shoppe and Locksmith, jiggling the doorknob the way the boys and I used to do when we were kids. Romulus, Remus and me were closer than three believers in a cape. We did everything together. Even though they were twins, they didn't leave me out of nothing. Not that I would have let them. Just one year older, they got to do everything just that little bit before me. They'd let me tag along even when folks warned against it.

* * *

I'M rattling the doorknob but, looking down, it's Remus's young brown hand that I see.

"Let's hurry inside," he's saying. "So no one sees us." His face is large brown eyes, big grin and life.

"We should have just gone in around the back and climbed through the window. Wouldn't nobody see us." Romulus keeps careful watch. "Maybe we shouldn't do it. If Mother finds out—"

"Get out of the way," little me says. I push past the two of them to make my way inside. The shop is filled with music. It's coming from inside the back room and all around us. We're surrounded by trumpets, trombones, pianos, organs, drums, flutes, clarinets, a harpsichord and music stands of all shapes and sizes. There are stacks of music sheets and books scattered on the chairs, piano benches and instrument cases. I lose the boys, who are pretending to play instruments too big for them to carry. I walk up to the counter to see the handmade violin Fleming keeps in its case behind the glass.

It's beautiful. One day, I tell myself, it will be mine. I don't mean to but my fingers are pressed against the glass and then on top of the counter and then inside. The case is in my hands and if it weren't for its intricate little lock it would be open and I'd be plucking the violin's strings till I yanked a tune out of them.

"Your parents know you're here?" Fleming asks.

He puts out his hand for the violin. I run my fingers along the case then wipe the streaks and smears they leave behind with the cloth Fleming gives me to do it. He's shorter than Daddy but sort of takes up more space. I have to look up at him when he talks. His denims are hitched up by his favorite suspenders, the plaid ones with musical notes going up and down them like a song.

"No, sir, they do not."

He smiles. "Good, then it's time for your lesson."

Fleming flips the sign on the door from *Open* to *Closed*, pulls down the shutters and draws the curtains, and for the next hour the boys and I take turns practicing scales the way Fleming's been trying to teach us to for months. We're getting better at it. One day we'd be good enough for a concert if we wouldn't get in so much trouble for being here in the first place. Mother and Daddy don't approve of Fleming. He's always singing, writing and playing music, cavorting with his wife, Charlie Ann. She makes the best sweet potato pies in all Curdle Creek, but that doesn't stop folks from whispering about the two of them.

"You should be on the road, playing for a big band, traveling around the world," Romulus says. He's been banging out the Curdle Creek anthem and this time it sounds recognizable. "You have a gift."

"Folks from Curdle Creek do not go on the road. My gift is *teaching* music, not *playing* it."

"That's not true," I say. "Didn't we hear you playing before we came in?"

"Please don't spread rumors like that." Fleming stands up,

snaps the piano lid closed, pushes out the bench. It scrapes against the floor but he doesn't mention it. "It's time for you all to go. I need to tune all of these instruments. The band needs them for tomorrow. I can't keep them waiting."

Fleming works so hard for the town. Music makes him happy. If Mother knew how happy it made him, she'd speak to the Council and get him put into the band. Maybe he'd end up directing it. I talk to Mother about it as soon as the boys and I get home. She agrees. Fleming would be happier if there was a change and she has an idea of what that change could be. She'll talk to Mother Opal and the Council about it. Just leave everything to her.

Charlie Ann's name is called the next day. There's been no music in Fleming's ever since.

*　*　*

I let go of the knob and walk away. I won't bother Fleming with my burdens. I could call on Mae or Jeremiah. There's no reason not to. No ordinance against visiting before the Moving On. As a widow and now a daughter of a soon-to-be Moved On, it would be bad luck for me to be turned away on the evening of their nuptials. But we're friends, and friends take risks with luck from time to time. If anyone would understand how I feel, it'd be them.

But they are honeymooners first. Any conversation with the two of them would turn into a discussion with the four of them and, even though I know the good doctor and Florence too, that don't make us friends.

If I go home I can at least be with Daddy, but I wouldn't

know what to say to him. The more I think on it, the less certain I am the message came from the ancestors. *One by one before it's done. Two by two until it's through. Three by three just wait and see! More and more will grace death's door!* It could have been just wishful thinking. Ending the Moving On would ruin us. Wouldn't be long before we turned against one another, seeing danger everywhere, in everyone. We wouldn't be no better than anyplace else. Curdle Creek wouldn't feel like home. Wouldn't none of us belong to it. If I'm wishing on an end to Curdle Creek, I'm not the true believer I thought I was. I can't admit I have doubts so close to his Moving On. That would be wrong. What Daddy needs right now is a plan. Preparing for the Moving On is everyone's responsibility. If it's going to go ahead, it's meant to be, and if something or someone intervenes, that was meant to be too.

The mist is thick like fog. I keep walking to the end of Main, turn right and I'm on the overgrown path heading to the Curdle Creek sign.

The counter whirs like a clock and I settle down on the back ledge hidden by tall grass. Other than a few kids, the occasional lovers and the official counter, no one really visits the Curdle Creek sign. It's tall and wide, a wooden billboard with a new-fangled counter in the right corner. The scrolling is automatic, connected to a device managed by the counter that ticks after each birth, death or Moving On.

When the children left there was an uproar. "Three Curdle Creekers Abscond in the Dark of Night," the headlines read. For weeks, the editor of the *Curdle Creek Gazette* interviewed former friends, neighbors, teachers, employers, lovers. Wasn't a soul alive they didn't talk to about the children, Moses or me. Everyone gave an interview too.

The party line was the worst. The whirring of the counter waiting to tick over sounds like the Curdle Creek gossipers. Couldn't pick up the phone without overhearing folks speculating.

"I heard the Deacons found them three towns over. Dragged each of them back for a special Moving On, bless them."

Followed by gasps or cackling.

"Serves them right."

"Where do you think they run off to?"

"Somewhere that's making them wish they were right here."

Cackling.

"Osira, is that you?"

To this day I won't pick up the party line without saying "Osira here," so folks at least have a chance to consider what they're about to say before I hear it.

Residents wanted the counter to reflect the leaving. The timers said that was the way it'd always been done and that was the way it should be done now. The counter was sent out. Deducted three, *tick, tick, tick*, and went on his way. The nonbelievers said since they hadn't been Moved On and could not be counted as dead without proof, they should be counted as still here, with the number reflecting the population before they left. The counter was sent out. The three were added again.

Moses disagreed. "Take them off and leave it there. They're as good as Moved On." But as good as Moved On is not

Moved On. I wanted the numbers to stay. Maybe it let me think that one day the children might come back, one day they'd be forgiven.

"They will be Moved On in absentia," the Council declared. Three effigies were created, one for each of the children. They dressed them in their clothes so that Jasmine's wore a pretty teal dress and roller skates, Cheyenne's wore a pleated pant-suit with sensible shoes, and Moses's wore the zoot suit his great-grandfather wore on his first day as a lawyer. They even collected yarn to use for hair. They hauled them all through town like they would do if they were Moving On. Did the Warding Off too. I wanted to stay home. My stomach couldn't take it. I couldn't keep anything down. Moses made me go. Threatened to tell the Council that I put the kids up to it. Me and my hand-me-down stories about Well Walkers.

After the Moving On, the sign was corrected again. *Curdle Creek, Population 199.*

* * *

THE fog is thick. I've been in it for hours. Mother must be worried. I make my way back to the path, ready to turn onto Main. Sweat and humidity drip down my face, my arms; my blouse blooms with it. The Sisters swoop in. They sidestep the puddles, gather me in strong, bony arms and push me into the car.

"I'm on my way home for the Moving On," I say. I smile to prove it. "Don't want to be late."

A wannabe Mother purses her lips at me. She shakes her head. Makes the sign of the holy bells.

"Only the wicked would rejoice at a time like this," one of them says.

Mindful of the advice, I purse my lips too. There's no sense in explaining it to them. I keep my silence to myself. I'll leave them to make up stories about how they had to drag me back home to make me participate in my own father's Moving On. How ungrateful I am. How far I've fallen from the believer I once was. We're puffing our way toward my street. Mother will surely hear the loud pops and groans as the Sisters' "hooded beast" shifts gears, making its way up Pleasant Mills as if the house is on the top of a hill it can hardly be expected to climb. The car will sputter up the gentle slope, gears slipping, tires spinning every so often for no reason at all. If there's any luck in the sky, we'll at least get stuck at the red light. It's always red. As the only traffic light in Curdle Creek, red was as good a color as any.

There are only four cars in Curdle Creek. This one is wagon-like and too long. The seats are hard perches good for the bursts of spontaneous worship the Mothers-to-be are often guilty of. They catch the spirit like it's a cold flowing from one to the next until they are all burning with love for Curdle Creek. Bugs and air hit my face. I do not complain. I know not to mistake this ride for goodwill. The top is down so they don't catch something in case bad luck's contagious. Even if the top were up, everyone would still know I was inside. Everybody knows when the Sisters take you home. They broadcast it on the AM radio then print it in the *Creek News* under "Creaks" so everyone knows it's gossip and not to read it expecting verified facts. That keeps them from being accused of printing stories and not news again—and keeps folks from hounding them for retractions they won't print anyway.

There's no speed limit in town, and if there were, the Sisters wouldn't follow it. Everything is an emergency when you're one good deed away from being a Charter Mother. We hit every bump. My body lurches and slides across the bench between them, pushing up against one then the other. Try as they might to move out of the way, my arm brushes against one's chest and she hisses like a mourning balloon letting out air. I dig my nails into the hard leather cushion, tuck my feet under the front seat, sit straight and play coffin bride in my head. I sit stiff as day-old bread.

We glide down Main and, too quick, we're turning onto Pleasant Mills. Pebbles ping beneath the car, popping like corn kernels. The Sisters must be used to it by now. All streets lead to Main and they all, except for Main and one quarter of Pleasant Mills, are dirt roads. The timers say *Country roads know the way home*. The idea of changing anything gets them riled up. It was hard enough to get the town to agree to have Main paved. Folks hemmed and hawed so long I thought for sure the answer would be no. But then the Charter Mothers started scroll reading and deed searching and the paving started as soon as somebody could be trained to do it.

It would have been faster if they'd brought someone in from out of town. One of the ushers recommended that very thing. *Do you have spare luck to share?* This was the timers' favorite question. They rolled it out every chance they got. Sometimes, they posed it even when it wasn't true. There's plenty of luck to go around. Just not all of it's good. Luck had nothing to do with the cleansing of '44. Our best plumbers can only be in one place at a time, which was fine until the pipe backed up, spewing *Lord have mercy*s all over the town square. Of course, some of the children thought it was a chocolate fountain. That only added to the emergency. An outsider was brought in to create a sewage system. A more complex and reliable puzzle of pipes. Soon, every house had its very own toilet indoors. That man never did leave. I'm just as happy about it as anybody but someone's got to do something about that Creek.

There's a bang and a pop. The windscreen could crack wide open any moment, but of course it doesn't. It's Mother. She's at the side, tapping on the door. Sister Two springs it open. I'm not even sure we've stopped fully when I'm pushed out. The door bangs shut behind me. They didn't even bother to stop the car.

"I was on my way," I say.

The tires kick up dust. With a screech, the Sisters pull away. I've thrown them off their schedule. They aren't meant to visit until after we're prepared to receive them. It's bad luck, like seeing the bride before the wedding or saying *I love you* before your name's called. There's no time for foolishness like bringing home wayward girls. They'll have to steal time from somewhere else to make up for this.

I tense my body for the slap and rush the words out so at least they'll be the last thing she hears before she strikes. "I was blessed or I was cursed, I'm not sure which, but I know the Moving On has to end. The ancestors said so or I think they did and it's not because Daddy's name's been called. It's not because I can't stand to lose one more person to that Creek.

It's not because it's not fair even if it isn't." My words are muffled into Mother's chest.

She's hugging, squeezing me tight right here at the gate in
full view of anyone watching. She hasn't held me like this in
years. I can't move my arms to hug her back so I mouth *I love
you* onto her skin. I feel her heart stop, start again.

"Mother Opal died," she whispers. "This changes everything."

Moving On

Mother Opal's death changes nothing, and nor does my visitation, if that's what it was. The Charter Mothers decree that Mother Opal's rulings during her tenure were true and just and that there is nothing gained from delaying the Moving On to investigate further. The Moving On will take place just like it always will, tonight.

The Messenger wears three wigs, one for each Council member, to deliver the news. Daddy's hands tremble, tinkling the cup against the saucer in his hand. Mother paces back and forth, asking the Messenger questions she does not have answers to.

"Which one of you decided this?"

The Messenger looks to her notes. There is no information about who declared that the ritual would take precedence. She shrugs, as indignant as she would be if she were a Charter Mother. "I do not need to answer that," she says. Lines spent, she turns to go. "If there is nothing else—"

"Why wasn't I consulted about this before it was voted upon?"

The Messenger shrugs again. Wraps all three shawls around her shoulders. Gathers her bag. "You will be pleased to know," she says, repeating the line from earlier, "that you have been nominated as the new Head Charter Mother according to Book V on Emergency Situations. You will assume your post immediately after the Warding Off. We look forward to working with you in this new capacity."

The Messenger tips her church hat prop and is on her way. I tip her again on the way out.

Daddy sets down the trembling cup. He hasn't taken a sip anyway.

"Would you like some more tea?"

"No, but thank you."

"Is there anything I can do?"

"You can help me pack," he says. "That'll free me to say my goodbyes. I'd like to say them now instead of—" His voice breaks. "I won't be able to say them during the Moving On."

Daddy wraps his fingers around mine. His palms are rough, his fingers warm. He's not the only one shaking. He must be wondering what he could have done, who he could have offended. How unlikely this thing called luck is.

He's already up the top of the stairs by the time I shut the door. I'm not supposed to, but I lock it. The Deacons will be gathering outside, lined up, heads bowed.

"It isn't fair," Mother says as the latch clicks.

The windows are closed, curtains drawn. It's dark. Heat's trapped up with nowhere to go. It feels as though the whole place is going to crack open. Daddy doesn't answer her. He tells the girls and me to gather around in a circle. We hold hands. Hum the family song. Before we're even at the chorus there's a knock at the front door. Dread and them don't usually knock.

"Looks like we'll have to put off that packing for some other time," Daddy says.

We drop hands.

"Just go out the back! Go out the back! Who would see you?"

Daddy looks at Mariah and Rumor. They're swinging hands and singing, "We would! We would!"

"Don't pay them any mind, they're babies!" Mother's practically yelling.

I've never seen her this way before. I almost want to close my eyes but I need to witness in case there's a trial. She's standing between Daddy and the door, blocking his path. It's a *violation*, surely. It's either in Book XIII or Book XXII. Unless it's even worse. If it's *impeding*, it'll be in Book VIII. If that's the case and I have to swear hand on heart at Town Hall, she'll be called to take his place unless she's Moved On with him.

Daddy turns to me. I stand straight. My mouth's so dry I don't think words would come out even if I knew what to say. Mother is *courting chaos* and *conspiring to seduce into temptation*. Breaking two ordinances in one throw. There are whole books dedicated to it. Papers written about it. Pastor led a sermon about this very thing, temptation. It's a thou-shall-not-er. I step back in case the girls—in the telling of the version they choose to tell on the stand—put the words in my mouth instead of Mother's.

I should have tried to save my brothers; Moses too. I should have done something. I kept quiet then. I'll keep quiet now too. "I wouldn't see a thing," I whisper. I close my eyes to show that I mean it. Mother's offering him a way out. Please let him take this way out.

"Constance, you know better than any of us that if I run out that back door you'll be bound to tell them which way I went. What would you say? That you don't know? Didn't see me? You're a Charter Mother, woman. What would that look like? Anyone called to lead the town at least has to follow its rules."

"You aren't going to be here anyway. I'll be all alone!" Mother's crying. Her chest heaves. Her words come out broken. I don't think I've ever seen her cry before. Her lips are twisted upward in a painful-looking smile, her eyes squeezed shut, her cheeks puffed out; red patches grow beneath her otherwise smooth brown skin. She looks unnatural, close to popping. I don't ever want to see her look like this again.

"Forgive her, she knows not what she speaks." I whisper the apology on her behalf. "Her mouth is full with the tongues of grief." I hold my breath for sixty seconds. They don't have clocks in Heaven, Hell, or wherever the ancestors are, so a one-minute apology will have to do. I skip ahead. "Humble, most honorable, all-knowing and all-seeing Mothers of Curdle Creek, her head is firm but her heart is swollen. Please give Mother the strength to endure without question, or to question and find a way to endure. Amen." If it reaches them, there's no harm in asking a favor, is there? "And please, in the spirit of mercy and the thanks that is my birthright as a citizen of this land, follower of ways, believer in traditions, etcetera, etcetera, please grant Daddy luck everlasting, life abundant and time enough to die from old age. Please keep him from the Moving On."

"When we got married you told me if it came down to this town or me, I wouldn't stand a chance. You swore an oath. Took a vow."

I want her to deny it. To tell him it's not too late, to beg him to ask her now so she can declare her intention to leave. Black folks ain't safe anywhere but here. Beyond Curdle Creek it ain't nothing but lawlessness and running. Always running. It's awful. Fires flaring up. Homes combusting. Air thick with smoke. Floods. Locusts. It's like the End of Days, they say. It was prophesied. We're safer here. But maybe *safer* isn't *safe*. If we all leave together, at least there's no one left to pay for us. At least we'll be together. Maybe then we can find my children.

My heart's beating loud. It's in my head, my fingers. Everywhere. I cover my mouth to keep from screaming *Say it!* If she's going to say it, it has to be her choice. Otherwise I'm inciting her to commit blasphemy. It would be almost worse than getting Rumor to take the town's name in vain again.

Mother says nothing. She looks at me, at the girls, back at Daddy.

Daddy nods. He's right, but doesn't look smug about it. He hugs her. It's all right since even if they are both Moved On they won't be buried together. Mother will be buried next to her new or last husband. If there is one. Daddy will be buried in the same plot, though. He'll just be beside the husband after him. So a *till-death-do-us-part* hug now won't cause any harm. He squeezes the girls. They both wriggle and complain. They can't wait to go and gather more stones with their friends. They whine that it isn't fair. Their friends will have more time than they do. They'll get all the good rocks, the black ones with jagged edges. Daddy kisses me on the forehead. His lips are chapped. I try not to focus on them. I couldn't stand for my every memory of him to be tainted with the image of his lips dry and puckering, wanting. I make pictures in my head. A snapshot of his hands, slender and wringing. His dark eyes, nestled in wrinkles. His gray hair and salt-and-pepper beard. If I could, I'd snap a picture of his smell. His voice too. Bottle them for later. The scent of smoked meat and mint, the rich sound of kindness saved for a day without rain. Or another time I'll need it.

There's another knock. I picture the woodpecker bursting through the sitting room of a family of fat, wriggling grubs midway through supper. Mother wipes her face. Straightens her dress. Pats her hair. A few deep breaths and she's a rule swigging Charter Mother again, as predictable as a clock stuck on three.

"Ready?" Daddy asks, as if it's up to her.

"Ready," she says. Even though it's not up to her any more than Moses's going was up to me.

Daddy opens the door. The men rattle off something about deeds and rules, names and blessings. Mother mouths the words as they speak; she knows them by heart. Daddy steps outside.

"Wait! They didn't say the Warding Off prayer. You heard it!" She turns to me. "They didn't do it right so it doesn't count. Osiris, get back in this house! Get back in!" She's pulling at Daddy's shirt. "If they're all set to do it, make them do it right!"

Daddy shakes her off.

The men look like they want to be anywhere but here. They look to the sky, the ground, one another. Finally, they turn their backs on Mother like she's a stranger destined to be gone before the morning bell too. No one wants to see a Charter Mother behave this way—it's not decent. As if it's a sign, three women swoop in—the Mourning Brigade. I should have known they'd come. They'll tell the Deacons to move along and leave us be. That it isn't Daddy's time. There will be parchment. It was all a misunderstanding. Some sort of official paper sealed with Mother Opal's signature confessing to having misheard. It will be the first annulment, the only one in history. I know because the Book of Annulments is filled with blank pages.

Of course the Mourning Brigade does no such thing. They don't say anything at all. The men don't seem to look at them; they sure don't say anything to them either. They part to let the women through and quickly close the gap. The Sisters march toward the house. Their coats are crisp, held in place by years of starch and practice. Their faces, though they'd all tie in a race for the oldest alive, are smooth. They are quick. They bundle Mother and the girls back inside the house. They hush and coo, click and murmur. They don't waste empty words.

Instead, they whisper in unison, all singing the same hymn. Daddy is Moving On. Even the faithful falter. The sun will still rise in the morning. The tune is without warmth or mirth. There's not a wrinkle of kindness between them.

*   *   *

THERE'S dust everywhere, and smoke. There's always smoke lately. The town north of us has been burning for three days straight. For now, it's too far away to hear much of anything but the occasional engine buzz, rifle shot, scream. *As long as they keep their troubles to themselves, we'll keep ours too*, the timers say. There's rumors that other Black towns didn't survive the razing of 1919. Couldn't pick up the paper without a headline. As kids, we used to stay up late at night, Mae and me, reading the town newspaper and imagining what went on outside Curdle Creek. The sin, the absolute sin of it. Robbing, killing, cheating. There didn't seem to be an end to the things people were willing to do to their neighbors.

Without the Moving On and the Warding Off, Curdle Creek would be just as bad. Lawless. Streets flooded with ghosts. The dead bumbling and unholy, grudge filled, taking up time and space. The living, reckless. Coming in and out of town with one foot here, one someplace else, as though home's a revolving door. Moral compass swinging every which way. Our ways are what save us—protecting us *from* them and from being *like* them. I know it and I don't care. I don't care about any of them. Not the Mothers, the Sisters, the town, its secrets. How long can I afford to stay here? To keep sacrificing us to save them?

"Stop!" I yell, ordinance be damned. Book XXV forbids yelling except in an emergency. Only Mother Opal and Charter Mothers can declare an official emergency, let alone sound the alarm. But it's not like I'm running up the hundred and thirty-five steps to the bell tower, toppling over the ringer, yanking the bell thirty-three and a half times to warn of an attack. There's no time for that right now. I just want this—this taking of my everything—to stop.

It doesn't. I could yell until I'm hoarse. The men don't pay me any mind. They probably can't hear me. The procession has begun. The Curdle Creek marching band, an award-winning troupe full of drums, flutes, clarinets, tubas, saxophones, trumpets and of course bells, steps in double time, making its way closer and closer to the house. What sounds like a hundred pairs of feet pounding on the pavement is really twenty-five of the town's finest believers. The band is almost sacred. Not one member's name has ever been called in over a hundred and fifty years and that's older than the town and everyone in it. They halt their melancholy tune—some number designed to make your heart beat with it while you're crying and silent-wailing—and descend into a drum roll to wait.

The band marches in place in front of the gate.

The drum majorette high-steps, arms raised, shiny whistle between her red lips. Her head bobs in time with her tweets. Her hat, pristine black, with a plume of feathers, perches high atop her curly black hair, pin curls practically starched to death to keep hair and hat in place. The drum majorette says she wants the Moving On to be perfect. Not so much for the town, but for those Moving On. It's the least she can do, she says. She tweets the customary seven blows: four for the thanks and one for each of the Moving On. At the last tweet, the drum roll gets faster, louder. One minute of musical celebration. Then it's twenty-four seconds of the cymbals. Then, God help us, the bells.

Two minutes later, the drum majorette claps her gloved hands. Instruments are readied. She gives the signal. The marching band high-steps, the majorettes twirl and spin, the drum majorette whistles trill and sharp. The drumming starts. The other two Moving-On-ers are already in line, solemn, heads bowed, marching in time surrounded by volunteer marshals— townsfolk nominated by the Dedication Committee.

Arms back, knees straight, one of the marshals bows to Daddy. It's a sign of respect. At least he has manners—or a good memory. Whenever Daddy's been a marshal, he's been kind. Always allowing the Moving On a moment of dignity, a blindfold if they asked for it, a bit of a shoulder to lean on if they needed one.

Daddy doesn't look at me. He straightens his shoulders, takes his place in the middle row. It breaks my heart to see him marching in place, half a beat behind the others. As if she just can't wait to get started, as soon as he's in line the drum majorette trills. It's loud and close; it pierces my ears. The parade is in motion. The Moving On has begun.

The band, the marshals and the Moving On march straight down the middle of the road as they've done over a hundred times before. They kick up clouds of dust, making their way down Pleasant Mills Road until they get to Pleasant Mills Lane, where they will turn and be out of sight. The Deacons follow close behind. They're sort of their own band though: no instruments, no high-stepping, just marching. Each of them holds on to something. Some have ropes, there's more than one Bible, one sack of rocks. They all carry sticks.

Mine's in the house. I clench my fists, dig my nails into my palms to keep from swinging them. Nothing good would come from attacking the band, pulling Daddy out of line, or crying. Instead, I follow them. It's forbidden. Families aren't meant to take part in the procession. It's bad luck for anyone else. I know it's just superstition, but my skin tingles anyway. Mae would laugh at me if she saw, but I cross myself like it says to do in Book XIX. In case that's not enough, and so as not to completely break the ordinance, I'm careful to walk out of step with the others, out of time with the music. It isn't too hard. Though, every once in a while I'm in step with Daddy. He must not be thinking straight. He's marched in many a procession. He should know the rhythm by heart. It never changes.

They march straight through town without faltering or wavering. The street is lined with men and women doubled over, arms outstretched in thanks, one palm up for forgiveness, eyes down for respect. In their other hand, they clench a pipe, stick, or rock. Those with large hands hold more than one weapon in them. It's only the families who don't give thanks publicly. Husbands, wives, children—the left-behind family— take turns praising and thanking, singing remembrances, in private. While the town Moves the body of the living On, the family, later, moves the spirit. The Warding Off is all about the soul. It's a celebration with candles, incense, mourning, running. I praised dear Moses from the moment he left the house until the Moving On bells rang. Then, just like everyone else, when it was time, I chased his spirit through town. My heart wasn't in it. If his ghost wanted to come back to visit, it wasn't my place to deny it.

Folks stay doubled over until we pass. I know they don't mean any harm but I wish they'd look the Moving On in the eyes. Instead, they bend so close to the ground they could topple over with a good wind, hand already outstretched to save them. It's uncomfortable. Their backs must be aching, heads swimming like they might pass out. Imagine! Falling out when the Moving On pass by. So disrespectful to make someone else's last moments all about you. The whole town would be out for you. Even still, I'd switch places with any one of them right now.

Those we pass fall into the procession seamlessly. They are in rhythm, in step with the Moving On. From time to time one gets a little anxious, tries to rush the proceedings. The drum majorette stops us all, tweets until we fall back into step before she starts again. We will march until we reach the Town Hall. Then, we run. The Moving On will get a two-minute head start before the town descends on them, pipes, sticks, rocks and all.

Other than the music and the marching, the occasional muffled gasp, the town center is quiet. Go down any side street and there's sure to be mayhem. Children running wild, playing rude games like Move-On-Already-Mary and Too-Slow-Joe. We walk past the church, the Grand Hotel, Carter's Everything Store, straight past the library, and Penny for Your

Thoughts Beauty Emporium. At Fleming's, my father slows. The band does too. They're at the section where the bass drops and the drums beat like a heart to inspire the Moving On to the next step. It's almost beautiful. It sounds better when the orchestra plays it on Memorial Day but the marching band doubles as the orchestra so it isn't worth complaining about.

Sister Mildred looks pale. All of the beautiful brown has seeped out of her face and arms, leaving a grayish-looking woman in an oversized dress that sticks to her back. Brother Isiah doesn't look much better. His suit bunches when he walks. His tie is too tight and he looks about to faint. His forehead is dripping with sweat plastering his hair to his scalp. Daddy's breathing through his mouth. He can't seem to catch his breath. His body is stiff. Every so often he twitches. It's almost like his feet want to move faster than his body knows how to. It won't let him move all at once.

It's almost invisible, the motion, but one minute he's standing still, the next his back is sort of rippling. He's getting smaller, shrinking like a silk shirt on a washboard. It's so quick that it takes me a moment to figure out that he's already running. He's always been fast, and the men—even though they've trained for moments like this, moments when the Moving On decide they don't want any part of the town or the traditions or maybe they just decide they can't wait any longer and now is just as good a time as any—don't seem to know what to do. They bump into each other, bumbling over rope; one reaches for the sack of rocks. Daddy has about fifteen seconds' head start.

Like an old picture show, the crowd springs to life. It's too late for Mildred and Isiah. The crowd is already upon them with objects ready. They get a head start but it's not two minutes before the bells are ringing and clanging and the pipes are clanging along too. They sort of stumble together even though it'd be better if they split up. They make their way to the Creek. It's the last place they should go. The banks are always slippery this time of year and the tide is at its highest for the Moving On. Meanwhile, the Deacons are chasing Daddy down Main Street. Rocks rain onto buildings and signposts, backs and heads without reaching their intended target. Daddy slips through an alley with the Deacons not far enough behind.

The screaming. I can't keep the sound out. In my head, the men sound just like the band marching with their stomping feet. The marching band's still playing, the bells are still ringing, above a hawk screams. I guess I do too. My heart is drumming so loud it almost drowns everything else out. I'm running like I'm chasing after the devil. Faster than I've run in my whole life before now. Trespassing through yards, trampling over flower beds, bumping into sheds, tripping over cows, traipsing through fields, I'm breaking hundreds of rules as I go. My side's cramping, threatening to seize if I don't slow down. No matter how fast I go, I can't outrun the sound of Daddy running away. This must be what goodbye sounds like.

Mother's

I run all the way back to get to Mother first but I'm too late. She's in the sitting room, leaning back in her chair, one leg crossed over her knee, finger twirling the phone wire as she talks. The party line—I should have known. "You don't say," she says. "Before the others had a chance to run? He has always been ambitious. *Mmm-hmm*. I bet Mother Opal didn't see this coming. It can't be helped. We'll bury her in the Creek."

Mariah squeezes my hand before leading me into the house. She nearly skips up the steps. Rumor locks the door. The click sounds out of place, loud and obnoxious. It shouldn't be, but, from the sound of Mother's voice, Mother Opal dying is about the best thing that could have happened. Charter Mothers are holy in Curdle Creek. They don't just die like normal people. Their names don't get called. They don't slip on sheets of ice and crack their heads wide open, or tumble down stairs reaching for light switches. The rest of us get Moved On or have accidents. Charter Mothers are supposed to die from old age. Mother Opal always said we'd know when it was her time to die because she'd tell us, not because she'd wake up dead. We've never not had a Head Charter Mother. Not even buried yet and Mother's already holding office.

I don't even have time to stop them. My fingers are popping and cracking and it feels so good even with Mother staring at me, mouth wide open, shuddering as though each pop is a touch and I just have one more left and *ahh*. It's like every bad thing is a bubble, a big old wad of chewing gum, and cracking my knuckles sort of sets them loose. My hands settle. I let out my breath. The look in her eyes dares me to smile so I bite my lip to keep from doing it. I'm smiling inside though.

"I better go, Osira's here. We have plans to make, especially before the Warding Off."

Mother presses the connector before replacing the receiver in the cradle. She reaches into her blouse, pulls out a Moving On jubilee flyer, a change purse, and then, tucked close to her chest and still warm, smelling of her favorite scent—mourning and ginger—she pulls out a pair of misshapen gloves.

I'm a grown woman. There's no use in saying it out loud unless I want to hear about my being a big beast of a baby who almost cracked her like a walnut clear in two at birth. A baby born to wail, or born wailing and wailing until Daddy scooped me up, cut the cord, cleaned me off, named me, and welcomed me properly into the family like a stranger. She'll eye me again as if, even though I came from her body, she's not a hundred percent certain I'm her child. She leans forward, eyes looking where my hands should be, holds out a glove. They are stiff, made with twined hay and cord, heavy and uncomfortable. I put my hands out, palms up, fingers stretched. They are big enough to slip right on but she wiggles and jiggles them, scooches each finger in an inch at a time so the hay scratches against my skin. I would close my eyes and pretend I'm somewhere else but the last time I did that, she forgot herself and slapped me across the face with the hand holding the glove and the hay scratched my eyelid. It was that and not the slap, she said, that caused my eye to swell. So I keep them open, watch her twirl the cord around and around my wrists to bind them.

"Ten minutes," she says. She walks away, *tsk, tsk, tsk*ing, to go and check on the girls.

"Daddy ran off."

"Good, then he won't be around for the Warding Off."

"I mean before the Moving On. He left—"

"We'll talk about this in a minute."

She leaves me standing in the vestibule. I can see outside from here, which means outside can see in. Nothing would make her angrier than a neighbor knocking on the door to find me fumbling around trying to unlock it. They'd surely be wondering what we were trying to hide, since everyone knows only the guilty need locked doors in the first place. I imagine I would use my chin to unlock it somehow and then my mouth to turn the knob. Mother would have a fit. The first thing they would see, once I opened the door wide enough to push it the rest of the way with my toe, would be the devil gloves. The shame. They'd know I was up to something I shouldn't have been up to and they would guess at what it was. Their guesses would be far worse than my cracking my knuckles and getting on Mother's *one good nerve*.

If Mother Opal is truly dead—and it isn't the sort of thing Mother or the Council would joke about—then Daddy running away is the least important thing to have happened today. That, and my declaring we should end the Moving On loud enough for anyone to hear, maybe. That doesn't mean I won't be punished, though. There won't be any point in a trial, but they'll hold one just to show how fair they are. It'll be there in Book XIII. The trial will be public. Mae will be all dressed up, holding the good doctor's hand. He won't know me well enough to be a character witness but it won't really matter. Jeremiah will be there too. He won't hardly look at me. He'll be too busy worrying if he's crossed out all of the double-grave signs he's scratched into trees around town. Those were long-ago days. Before we were old enough to court, so what felt like love then wasn't. He'll have missed one though so he may as well not even bother. He'll be a suspect too before the night ends. Mother will bring out the lavender. It's good for situations like these. She'll weave a garland or something for the girls' hair, put one in her buttonhole and pin one to her scarf, to show she's grieving two. Mr. Jacobs might not be in such a hurry to take Daddy's place then.

Mother comes back with the Book of Sorrows. I'm in for it now. I can't imagine what other folks keep theirs for but ours seems to be just for me. Mother would say I'm stuck-up for even thinking that. Anything I do that rubs her up when it should smooth her down goes in the family book. Use up too much hot water? In the book. Invite a weak ringer around for tea? In the book. Paint the girls with glue so they'll really be "joined at the hip"? In the book. Even Romulus only made the book when he ran off. I have pages and pages. Maybe even a whole chapter. If she were creative she'd call it *The Least Likely Among Us.* Knowing Mother, if anything the title's *There's Always Been Something About That Girl and I Saw It Coming but Who Would Believe Me?*

Mother settles down in the front room. She motions for me to join her. Not to sit down, to stand before her. Across from me, she spreads the book out. It should be stiff—the spine is meant to crack to show we don't harbor trouble here—but ours just flops right open. She leans back into her armchair. Closes her eyes as if she's thinking of what to write. She sits there for a full minute. It almost looks like she's asleep. If she were, she'd be snoring, although, to hear her tell it, snoring isn't something ladies like her do.

I'm not supposed to be looking at her, but since I am, I see her eyes snap open. Her back straightens. She lifts the family pen out of its sheath. It's brass, polished and practically glowing. Mother presses the nib against her tongue. Sucks her teeth. She's been hit by an inspiration. She dips the spitty pen into the ink. *Let it be empty, let it be empty, let it be empty.* She slides the pen from the well. I can practically see the words dripping off it even from here. I won't even be able to sneak a peek at the passage until the ink truly dries. By then it will be too late. Whatever is written will be there for life. That's not because it's holy or anything. I know it because I've tried to smudge a deed or two off of a page. I was only twelve.

How was I supposed to know lemon juice only made the sins shine—and stink?

If she writes that I had something to do with Daddy leaving, I'm as good as dead. It won't matter that it was her idea in the first place. All that will matter is that I was in the procession and shouldn't have been and now Daddy hasn't been Moved On and should have been. Once it's in the book, anyone from the Council can call it in for a reading. The only thing worse than having to kneel on the cold marble floor and read out my own crimes in my mother's voice—since she'd be the recorder—will be the atonement. They'll be up half the night, each Council member trying to outdo the next to suggest the most severe punishments. If they don't outright kill me, it won't make a difference. I could atone until I can't atone no more; my name will be called next year either way.

"Is Mother Opal dead because of me?" I ask. I don't know what makes me think it's my fault but maybe my doubts killed her. The true believers have always said that doubt will be what topples Curdle Creek in the end. Maybe, instead of fire and brimstone, a forty-five-year-old widow will be what divides Curdle Creek once and for all. I just wanted Daddy to be here. I didn't mean for anything to happen to anyone. Least of all to Mother Opal. The tears spring and I let them slide down my face straight into my mouth. I don't swallow them, though. Mother says I look ugly when I swallow tears and that's the last thing she needs to be thinking about right now.

Mother sets the pen down. "What foolishness are you talking now?"

My throat opens up. Everything, every deed, flows out like a fountain. I'm sobbing and boohooing and just confessing right there and then. I don't bother to get on my knees and apologize. She can't forgive me.

Mother lets out a grand sigh. It's her practiced one. The one she uses to show you've worn out her patience or your welcome. "I'm trying to write about your father. Not everything is about you."

Of all the great sins against the town, arrogance is one of the top ones. It's smack in between failing to come to the Calling and not participating in the Warding Off.

"But Daddy's gone."

"It was his time to go." She taps the pen on the palm of her hand.

"He didn't wait for the bells to ring. He didn't wait for the call to run. He ran. Not *in* the Moving On but *from* it."

Mother closes her eyes. She rubs her temples. She likes to do this when she wants to look thoughtful. As though she's measuring words before dishing them out.

"That's simply not true. They collected your father. He marched with the others to town. As he approached the Town Hall, he ran, just as he's supposed to do. The bells were rung."

"Mother, they rang after he left, not before!"

"The bells were rung. I *know* you are not standing in my house accusing my husband of running off today on the day of his great sacrifice when no one but you is saying it. Now, if you're saying the bell ringer was late with the ringing, that is another matter. We can take that up at the next Moving On. Is that what you're saying?"

Of course not. I know what I saw, but if no one is accusing Daddy of deserting then it's my word against that of the Deacons and everyone else. If Mother told them I wrongfully accused Daddy, I'd be compelled to offer a lifetime of sorrys. Each time she entered a room, I'd be forced to drop to the floor and sing a litany of apologies. It would take hours. She wouldn't even have to listen. She could read, eat, sleep. Even if she left the room, I'd have to stay there until it was finished. If she came back I'd have to start over again. She would rather be stoned than let me have even this one thing. She'd have the bell ringer called just to prove I'm wrong. I can't let an innocent person be punished for what I know happened.

"No, ma'am. I must have been mistaken. It happened just as you said. I have no call to accuse or falsely accuse anyone. Book VI says—"

"Please don't recite those damned books to me."

It's not the first time she's said this, but blasphemy today doesn't feel right.

"You were just tired. There was the Running, the excitement of the Calling, the Moving On, and not to mention the rain. It's natural. You can hardly be trusted to know what you saw or when you saw it."

Maybe she's right. She must be. Mother doesn't even think before the words pop out of her mouth, she's that sure. It was all in my head. Even if he wasn't a Deacon, Daddy knows what happens to families once someone deserts Curdle Creek. He knows how a broken heart feels afterward. He would know that after Romulus, my own children and him, I'd be the one left to pay for the leavings. Of course Mother's right.

I change the subject. "How can Mother Opal be dead? What happened?"

Mother drums her finger on the table as if she's playing the piano. "Who's to say anything happened? Sometimes people just die."

"Not Charter Mothers." My mouth is dry. I feel sick.

"Even Charter Mothers. Our names don't get called but surely you don't think Moving On is the same as dying." She twirls the pen in her hand like a wand. She'd have made a beautiful band leader.

"Of course not, no. I just mean, she was Mother Opal. Who would kill her?"

"Who said anyone killed her? Accidents happen all the time, and old age—though that's no accident . . ." she chuckles; they are the same age ". . . old age happens to the lucky ones. Sooner or later everyone runs out of luck."

"But we just saw her!"

"The last time anyone saw her was at the Calling." She closes her eyes. As if she's imagining that last time she saw her, she smiles, savoring it. She looks down at my feet, still covered. Frowns. She traces my footsteps from the top of the stairs to where I stand. I look too. A pebble or two, a smudge of dirt. Nothing that won't come off without too much trouble. It's the indentation that will drive her to distraction. The stamp of soles crushing her good plush carpet. I lift my leg to nudge one shoe off with the other. Not like I can unclasp the latch around my ankles but the effort, the *shh shh* of leather against leather, then leather against clasp, might wiggle it free enough to push off. Then my toes can undo the other one.

Mother hates the sight of naked toes. For a moment, wrinkles crease her face. My fingers stick to the hay.

"The Calling." She shakes her head slowly from side to side like the tongue of a bell in need of oil. "We were all there when you gave her that little something to drink. I sure hope there wasn't anything wrong with it." She taps the pen again. "I have been thinking about the Running of the Widows, though. Not so much the running but the *outcome.*" The word sounds like a curse coming from her lips. "Letting your *best friend* beat you to the church like you don't give a damn about protecting me, your poor darling sisters, the town, or anyone in it. As if you don't have an ounce of Turner blood flowing through your body and you wouldn't know winning if it hit you in the face. I would have thought surely you would know about running, though. You are your father's daughter." Mother's lips twist in her *poor Osira* look. "Girls!" she calls.

Never far away, Mariah and Rumor trudge into the room, holding the hourglass between them. It's glass and wood, inscribed with the family name. It's been with us for generations. Outlived many a Turner. It's nearly bigger than both of them combined. They each hold tight to a curved wooden handle. They know better than to drop it or let the sands dip. There's nothing worse than wasting time around here.

It's eerie how they know what she wants without her saying. They slide it onto the table next to her. On either side, they both lean their cheeks toward her on cue. She pecks each one. Rumor first, then Mariah. The girls skip out of the room. When they're gone, Mother turns back to me.

"We'll start your punishment from the beginning so there are no distractions."

She flips the hourglass over, picks up the pen, and writes, and writes, and writes. The *scratch, scratch, scratch* sounds like nails in a coffin. Not that anyone has much use for coffins anymore.

*   *   *

BY the time she finally closes the book, supper is underway. I've made Mother's favorites. The ham hocks are just about done so it's time to put in the greens. I take the lid off quietly. The heat feels good on my skin.

"Did you wash them?" she asks from the next room.

"Yes, Mother." They're still dripping from their bath in salt and vinegar water. It took a while to ease the gloves off and still my fingers were near raw where straw had scraped away skin. Careful as I tried to be, dunking my hands in a pot of that concoction for the sake of clean greens was almost my undoing. My fingers still tingle.

"Dry them?"

If they could talk they'd start telling on me right now. They might be trying to. The dripping gets louder and louder and—I pop the little traitors into the pot. "Yes, Mother."

I fiddle with an empty pan so she can't hear me checking the roast. My mouth waters as I open the oven door. I stick out my tongue to taste the beef-onion steam. The fork slides right into the meat. Juice oozes out. It's tender and near-perfect.

"Leave it in a bit longer. I like mine well-done," she calls without looking at it.

"It's finished. I'm going to leave it to rest."

"You are going to leave it to cook until I say take it out. That's what you're going to do."

I slice off a chunk. Wave goodbye to the roast. The next time I see it, it will be thick-skinned and dry.

"Put that right back in with the rest of it," she says. I'd swear she has eyes all over her head. "I won't have you getting sick before the Warding Off."

As if she'd let me miss the Warding Off even if I was. I dig my fingernail into the chunk before sentencing it to the same fate as the rest of the roast. Ashes to ashes. I close the oven door, suck the juice from my finger like I'm ten.

*   *   *

ONCE the smoke fills the kitchen, Mother comes in to finish supper. She sets the roast, still smoldering, on the countertop to rest. Mostly she's tasting everything I've already cooked while waving a tea towel around to clear the air. "Cooking wears me out," she says. "Go sit at the table for a spell. I'll make us some fruit punch."

I do as I'm told. Maybe it's the smoke but Mother doesn't seem to be able to find anything without banging, clanging and slamming pots, pans, lids, and cupboards. A few minutes later she sets a pitcher of what she says is *special fruit punch* in the middle of the table. I'm not sure if it's special because there's alcohol in it or because there's hardly any fruit in there at all.

"If Mother Opal's gone, what happens to the Warding Off? We can't hold it without her. Does that mean Daddy can come back?"

"Oh, God, no!" Mother cackles. Doubled over, she holds her sides. Her laughs turn to coughs. I could pat her back. I don't do it, though. "How could he?" She takes a deep breath, shakes her head. She sits in her chair at the head of the table. "No, that's done. I wouldn't know how to bring him back even if I wanted to."

Wasn't it her idea in the first place? Daddy was probably standing there about to do the right thing when her words came back to haunt him. So, he ran. It's almost like she rode the getaway horse, if there'd been one. It can't be too hard to convince whoever needs convincing. But then again, I'd be up there too. I heard her and didn't record it, didn't tell anyone at all. They could call both of us. Leave Mariah and Rumor orphaned. Unmarried and not yet thirty, they'd be split up for sure.

If it's really just the right name at the wrong time, next year I could sneak down a few nights before the Calling and write her name on one hundred slips of paper. There would be no room for hardly any other name. The Law of Probability says Mother's name would be called. That don't mean it would be. Even Callers have families. They could show her the slip with her name written across it and she could say another name. No one but them two would know. Them two and me. Mother would know my handwriting and would let me know she knew it was me.

All this plotting. One way or another, Daddy's gone, and here I am breaking ordinance after ordinance like I don't have any home training at all.

Besides, I know it won't happen. The last place I'd want to

be is in that smelly, creepy well. I'd swear I hear the ghosts of old Callers wailing on clear nights and holler until someone came to get me out. I'd get my own self caught. I'd have to get someone else to do it. There's no shortage of people on Mother's bad side. And thanks to her high-and-mightiness, if only in public, I can't imagine folks like her any more than she likes them. With Mother Opal gone, there's no one she can *have a word with* about discrepancies of one kind or another. There's no way she can have the entire Council in her purse just waiting to do her bidding. Mother Opal might not be the only one out of luck.

I don't say it out loud but it's on my face, though. I can tell by the way Mother's looking at me like I'm a photograph she wishes hadn't developed.

"He'd be different if he came back now." Her lips twitch. It's just a little smile, but I see it. "Angry, dangerous. I couldn't have him around my babies." She raises her glass to her lips. Puts it back down. "Around you either." She bats her eyelashes. That innocent look has only ever worked on Daddy, and of course on Mr. Jacobs. She bows her head.

I'm sitting next to her, staring down at the top of her head and her fresh-permed hair still straight despite the rain. Newly dyed, here and there a curly gray strand breaks through. She'll have plucked it out before her next appointment. I feel like a priest. As if I can see all of her sins.

"I could protect us," I say.

Guilty. The word pops into my head from nowhere. It nearly comes out of my mouth. She looks small in Daddy's chair. But why is she in Daddy's chair in the first place? There's always been six of them. Moses's chair is still empty. Mother tilts her chin, motions for me to take the seat across from her instead. To sit in her chair. I do it, but looking at her makes my eyes water so I look at her reflection in the mirror. The dining room mirror is a puzzle of glass. Daddy got the fitters to do it just for Mother, so he could *see the million pieces he loves about her.* There's nothing worse than watching a million yous with a fork. The sight of all those mini-mes stuffing their tiny mouths fills my stomach right up. I couldn't wait for the girls to get old enough to sit at the family table. I almost wish they were here now instead of picking out clothes for the Warding Off as if they're too excited to eat. Since I'm the oldest, my back's normally to the mirror now. Now when I visit it's just the horror on their faces that makes it hard to keep food down. Hard, but not impossible.

Daddy must have really loved her. It must be the light, but sitting way at the other end of the table makes Mother look like death to me. Not like she's dying or sickly but like I'd imagine death would look like if it were sitting across from me sipping a glass of bloodred punch and wiping its mouth on a freshly laundered napkin that I'll have to wash later. Pleased. It's like there's two of her. One sitting in front of me and one shadow mother standing over her staring down at me like I'm next. When I look away from the mirror, she looks away too. My heart's beating so fast that my fingers are tapping. My throat's so dry I think I swallowed the same spit twice. I lean forward and reach for the pitcher.

"I'll get that for you, sugar," Mother says. She's not sitting across from me anymore, neither one of them. I didn't see her get up. Growing up, I could hear her chair scraping the bare carpet when she pushed back, leaned forward. But she's standing next to me now. I smell her peppermint soap, vanilla baby powder, cherry-scented hair grease, rose-infused sweat. She has the pitcher in her hand, nods to my glass. My hand shakes as I hold it up. She leans close, wraps her strong fingers around my wrist, squeezes. "If I ever hear you talking about your father ran off again—" She pauses. *Mmm*s. Mother is a hummer. She punctuates silence with sound. *Mmm* can mean anything, really. Sometimes it's good, like *Mmm, that pie sure is tasty*. Or, *Mmm, that sounds interesting*. It's one of her could-mean-anything phrases like *I didn't know that about you*, *have a good day*, or *Watch your step*. "I'll give you something to cry about."

I nod to show I understand that here *mmm* means she'd enjoy that.

*   *   *

I sit for ten minutes watching her watch me not take a sip from that glass. It's not that I think she'd poison me. I just don't want to take a chance on dying before my time. Every so often I raise the glass to my lips. She leans forward. I put it down.

"I can't think straight," I say. "First Daddy, then Mother Opal."

"The harvest will be full this season," she says.

Timers and their sayings. Seems no matter what position they get, some people just don't change. Here she is, a Charter Mother, and she can't stop herself from sounding just the way her own mother and father probably did. Anybody can be a timer if they believe and live long enough. I guess that's why they have sayings. Helps them pass the time. They have one for just about everything. They say the traditions will die out when the timers do. Like timers don't just birth more timers. That's silly talk. You can't pass down time. Just beliefs. Timers birth believers, mostly.

She's already opened the windows. They say it helps Move On the spirits. I suppose it does. That and packing up their belongings. Gusts of wind carry damp air like news through the house. The dining room is thick with it. The girls are still in their rooms trying on outfits. It's just like them to want to look good even on a night like tonight. They're singing "Move Along Harry," a duet usually reserved for courting. But since there's only two of them and neither of them ever wants to be Harry, they've changed the words. They sing: "Somebody's daddy's not coming home, somebody's daddy's stayed too long, somebody's daddy's done something wrong, somebody's daddy's Moving On." Their voices trail off into a fit of giggles.

The room feels cold all of a sudden. "Should they be singing that?" I ask.

Mother's been snapping her fingers to their song as if it never occurred to her that that *somebody* is them. "I don't see why not."

* * *

I won't look up at her so I just stare at her fingers. The way her nails click slightly when she taps them together. They are short and strong. They left dents in my wrist. I wonder if Mother Opal has them too. I should tell her I was there. Heard her and Mother Opal. But asking questions is just what always gets the girl killed in the books the library's always displaying for Ordinance Awareness Month. The heroine's always some Inspector Suzie–type cozying up to the killer talking about *I know you killed him and I can prove it*, just before she ends up at the bottom of the Creek or holed up in a mineshaft or just everyday dead. No, thank you. I close my lips tight so nothing I can't take back slips out.

"I hope your sisters aren't as hardheaded as you are," she says. She grins like she really hopes they are. I picture her pinching their slender arms, making heart-shaped welts on their soft brown skin. Mother's never been much of a mother. More a fickle friend I could trust from time to time. I'm grown and I still can't look at her without shaking. She's prone to turn her back on me. Again.

"What will be your first ordinance as Head Charter Mother?"

"We'll just have to wait and see, won't we?" she says. And she giggles like a schoolgirl.

*   *   *

I get up to clear the table. The bells. Without being told, the girls come running downstairs. One grabs Mother's hand, the other mine. From the top of the hill, the bell rings. It's loud and sharp. The echo reaches each corner of Curdle Creek. *From house to home and hill to knoll, all shall hear the bell's true toll.* According to Mother Opal, the first set of townsfolk, the Founders, forged the famous stalactites and stalagmites of Bell Cave so the ringing could be heard all through the town.

Because Curdle Creek's at the butt of a mountain, the ringing bounces off rock back through brick, wood and window so that each tone answers its own prayer. There's one for all the Moving-On-ers. Even one for Daddy. My heart aches when his rings. The return one, the one that's supposed to be him blessing the town, is hollow and offbeat. It doesn't sound anything like him. I hope he got away and he's still running.

After the chime, lesser bells including Old Glory peal into "Ten Minutes of Glory" and, finally, "Thanks for a Plentiful Year." I keep my eyes closed for the minute of silence. I can't see them but I know Mariah and Rumor and Mother are all staring at me. My forehead burns, then my ears, neck, chest, arms, waist, legs, feet. They are wondering if I'm strong enough to carry the family name, fast enough to get away with it. Not everybody makes it back from the Warding Off. How could they? Accidents happen and in the dark, well, the Moving On blend in, hide, and sometimes a family member with too close a resemblance ends up being chased clear through town before someone recognizes the mistake. Once it's done and the body is declared dead, it's time for the Warding Off of the soul. That's worse. Anything's liable to happen at the Warding Off.

When the Thankful ends, the girls go back to their rooms. They have too much energy; it's been raining all afternoon so they couldn't go outside. Small creatures all over Curdle Creek must be rejoicing. I am too. Those girls hunting squirrels and dressing them up in little pinafores and ballet shoes is about the scariest thing. I can't handle it right now. Just the thought of the things they get up to makes me cold all at once. I can see them singing and laughing while cornering one, scooping it up by its tail and then, just when it thinks it's going to go in a pot, contorting it into shapes not befitting a rodent. Arms in the air, legs akimbo, tail mid-flit. It is primped and pressed into poses and snapped. The picture is all the girls seem to want. They undo and unbutton, unfurl handmade outfits and set the dazed squirrels free. I wonder if they talk about it. Little squirrels plotting my sisters' downfall. I hope they know I'm not one of them. I would never do to an animal anything I wouldn't do to a man. Daddy taught me that.

Mother's on the phone again. I imagine her whispering to her one good friend but even telephones can't summon the dead so it's most likely Mr. Jacobs. She's reminiscing. I recognize the tone. It's her *you should have seen me then* voice. Sultry. When she talks about how she and Daddy met she always adds, *There he was when I wasn't even looking. I wasn't even thinking about getting married when love tapped me on the shoulder talking about try this one on, see if it fits.* She's always like that. If she talks about love at all, it's like she could eat it or wear it.

The Warding Off

Mother's in the kitchen slamming pots and pans for a good ten minutes. She isn't really going to cook. Soon, the Sisters will be here with lunch. Mother's still not over having to cook our own supper last night. It's unheard of for the family of the Moved On to have to cook their own meals for the first seven days. I imagine they're busy with Mother Opal passing. Mother won't talk about it but I know she's annoyed. Imagine, dying on a day meant for the Moving On. Selfish, she would say.

There's a knock. On cue, Mother sits in her big leather chair in the front room. It's still raining hard outside, the curtains are tightly closed for mourning, and we have all the lights on indoors. The girls shuffle down the hall and plop down beside her, one at each of her feet. Mother taps each of them on the head in a familiar rhythm. The look of them sends shivers down my spine.

I get the door. I barely have time to move to the side before the Sisters slip in, heads bowed and covered. They shake off the outside and leave the rain on the front porch. They march to the kitchen with steaming plates and bags bursting with fresh fruits and vegetables, wrapped parcels of meat, packets of buttons and fabric, bundles of books and paper.

"Gifts from town," they say.

"It's the least the town can do, since—well . . ." I begin.

"Since what?" Mother asks.

Nobody owes us anything for the Moving On. It's our duty to do it. Our right. Lightning flashes and before long the sky splits open. It's a long drum roll stretching for what feels like hours. Of course, no one moves. If I could turn my head, I would see them frozen mid-step, some reaching for plates, one in front of the refrigerator, one wiping Mother's brow, all of them probably staring at me. Like I would say it. The thunder rolls on and on. Since Mother's not going to do it, I go to the utility closet. It's a sliver of a space cut out next to the bathroom. I slide my arm in, reach past the cobwebs. My wrist brushes up against the water pipe. Still hot. It burns but there's no sense complaining about it. Nobody's going to help me. I pull the switch. The house goes dark. If Daddy was here he'd turn off the boiler too but he isn't here anymore and I'm not about to fiddle around trying to convince it to light back up later. Turning the lights off will have to do. Superstitions.

It's pitch-black and I can hear everything in stereo. If this was one of those old movies we watch once a month, this would be the time when I die. I hear my blood rushing through my body. Someone swallowing. Breathing. There's a slight buzz in my ears. Electricity. It's off so I don't know where it's coming from but it's so loud I feel it. Someone's moving close to me. The air around me is hot. It's like someone's taking up my space, moving into my skin. Each time the sky flashes, I see a foot, an arm, a step closer to me.

There's a low rumble. It's not the thunder but another kind of storm. A flash, a grin. I don't wait for the rest. I run down the hall to my old room. I close the door lightly. It still sighs and clicks into place like a book dropping on a hardwood floor. I know I have about a minute before whoever it is finds their way in here with me. If Mother hadn't complained *There's no need for locked doors when everything in here belongs to me*, I'd have a bolt on the door and be safe. But, no. I roll halfway under the bed. Thankfully it's still there. My first Moving On stick. The stick's in my hand by the time I hear the soft push of the door opening a crack, a foot sliding across the floor. A toe snagging in the rug. I'm on my feet, stick beating as fast as my heart, raised high above my head. A flash, a smile, a shimmering thing.

"Your father would have wanted you to have this." It's a Sister. She's whispering close to my ear. "Don't tell anyone you have it. You'll know when you need it." She presses something small into my hand, warm from her fingers. My fingers curl around it. I'm thankful she doesn't mention the stick so close to her head. I nod. I doubt she can see it. She taps my wrist. In reverse she shuffles from my room, back down the hall. I stuff the warm thing in my pocket. I hold on to the stick. Sooner or later, I'll need it.

* * *

FOREVER later, the storm passes. My legs are stiff. I light a lamp and we go about the business of grief. The Sisters find places for things, set the table, and sit the girls and me down on the back porch so they can talk to Mother in private. They will thank her for the family's sacrifice, offer to pack Daddy's things—she has to decline this offer, it's in the ordinance; that won't stop them from offering, though—there's an ordinance for that too.

The girls play Diamonds on the floor. The scraping of the metal against the wood grates on my nerves. I don't mention it to either one of them. That's the last thing I need. Grudges.

"Mariah's cheating," Rumor says.

"How can she cheat at Diamonds?"

"I don't know, she's not bouncing the ball up high enough. Of course she'll catch it when it comes down."

"I don't think there's a rule about how high you have to throw up a ball."

"Don't be stupid," she says. "There's a rule for everything."

She's probably right but I want to slap her anyway. "I think the rule is that you throw the ball in the air and if the other player can't throw it up as high as you can, the other player is destined to lose. Fair and square." I'm making that up.

Rumor shrugs. "If they don't break it, can I have your stick? It's real pretty."

"Who would break it?"

"Your friends, silly," Mariah answers. She puts her hands on her waist, squeezes. She's so full of answers they overflow out of her mouth. I picture her not even trying to swallow them down. I should have known my little sisters wouldn't be innocently playing anything, least of all Diamonds. "Now that you're a weak ringer, you'll have to prove yourself."

Rumor shakes her head. Her braids shake with it. "Oh, Osira," she says. "Just like your daddy."

It would look like an accident. I could say I saw a snake slithering up the steps, mouth gaping, aimed at the baby of the family. The baby, of all things! That just before it made to swallow her whole, I swung my stick and saved her life.

Like I would do that. I lower my voice cuz she hates that. "He's your daddy too."

They both laugh. They stop at the same time. I'm shivering.

"Not anymore. *Our* daddy's going to be strong and fearless, Mother promised."

I tap my stick on the floor to drown it out. *Our daddy.* There's something about the way they say it. The lilt in their voices, the singsong cheeriness, the hope, that lets me know I'm not included in *our.*

"Who called me a weak ringer?" I don't know who it was who gripped my wrist, forced me to start ringing the bell yesterday after the Calling, but news travels fast in Curdle Creek. Each house has one phone, that's really all you need according to the Charter Mothers. They share the same number so if you call one house, you call them all. Nobody with any sense would use that phone unless they want the whole town, as Mother Opal would say, *rattling around their graves.*

"Everybody," Rumor says.

"Even you?"

"Who are we to call you out of your name?" From the grin on her face, the way she's looking up at the sky, head tilted as if she's trying to remember something, I know who started the rumor. They have a script, the two of them.

"I wonder who will be Mother's favorite when I'm gone." I turn to go inside.

I don't get far. Mariah doubles over laughing. She nearly rolls off the porch, she's laughing so hard and hugging herself like she doesn't have an ounce of pride. Rumor stands in front of the screen door, hands on her hips. "It won't make a difference if you come back or not, I'll always be Mother's favorite."

I lean down close to her face, look into her spite-flecked brown eyes. "You *would* think that. If it were either of you, I'm sure Mariah would be the one." I brace myself. She jumps up, bumps her head into my chin hard. I bite my tongue something fierce. Flashes of light dance across my eyelids. I close them. She waits. If I touch her, she will scream. Mother and the Sisters will swoop to her rescue. I suck my tongue, rub the cut with my teeth. "Always a sister, never a mother. Always a widow, never a bride." I sing the childhood taunt as though her fate is just as sealed as mine.

"*I am nothing like you.*" The words are a whisper. "That's why they're planning to jump you tonight." Rumor's practically singing. "While everyone else is busy with the Warding Off, you'll be sitting in the well. Nothing but that horrible stench and your own heathen thoughts to keep you company till morning. Guess you'll be able to see what names are left over down there. Everybody's talking about it."

I turn to Mariah to check that it's true. She nods. All right then. "I guess there's nothing left to do but pray."

They're still giggling as I walk into the shed. I imagine them racing to the phone as soon as Mother's back is turned.

A moan rolls across the sky. It is intense, soulful. As beautiful as the sound of screaming seagulls. The wailing. Mother must have accepted the position. It's official. She's the new Head Charter Mother. She will have fifteen minutes to mourn.

I close the door behind me and go to Daddy's boxes. There are only six of them. He didn't live a long enough life. A full life means stacks and stacks of boxes. Some people have so many of them that they have to rent out rooms in other people's houses just to store them. Mother must have started packing even before the Calling. She's used last year's boxes, tape, markers, *Waste not, want not*, and all that so that his boxes are headstone-gray instead of this year's earthy brown. Anything that's not in here will be handed down to the girls, left to me, burned.

I know what I'm looking for and where to find it. Everything I need is right here in Daddy's tackle box. Tucked between the stacks, I pull out the key the Sister slipped me. Slide it into the lock. Jiggle it the way Daddy used to do. From the box, I take only what I need. I bind the stones, candles and matches, knife and water pouch close to my chest. I stuff my pockets full of things like oat bars, a pocketknife, some beans, and a half-empty flask with more water. I set aside last year's *Curdle Creek Almanac*, fishing cards with fish in bright colors hand-painted on the front, and dig below the rocks Daddy collects. Beneath all of his treasured things there's a small, worn leather pouch. Inside, there's a Well Walker stone. I recognize it from Book XIX. Superstitions. Don't tell me

Daddy really did believe in that old tale. If he did, he would have used it. Unless he thought he wouldn't need it.

I close the box, restick the tape, push Daddy's life back where it belongs. Three minutes later, there's a click, the twist of the knob, the creak of the door. Light. Mother's early. I can't reach my pocket, can't leave it here for nosy mourners to find. I slip the stone in my mouth. It's chalky.

"You don't want to be late," Mother says. She sounds giddy, almost drunk with excitement.

My tongue feels thick, coated with a gummy paste. I keep my back to her. "I wanted to say goodbye to Daddy." It's just the sort of thing she would think I'd believe. Like his soul is packed up tight in a waterproof box just waiting to be of use again. I move toward the doorway. If I leave, maybe she'll follow. The last thing I need is to see her picking through Daddy's things like some sort of buzzard.

She moves to let me pass. "Did you hear me wailing?"

"Yes, Mother, you're very good at it." We are nearly shoulder to shoulder. Just a few more steps.

A smile flashes across her face. I want to say, *You can do it, little smile, you can do it*. To coax it out like a stubborn mule. But I know better. It can't do it. A smile doesn't stand much of a chance with Mother. It doesn't hold long before slipping into a thin line. The stone sucks the spit from my mouth, dries out my lips. I feel them puckering.

Her breath is hot against my face. "Put some balm on your lips. You look like you've been kissing a chalkboard." She hands me a compact. "You've got your Daddy's lips. Keep it."

I slather my lips with it. They drink it up. I know they are brown and smooth like hers. Quick, I spit the stone into my hand. "I know Mother Opal meant a lot to you. I'm sorry for your loss. Do they know how Mother Opal died?"

I'm close enough to hear her swallow. She sucks her teeth. "I have a feeling they know." Mother winks. Her voice sends chills all across my arms. "Come get something to eat before you go."

I put my hand in my pocket.

"I don't think I have time." It's not that she would poison me, kill me so close to the Warding Off. But maybe a touch of castor oil to slow me down. She's always been that little touch of spiteful. Mother Opal tried to warn Daddy. He didn't listen.

"I've already packed you a bite."

She's so close to me it's like we're taking the same steps. She must know what my friends are planning. If I had somehow raced Romulus and Remus to the gate and been the firstborn, she would have loved me more. She's snapping her fingers, doing a little bop when she walks. It's as though she can hear my heart beating and it's playing her favorite tune.

We're just in front of the house. Mariah, always waiting, slips beside Mother and hands me a steaming bundle. "Can I have Osira's dinner?" she asks.

Greedy. Instead of saying goodbye, she's eyeing my food as if she and Rumor haven't already halved Daddy's portion and agreed to share both of our desserts. Mother tells her not to be rude, that she can have my dessert after the Warding Off. It'll be a treat. Mariah whines until shadows creeping across Mother's face tell her enough is enough. She runs back inside the house.

With this bundle of could-be-poisoned food warm in my hand, a pocketknife, the supplies I've tucked away, and Daddy's stone, I'm as ready now as I can hope to be.

"Wait, let me do your hair," Mother says. It's just like her, wanting to send me off to my doom looking good. She's already pulling me to the porch, settling herself on the steps before I can remind her that I don't have time. I couldn't get the words out if I wanted to. It's nothing like the hairdresser's hands moving quick, quick across my head, or Mae's tugging and pulling so I have to twist my neck in awkward positions to be halfway comfortable. The feel of Mother's hands working through my scalp, massaging, pulling and prodding my head is everything. The warmth of her hands winds curly hair around her fingers. Slender nails craft delicate parts, smooth sides, tease puffs into baby hair I haven't had in decades. Even if the whole town never talks to me another day in my life, if I'm no longer slightly blessed, forced into being a farmer and trying to learn a job even a last-chancer wouldn't want, this moment will be worth it. Mother braids my hair. I can't see it but I know I look like a princess or movie star. I'm tempted to ask her if she knows about Daddy's stone. Believes in Well Walkers. But she'll say there's no such thing, and I'd hate to waste this time with make-believe.

"Go on now," she says too soon. "Don't forget that food. It's not for you, though. It's for *them*. And don't fuss with your hair. I'll catch up with you after the Warding Off. If you see your father, give him a gentle send-off."

"Yes, ma'am." It's really all I can say. Any more and she'll know that I know she knows that if Daddy did run off before the Moving On and if by some chance he didn't get away, the town will make him regret it. If I get to him first, I can be merciful. Send his soul off quick, almost without pain.

Since I'm the oldest, I get to set up earlier than Mother and the girls. Moving-On families always get to choose the best Warding Off spots. It's only fitting. As you should be for the Warding Off, I'm dressed for flexibility. Plain blouse, long skirt, Daddy's stone now hidden in an inside pocket, Mary Janes. I'm like a whisper. No one will see me coming or going. I walk down the path, trailing my middle-school stick behind me for good luck. I know she's still there watching so I don't look back. Mother Opal used to say *The only way to move ahead is to turn your back on everything.* Well, the only way I'm going to survive tonight is if I remember everything she taught me. Not that all that wisdom did her much good in the end.

The Well

As soon as I get past the fence post, I'm in. Tonight is a long game of hide-and-seek—according to the flyers. The townsfolk, young, old, sick—well, everyone who isn't Moving On—are expected to contribute to the Warding Off. In the olden days, before the population boom of '54, families had to Move On their own kin. Imagine Moving your own family On and Warding them Off in the same breath. It's unnatural. It took Mother Opal to put an end to that.

On the breeze, I hear snatches of music. One of the marching band's tuning up. They'll be playing all night long. Each of the Moving On is assigned a small band. Never far behind the chase, led by a tireless conductor and creative drum majorette, each band will match the mood with joyful or suspenseful tunes composed especially for the Warding Off. Just last year, the pelting and screaming, hooting and hollering were accompanied by a catchy tune that became a top-ten hit by the next morning. The music sort of adds to the festivities. It lifts everyone's spirits. The Moving On appreciate it as much as everyone else—dead or alive—would do. Even if it is loud enough to raise the dead.

When they can't take it anymore, the ever-rising crescendos, stones, chants, hisses and screams will lead the Moving On to the Creek. The blows of mercy send the soul from the body. There's worse things to come. Once the soul is freed from the body, the townsfolk really get to work. Along with everyone else, children, little clubs in one hand, some sort of candy in the other, will be up hunting ghosts all night for the Warding Off. If it weren't against the rules, they'd be sure to keep one for themselves to dress up in see-through getups and twist into indecent poses while they take pictures that no camera could capture anyway.

Once the souls are set upon and dispersed, the prize ceremony can begin. The little ones get participation badges so even if they don't hit a Moving On earlier, they have a souvenir of the night. Everybody needs something to hold on to. There are trophies, prizes and ribbons for the older folks. Fastest Mover-On-er, quietest chaser, terrorizer, hell-raiser. *The Moving On is getting too commercial*, Mother Opal used to say. *Before long they'll be selling postcards and key rings.* Like she'd be caught dead without her Moving On satchel. Bless her soul.

There's not a star in the sky. It's just past six and dark as midnight. Just like the Warding Off should be. The street's littered with shadows. It's going to be a good night. I can feel it. If I'm lucky, I won't see any spirits at all. Won't even be a need to use my stick. I'll use it anyway, of course. I'll run just as hard as usual, swing just as wide. I'll make a show of it. *Osira the believer*. Everybody will be talking about it: how I cornered some misguided returned soul. I might even win another trophy this year. There will be no limit to my commitment—no doubt either.

The wind's rushing through the streets like it's got the good sense to blow on through this place without coming back. I'm dressed warm enough but still shivering. Every now and then there's a muffled note. The bands are warmed up. Soon, the bell will ring. Families will file out of their homes, take their places in line. They'll march, left, right, left, right, left into town. There used to be pitchforks and torches but since the Council declared it uncivilized and voted to "move with the times," there's been an ordinance against it. I hear other places still carry them, though. Marching like extras in that old vampire film they used to rerun at the cinema.

All the streetlamps are out. Lights will be off all around town. Houses, shops, the church, the guesthouse, school, courthouse. *Not one candle lit or one switch hit*, the saying goes. I guess what happens in the dark, and all that. Rocks and dirt crunch beneath my feet. I'm echoing down the lane. I'm not the only one walking on it, though. Scouts from the other families will be out setting up viewing and hiding spots. Places to attack. Places to heal. They should have prepared before now but ain't that always the way? Some folks are just hardheaded. Last-minute Sallys. They'd probably be late to their own Moving On—if the town would let them.

Whoever is following me isn't very good at it. They breathe every three counts, hold their breath for ten, breathe out again.

I walk in place. Hold my breath. There's a gentle breeze as they rush past, trying to catch up. I slip off one shoe, cock my right arm, hook my hand slightly, and release. I imagine the shoe zigzagging in a crooked line.

"Ow!" The yell is soft, no need to draw attention. The voice and its owner seem to hit the ground at the same time. "No fair, you didn't have to hit me."

"No," I say. I catch up to where they fell. I feel around the dirt road with my stockinged foot. It's caked and cold. The rocks are sharp, jagged edges and angles. "But I wanted to."

Jeremiah's still rubbing his head when I help him up. We press our thumbs together gently. "Sorry," he mumbles.

"I know." I do. Betraying me like this will show the town that, unlike his mother, Jeremiah is one of them.

My friends, widows and newlyweds, swarm out of the trees like wet bugs. There's really only ten of us but they are a mass of chattering teeth and moans. It serves them right. They must have been waiting in the wet grass for a good hour for me to get here. They're not at all dressed for this in their bright-colored pantsuits, wide-winged blouses, dangly jewelry, hope. I tap my foot, steady my breathing.

"You gonna run?" Mae is always impatient. She would rush her own funeral if they didn't see fit to sew her mouth shut. I hope I get her first. She stands close to Jeremiah so I can see them together. It's how I know she's planning to marry him if something happens to the good doctor and Florence. He should be careful though. Wife or not, she'd turn against him even if she didn't have to. She's practically my sister and still

I trust her as little as I would trust myself if the rock was in the other hand.

"Nope." There's not much point to running anyway. Jeremiah's already told them where he thinks my hiding spot is. If they have even a drop of sense, one of them is waiting on me there. If I go to the real spot now, I won't be able to use it in an emergency. May as well let them think they know all there is to know. I'm glad I heeded Mother Opal's advice. *Never tell the truth to someone you love. It makes it worse when they turn on you.* Of course, her other piece of advice was not to love anyone.

"If you'd rung the bell, none of this would be happening," Ezekiel says. He has a handful of pebbles and I think of Daddy's stone, now tucked inside my pocket. He clacks them together like commas stringing his words together. Pharmacist by day. I used to like him. Not *like him* like him. But like him enough not to tease him for having a hand-me-down bell when we were kids.

I shrug. They need me to say it's my fault, that I deserve what's coming to me. None of them deserves anything but bad news over this.

"We'll give you a head start. Since you're practically family. Go on, take it." Florence pushes me.

"No, thanks." Anything they want to do to me, they can do in front of their own families. Especially their kids. Let them see what kind of monsters their parents are. Who am I kidding? They probably already know. Kids, parents, in-laws, lovers—most of them are probably peeking out of their windows, cradling their phones. *Did you see that? No? Me neither.* They should be minding their own business. Gathering clubs and sticks, tying hair back, oiling bare skin, getting their own houses in order.

"Even your father needed a head start," Mae says.

Heaven help her. She's expecting me to slap her and, as much I want to feel her skin beneath my nails, I kick her instead. It all goes dark after that. For a good five minutes it's nothing but pulling, punching, kicking, screeching and rocks. One of them grabs for a clump of my hair, curses the burrs they find instead, forgets and grabs again. Mother thought of everything. The burrs are sharp enough to prick but dull enough to look like decoration, an accident not a weapon. I keep swinging and kicking. My knuckles sting, my head throbs, my sides hurt. Someone throws pebbles. Some of the rocks hit me, some hit the others. They're in my hair, my clothes, around my feet. When I can, I pick one up and toss it back. They are smoother than I would have thought. This is a warning. I'm just thankful they aren't using the clubs.

The rocks that hit the others take them by surprise. Their yelps are as pleasant to my ear as their screams. Their voices crack then cut off sharp like broken echoes. Sooner or later someone starts chanting. "Weak ringer, weak ringer." Before long, they're all at it. Dancing around me in circles singing at the top of their voices. It's a shame to have a voice that loud and not be able to carry a tune but Mae sings louder than them all. Every now and then I catch the good doctor looking at her with this worried expression, like she can't be the same woman he married, when of course she is, and if he hadn't been so long studying all those bumps and bruises people kept mysteriously coming down with he would have already figured out that Mae sends him more patients than the common cold.

I raise my voice and curse like a last-chancer at a carnival. I string words that have no business going together one right after the other. Phrases like *discombobulated beau* and *rule-breaking-widow-making bride* flow off my tongue. Someone tries to cover my mouth, chants "Out-of-tune Osira" like when we were kids. I lick their hand. It tastes sweaty and dirty but their shriek makes it worth it. The rest murmur as if I can't hear them. "Where is she? What's she waiting on?" They've been expecting Mother Opal to stop them. To send some sort of sign or tell them to forgive me. To take charge. Lord knows she ain't coming. I'm better off praying for the ancestors to come break this up. Someone has to be the leader.

"Mother Creek, hear my bell, send these heathens straight to—"

The good doctor smacks me in the mouth. My eyes water, lips sting, I swish my tongue around my mouth to check for loose teeth. Before I can do anything about it or wish another bad deed, there's Mae. "Don't you hit her like that!" She's yelling and *pop, pop, popp*ing him until even I want her to stop. It's not his fault. While he was studying medical books, we were making up our own rules. Some hits are sanctioned, others aren't. He wouldn't know our ways. I don't say it though. He hits her back, sure does. Then it's everyone for themselves. Widows against widows, newlyweds against newlyweds, widows against newlyweds.

Some fool yells, "This isn't who we are!"

In whatever position we're in, hands raised, legs extended, knees up, teeth bared, we all stop. Turn. Stare. "You damned fool!" Ezekiel says.

We're laughing so hard we're hacking and coughing, spitting, ugly laughing. This is exactly who we are. We wear ourselves out. We're all panting and heaving. The night air fills with hot breath. Someone turns on a porch light in a house nearby. The next porch lights up. Then the next. It's a reminder that the whole town is watching. They're impatient. If there's a lesson to be learned tonight, it ends with blood. Always has. Until there's blood, Curdle Creek fights with fists, rocks, sticks and words. Only then can forgiveness begin. I'm not sure I can take being a widow for much longer. All this hitting on me makes me hate the whole lot of them. The whole town if I'm honest. I can't stand it here with rules for this and rules for that. Who can have babies and who can't. Who can be what. Who dies. There's an ordinance for just about everything in Curdle Creek.

The flickering of the lights seems to remind them they have a job to do. They circle me, all of them squaring up so close I can smell their deodorant wearing off. They raise the clubs.

I can't find my stick. It's the one thing I was supposed to hold tight to. The one unbreakable rule of Warding Off is to never lose your weapon. God forbid one of the Moving On finds it. Everyone will say I lost it on purpose. Aiding and abetting. There's an ordinance against it. And of course everyone would know it was mine. They would count the grooves, one notch for each knock. Even if I hadn't been vain enough to mark it with my initials, a quick tally would lead them back to me. Well, to Mother's. It's a childhood weapon. So before it led to me, it would lead them to the girls. But not to my girls. Nothing can lead them back to them.

My eyes sting from tears and dirt, pain, but I look each of my friends in the eye so they know they will die for this. I open my mouth to remind them. Jeremiah grabs my arm to steady me. I know it's him because he squeezes a bit too long. Then, *bop*. He hits me on the head with my own damned stick. I know it because someone laughs and my stick drops before I do. I don't see stars like I expect. Instead I see words. I hear myself mumbling "*One by one before it's done*," and I know one of us won't make it home tonight.

* * *

I wake up in front of the well. The bricks are cold against my back. I suppose I should be grateful they waited for me to wake up before tossing me in. I'm not, though. *Just following rules* or not, they should all be dead. *Fire! Fire!* No matter how hard I think it, none of them bursts into flames or any of that biblical stuff. The group gathers around my satchel, dividing up my things. From town, music plays. The Warding Off has begun and they've started without us. If we miss it . . . My whole body starts to tremble. Heaven save us if we miss it.

"There's enough food for all of us, if we share," Florence says. Even I almost laugh. Share? What are we, first graders? Well, I know that she won't be the leader.

"You all right?" Jeremiah smells like Mother's apple crumble biscuits.

I shake my head. Poor Jeremiah. Hitting me on the head

without even being asked should have moved him up the ladder a bit tonight. If there were one. I won't look up, so I only see his feet. He sits down next to me. Not close enough to be mistaken for kindness but close enough to be close. I shouldn't have expected anything more, really. He had to get tired of defending his mother's name. Proving himself trial after trial after trial. What better way to do it than to jump me, eat my mother's food, and sit beside me with the betrayal fresh on his breath?

He rubs his hands together, thinking. From time to time he looks at me, then back at the group with their cackles puncturing the air. They've lit a small fire to warm up. It won't stay lit because the ground's too wet. I won't tell them, though. They're bickering over who gets to toss me in the well. I would hate to interrupt that.

"You would have done the same," he says.

We won't know that. I wouldn't have been in his position in the first place. Mother would never have turned her back on the town.

There's a shrill whistle. Then, a cacophony of bells. They're all ringing. The Warding Off is in full swing. Mother and the girls must be in town with the rest of them by now. I can almost picture them in their ballerina poses, position one, arms raised, poised to catch a wayward soul before it slips into a house. They say once a soul gets in it's harder to get out than an old grudge. Just one ghost carries four seasons of chaos. A year of bad luck. People are liable to believe anything.

"You all gonna send me down there with nothing at all?" They don't know about what I have strapped to my chest.

"Just till dawn. We'll pull you up in the morning."

"It's uncovered already?"

"We couldn't toss you in with the lid still on." He laughs.

They've thought of just about everything. They must have come here this morning, pulled out the long nails, shoved the heavy lid to the ground. Plotted. Must have calculated how much air I'd have, how long I'd last after they sealed it back up, how they'd get me down there in the first place. I'm much bigger than Beth. I don't imagine they had time to refit the bucket she was folded into.

"If y'all toss me in the well, I'll probably die. Who gets to throw me to my death?"

Jeremiah sucks his teeth. "We're sitting you in the bucket. You can prove you're not a Well Walker."

Across from us, someone breaks the bucket into jagged pieces. They throw the shards of wood into the fire. The sparks are almost beautiful. The sweet scent of burning mahogany almost masks the stench of everything else. They whoop and cheer. Their shadows dance across the stones toward Jeremiah and me. It seems they have other plans for tonight.

"We took a vote," Mae says. She's lying, but no one corrects her. "There's only room for one of you next year. We don't need but one farmer in Curdle Creek. You can fight for the place."

"He can have it." I nod toward Jeremiah. Mae knows better. One farmer can't feed the whole town. There's only a few left as it is. More farmers means more choice and if nothing else, Curdle Creekers would want a choice.

"You'll fight for it," one of them says.

"Unless you're both traitors."

Even if we are, the ordinance clearly reads that we deserve a trial. We'd be found guilty either way, but a rule's a rule.

As if she's watching the words in my mind, Mae answers. "Did you know the good doctor was sworn in as judge this very evening?"

These heathens could say what they want and, because of yesterday, the whole damned town would believe them. Mother and the girls will be unprotected. Unless she marries quick, one of the girls will have to take my place. Mother would be so angry she wouldn't even use her fifteen minutes of mourning on me. She'd save them for herself and split them, seven and a half minutes each so the girls could mourn her extra.

"How's your mother, Jeremiah?"

That Mae, always stirring up trouble. She stands so close to the fire it's a wonder she doesn't burn up. Smoke might as well be blowing straight out of her mouth. She shakes her head, punctuates what should be silence except for the crackling of the flames with *mmm, mmm, mmm* sounds. My leg's twitching. Mae turns away, takes a few steps, stops, then, as if the words just popped into her head, she turns around a fraction, to barely face us. "Won't be too much longer before her name's called, will it?"

The rest of them are so giddy for a fight they bounce from foot to foot. With Jeremiah gone, his mother's name will be called whether she's a believer or not. There will be nothing standing between her and the Moving On. Unless they take his bride instead. Florence must be thinking what bad luck to be burdened with someone so easily swayed. He scrambles to his feet, kicking up dirt. With a toe he pushes my stick toward me. "Get up," he says.

It would be better if he growled, snarled, or something. But he doesn't. He's just my Jeremiah, fighting to save his mother over me.

"We're supposed to fight until first blood." I don't know why I'm reminding them. They're licking their lips, circling. I wish the fire would go out so I wouldn't have to see them.

Jeremiah pokes my foot with his stick—I'm sweaty. Sweat slips down my forehead, gets into my eyes. I must wink or something. "I'm not playing!" he yells.

He crashes his stick down on my ankle. The bone, or the stick, cracks. If I let him kill me, he'll have everything he's ever really wanted. He'll have the second-best job, second-best bride. He'll have three children, a big farm, a good house. If Mother weren't Head Charter Mother, they might even have my house. His mother will be given a role she will not want. And when they ring the bell, they will ring it four times. Once for all of us Warded Off tonight in the name of the town.

I leap to my feet. My ankle rolls. I wave my stick high, grit my teeth, Jeremiah braces for the blow. The stick pulses in my palm, guides me. Before anyone can stop me, I run to the well and curl my toes around the cool stone edge. One by one the rest of the group, my friends, double over in pain. The cramping. The only thing they're going to be watching over tonight is the commode. Mother put enough castor oil in that food to move a mountain. Not because she loves me, though in her own way I'm sure she does—but because she's already lost one person tonight. The more she loses, the closer she is to the grave.

The cramps aren't strong enough to stop them all. Jeremiah is one of the only ones still moving. He's determined to push me in, to claim his place. Not in my name he won't. The last thing I see is the shadows shrinking in the dwindling fire. There's the sudden crash of a cymbal, then the trill of a trumpet, booms of bass. The band's getting closer. The Warding Off is coming to an end. The Moved On have been subdued, Moved On. Their souls have been sent away, set free.

I hope Daddy got away and that he's far from this place. The bass thunders; its deep *boom, boom* makes my heart race. The band steps in time. Not too far behind, there are distant whoops, clatters of stones, footsteps. *May their souls fly over swiftly*, I pray. The sky is red. I don't know who's going to be around to pull me up in the morning or if they'll even bother to. Sometime after breakfast somebody's bound to come looking for me. By then, they'll have their stories straight. Ordinance has it that I'm supposed to forgive them. If I'm not dead. Jeremiah's hand grazes my leg. I close my eyes and jump in.

The Dark

I hit my everything on the way down. My head bumps on stones. My legs scrape against bricks. My fingernails snag on rocks. I'm sure to die when I hit the ground if not before then. My breath has left my body. My mouth is wide open. My scream has no sound, though. There's no air left for it. Just the *whoosh* of my body hurtling. The light from outside dims as I fall. The sky is covered in shadows. There's a scrape as one of the shadows pulls the thick cover across the lip of the well. A loud *click* as they clamp it shut and even from here, the hammering of the nails.

I thought I'd be praying in my last moments of life. That I'd list my wrongdoings and beg for forgiveness. But I can't think of one prayer that feels right. Not one saying that will save me except *If I should die before I wake.* If this is how I die, I hope it's quick and painless. Without being Moved On there's no telling where my soul will end up. My death won't be in service to Curdle Creek. What a waste. I'll be aimless, I just know it. Damned to wander for eternity.

I'm scared to die this way. Truth be told, the more I think on it, the more afraid I am to die at all. I just don't want to. Not for a bountiful harvest. Not for a prosperous spring. Not to keep the town safe for another year. I just want to see my sweet girls and my dear boy. And I want to be alive when I do.

When I hit the ground it is unexpected. The air returns to my body and I'm gulping and gasping at the rush of it. My neck is bent at an ungodly angle. My body is sore but I'm not dead. At least. I get up, shake the soot and lime from my dress, brush off my shoes. The bottom of the well is dank. The walls are slimy, dripping with gunk. There are leaves and slugs and living things down here. I slip on them when I walk. Beneath my foot, one shoe is long gone, I slide on what's left of folds of paper. There are mounds and mounds of them. The discarded. These must be the slips with the names of those who were nominated but not called. At least one of them is sure to have my name on it. They are stuck together by slime. I leave them. If my name is down here, I couldn't see it anyway.

It's still dark so I feel my way around. I light a match to see. I'm surrounded by bones, bones and more bones. Some are just skeletons, naked. Others still wear swaths of gingham dresses, patches of denim overalls, frays of cotton blouses. My hands are clammy. It's cold. My teeth are chattering, click-clacking like footsteps. Something drips, *plunk, plunk*ing behind me. I hope it's water. The match flickers and I stumble. My foot slips. I fall next to a little clump of nothing but bones. I catch myself before it starts. Swallow the wailing. I can hear

Mother Opal. *It's the living that you have to watch out for. The dead ain't nothing to be feared.* I wonder if she'd feel that way now, what with her being one of them.

I don't want to disturb whatever peace the dead have found. I pray that their final moments on this earth weren't painful, though I suspect they were. I make piles of the bones. I can't be sure but some of them are old. They could be the remains of the ancestors. There are no markers. There's no way to be sure, but it feels like the grave of the absconded.

The Glassblower's Hut

I make crosses out of slugs, leaves, rocks, and whatever else I can find. With my words back, I say a prayer, leave an offering, honor the dead. I can't give thanks fully, ring bells for them the way I would back home. It wouldn't be proper. Even if it were, I don't have my bells with me. For the first time in my life, I'm not prepared. Instead, I sing "O What a Privilege to Give," the song of thanks. The words feel out of place down here.

I feel my way around the well. There must be a way out of it. I can't die here. Mother and the girls will be all alone. They'll be called one after another. An unprecedented domino of Movings On. I never even got to say goodbye. There's so much I haven't done. If I make it back, I'll be a more faithful believer. There will be no doubt. I'll show my allegiance to Curdle Creek, to Mother, to the girls. I'll atone for Daddy. I'll pay what the town demands. I'll nominate myself for the Moving On.

I have to get home. I search for a rope to shimmy up. I

look and I look and I look. My back aches, my legs burn. My eyes sting. I can't seem to catch my breath. What would Mother do? I picture Mother pulling out a chisel, scaling the slick walls. Mother is always prepared, so she'll have a tool in that bag and when she reaches the top, she'll pull out whatever is required. She'll crack through the lid like it's a walnut. If Mae, Jeremiah and them are still up there when she comes out, they'll wish they weren't. I can picture her chasing them around the well, down to the Creek, into the water. She wouldn't stop, wouldn't give up. I won't either.

I crack my knuckles to loosen my fingers. I crack my toes. The pops are satisfying. My fingers are limber, ready. I stretch the rest of my body. Thank the ancestors I'm not as busted up as I would have thought I'd be. I climb. The walls are made of brittle rocks, wet clay and stones. My hands and feet slip in slime and moss. Where the walls are rough, my hands find purchase. I make my way hand, hand, foot, foot toward the mouth of the well. I hope.

I've been climbing and climbing and I don't feel any closer to the top than I was forever ago. It's dark all the way through. This is it. I will die here clinging to the walls of a well. Even now, I feel heavy. My arms are sore. My fingers are raw. The timers were wrong. There is no world beyond Curdle Creek. How could there be, without the Moving On to keep folks safe? I slip down to the ground, back against the slimy wall.

I'm crying when I hear it. Mourning the second husband I never got to have, wishing I had done right by my children. It's muffled but I would recognize the sound anywhere. Voices. Not inside the well but from outside of it. Wherever *out there* is. My heart stops. I'm not alone. Above me, there's a sliver of light. It's just a sliver but, as Mother always says, *Like mold, hope can make its way through the tiniest of places.* Of course, she meant that it's best to scrub it out before it can grow.

I take a sharp rock from the pile. Tuck it into a pocket. I press up against a wall and wait. If they come in here, I'll be ready for them. I'm waiting on them but the voices aren't coming any closer.

I'm sure they are young voices. Female. There's a sharp voice, a shout. Jasmine? Is that you? I move as quickly as the dark will allow. I could have lived my whole life imagining my children suffering somewhere far away from Curdle Creek. Even if it meant never seeing them again, at least they'd be alive. But that could be them. The well could have brought me to my babies. Maybe they're in trouble. I have to save them. I can feel the stone tucked away in my pocket. I wouldn't have thought Well Walkers were true or that Daddy would have been one of them but now that I'm in the bottom of a well, I'm a believer. "I'm coming," I say. I take a deep breath. There's no time to think of my aching back, arms, legs, heart. I'm on my feet and before I know it, I'm climbing my way up to my children.

Being inside the well is like being inside the barrel, only bigger. And darker. Thankful for the slime, I use my body to inch up. The voices are getting louder. I'm not far now. There's more light. I can see the sky. The lid's been removed. All this time worrying about the well leading me somewhere else and I've been in Curdle Creek all along. Of course I was.

Well Walkers don't exist. Mae and them didn't abandon me. Truth be told, I'm not even upset anymore. Rules are rules. Of course they had to teach me a lesson. I've learned it. I'm just thankful to be home. When they take turns to offer their apologies, *Bygones*, I'll say. I won't even nominate them for the Moving On.

The voices of young girls drifts down into the well. Folks shouldn't be playing here. Wouldn't want them slipping in, getting hurt. Their shrill laughter echoes off the walls. *I'm coming*, I think. *I'll save you.*

I pull myself over the top of the well and fall to the ground in a heap of leaves and rubble. For a second, I can't see. There's so much sun that it hurts my eyes. Even squinting, I can tell I'm not home. This isn't Curdle Creek. The girls are still laughing. There's no joy in it. I wouldn't have expected anyplace without the Moving On would have anything to laugh about but they're laughing loud and long just the same. Above, the sun is bright, cheerful and warm against my skin. It's not the burning ball of flame and damnation Book XXIII warns about. There's still time. For now, the sky is clear and blue. Hopeful. I shield my eyes against it. The girls, arms flailing, fists pumping, old-fashioned dresses swinging, see me before I see them. They are running toward me, arms raised in a welcome position. Before I have time to adjust to the light, the squealing, the fresh air, the sun, they are on me. Pummeling me with bony fists. Violent. Just like the ancestors said they'd be.

"She's mine!" one yells.

"She's mine! I saw her first!"

"Get your wretched hands off of me or I'll—"

Bop. I didn't see the stick in her hand but the smaller one hit me. Just as the headlines said, danger is everywhere out here. These two are proof. Rule breaking, plague carrying, deadly proof.

"Constance! You'll kill her. She ain't yours to kill!"

"Opal, I'll do what I damn well please."

Before Opal can complain or I can move out of the way, Constance hits me again. A place like this will kill you.

* * *

THE girls argue in high-pitched voices, low grunts and whispers for what feels like hours, but truth be told probably feels that way because I'm standing in a big black pot full of water and one of them is holding a match. Opal, the match holder, has lit at least one match and, according to the other girl, if she wastes one more she'll find herself in the pot right next to me. Like there's room.

It's not really her fault the first one blew out. When it lit, she got so excited about her "experiment" that she did a little jig. Of course, that blew out the candle. They both blamed it on me. The second match blew out because the other girl was whispering about trials and shouldn't they call a witness or a preacher to make it official. She pronounced it with a *shhhh* which obviously blew the match right out. They blame that on me too.

The girls are evil, I'm sure of it. It's not their fault. Everyone out here is. Their skin is the same color as mine but they ain't kin like the folks back home. At least in Curdle Creek we have each other. There's no way this place has a Moving On. It's like something from one of Mother Opal's ghost stories out here. Reckless, just like she warned us. Opal and Constance sort of remind me of Mother Opal and my own mother. These two bicker like sisters just like they do—did.

"I'm not a witch," I tell them for the umpteenth time. I try to keep my voice steady. Like dogs, they will be able to hear fear.

Opal shakes her head. "That's just what a witch would say."

"Just tell us how you got here, then," says Constance. "Did you take a train?"

"No."

"There's no bus stop for miles and miles outside of Curdle Creek. And you don't have no car. Did you walk? You all scuffed up. You look like you must have walked."

Curdle Creek? There ain't but one Curdle Creek and this ain't it.

"I was just about to say that." Opal twists her mouth in a pout.

"Sure you were, Opal. Sure you were."

"What did you say this place is called?" I ask.

"Didn't you see the welcome sign before you crossed over?"

"What did it say?"

"Welcome," Opal says.

"It don't mean it though," Constance says.

"You'd have seen it on the sign if you'd stopped long enough to read it before you started trespassing. Entering places you ought not to have."

"It doesn't matter where you came from or how you got here. You here now. Nothing in the Books says it matters how you got here. Just how you leave."

I'm shaking. Water seeps through my clothes. Fabric sticks to skin in places it shouldn't be sticking. But it's not just the water making my skin pimple. It's these girls and their *hush, hush* voices like whispering in a church. Girls like these can't be trusted. They might be Well Walkers for all I know. Could be a whole town of them.

"Where'd you come from?" Opal asks.

I look behind the girls. I wouldn't know what to say and I'm not about to explain myself to these children.

"Up yonder, just like I thought," Constance says, like she's translating my not-answers into answers.

"Look just like one of them girls. Wild. Y'all at least got the Moving On there?" Opal sounds hopeful.

Oh! Thank the ancestors! This place can't be that bad if they have their own Moving On.

"Of course they don't, silly. That's why she's here, trying to get away from some wicked, chaos-filled place. What you running from? Klan? Slavery? The law? You can tell us."

"You ain't sick, are you? Cuz Curdle Creek don't take in the sick. Sick folks ain't quick folks, I always say."

Mother Opal used to say that too. Just thinking about her now makes me smile. I miss her.

"Opal here says a lot of things," Constance says. "Got a saying for everything. You get used to it after a while."

Only superstitious people believe in superstitious things, Mother Opal would say. If there were enough room I'd make the sign of the bell to protect myself against old wives' tales and evil girls. Wherever I am, I'm in the middle of nowhere with these two wannabe witch-hunters and everything I say is wrong. I roll my eyes.

"Did you see that?" Constance asks. "Her eyes went clear up into her head."

"They did not!" I stomp my foot. The water sloshes and swirls. Above us there's thunder.

"Then what do you call that?" Opal asks.

"It's thunder. What do you call it?"

"Same thing, only it doesn't come when I call it." Opal smirks.

"How does boiling me alive prove I'm not a witch?"

"If you're a witch, you won't die and you'll owe us three wishes for saving your life," Constance says.

I laugh. It feels like the sky's laughing too, only it's thunder again. I see why the girls jump. It's getting closer. "Why would I want to give you two murderers anything?"

"How'd you know we were murderers?" Constance asks.

My mouth dries out. There's something about the way she looks at me. It's almost playful. Not like a kid playing with another kid but like a hunter toying with a deer. Or, even worse, like Rumor and Mariah would do if they were here.

"I don't know anything about you. You know I'm new here."

"Right, sprouted up a full-grown weed out of the well."

"I didn't sprout out of it. I jumped into it."

They stare at each other while I talk. It doesn't seem to matter what I say, only what they think I mean. Maybe they aren't Well Walkers after all.

"Where you're from, people jump in and out of wells all the time?"

"I jumped in because people were going to push me in."

"That sounds just like something witches would do. Wouldn't happen here, I can tell you that. The town's covering over all but one of the wells. Paving over them first thing in the morning. Seems some folks have acquired a fascination with them."

"Yeah, *some* folks."

"Don't you say one word about him, Opal. Not one more word." Constance's fists are balled up.

Opal takes a step back. "There you go thinking about that boy. I wasn't going to say his name. I'm just saying, be careful where you walk. And careful *who* you walk with."

"What about you two? Murder has to be right up there with being a witch." If they're busy fighting, they can't untie me. I'll be stuck here forever.

"Only a witch would know we did anything. Who would believe a witch over two little schoolgirls?" Constance sways from side to side, one hand toying with the hem of her skirt swishing left to right, the other propped beneath her chin, pinky finger tucked between pouted lips. I look harder at her. She's twenty if she's a day.

They might not have Charter Mothers but their little town has to have a sheriff or some form of law. Of course, from what I've heard, that might not be any better than these hellions are. But I'll take my chances. I open my mouth to yell for the law.

"Besides, who would trust a dead witch anyhow?"

I close my mouth, roll the words around in my head. Of

course they killed someone. But why? They have the Moving On, and the Moving On's supposed to keep us safe from people like them. They would kill me, sure as I'm standing in a pot of water they would do it. It's what would happen if the shoe was on the other foot and I was the one holding the match. Only, in Curdle Creek, there wouldn't be a pot, a match or water. It would be the well, the Warding Off or some other civilized calamity. One way or the other, these two would be Moving On. At least back home it would be in service of the town.

"What were y'all doing with a pot in the first place? Were you cooking? Maybe I can help."

They walk a few steps away and talk it over. They don't bother whispering or even lowering their voices.

"You said the ceremony would bring back the Moved On," Constance says.

"I said we had to say the words right. We must have gotten them wrong. It's supposed to cleanse the town, make a way back for a loved one."

"Well, it didn't work, did it?"

I've read about returning the Moved Ons. Can't believe they'd allow that here. Nothing good could come from it. Back home, there's an ordinance against it and everything. The water's getting even colder. My teeth are chattering.

"Want me to warm that up?" Constance offers. Her hand is raised, ready to strike the match.

I think I hate her. I grab the lip of the pot and lean forward. She jumps back as if I've hit her. "Opal, toss the match! Toss the match! The whole pot's floating!"

One girl pushes my head down; the other clamps the lid on top. It's dark. No darker than the well was, but dark is dark. "It's not floating, it's tipping." My words echo back.

It takes a few minutes for the water to heat up, but when it does, it goes from hot to hotter real quick. I try to squirm away from it but if it's not the water, it's the sides of the pot. If it's not that, it's the lid. I'm stewing in my own sweat.

"Stop moving!" one of them yells. My dying is such an inconvenience. I couldn't stop moving if I wanted to. I'm shaking and rocking and the whole pot starts shaking too.

There's a tap on the lid like I'm supposed to ask who it is. I don't ask and there's more tapping. It's louder now. It's not just on the lid, but the sides of the pot and under it too. It's not much cooler but the boiling's stopped. Maybe they've changed their minds, come to their senses, decided to stop this foolishness. Someone takes off the lid. It's pouring big plump streaks of rain. It's wetter out there than it is in here. Rain beats the trees, the ground, the girls. If I didn't know better, I'd think it was after them. Just in case it is, I stay in the pot.

"You coming out?" Opal asks.

"No, thank you. Please put the lid back on." I don't want no part of these girls or their rituals. I settle back down, tuck my knees beneath my chin. My back hurts right away.

"Please make it stop. We weren't really going to boil you," she says. She puts her hands out, palms up. "Promise." She makes the sign of something close to a cross around where her heart should be.

I would trust her if she wasn't still holding the match. If my back wasn't about to snap in half and my legs weren't cramped up, I would make her wait longer. "Help me out, then."

"Constance, grab a hold too," she says.

Constance sucks her teeth just like Mother does. It takes the two of them to get me out. I'm not really helping. For a while, I lean forward when they do and backward when they do. They slip and fall. When they are caked with mud and soggy, I stand, lean forward, and spill out, water and all. Serves them right. I want to show them the rain had nothing to do with me. If she's watching, Mother Nature is not helping any. The rain stops and, for spite, there's a rainbow.

"Aren't you just a well-dressed blessing," says Constance.

*   *   *

THEY argue while I wring out my clothes.

"We can't let anyone see her. We'll hide her at my house till after the Moving On. We can take the long way. Loop around the mill," Constance says.

"You just want Osiris to ask you who she is and what she's doing here. You'll do anything for attention."

I can't help it: hearing my Daddy's name out of that evil mouth makes me want to hit her. My daddy's the only Osiris I've ever known. I wouldn't have thought his name was common. But then again, I wouldn't have expected to meet another Opal or Constance either.

"It's not my fault that boy likes me. You just jealous," Constance says.

"Of that woebegone? He ain't good for nothing but stories and even them ain't his. He talks for hours and hours and hours about his father this, his uncle that. My, but that boy sure can talk." Opal shoves a book, plants and glass figurines into a satchel. Slings it across her shoulders. "Why you always around him anyway? You got Snow fawning over you, buying you presents, making up reasons to have a word with you."

"I'm a planner, Opal. Like to keep one man for a rainy day. I'm going to walk our guest through town so everyone knows she's ours. Won't nobody get to claim her before we do."

"No one is keeping me. I'm going home." The last thing I want to do is meet anyone else. With my luck, they'll be just as bad as these two. Even worse. I turn toward the well.

"I can see why you'd want to rush to get back," Constance says. "Who wouldn't miss a place so good that you jump into a well to escape it? Look, it's dangerous at night. Whether you're in Curdle Creek or wherever you're from. Wait until morning to go."

Of course she's right. It'll be dark soon and even if this place has the same name, it isn't home. I don't know my way around. I don't know how I'd get back. If there was a way home through the well, I'd have found it. Even if there is some way to get there, I don't know what's waiting for me. Mr. Jacobs could already be settling in with Mother and the girls by now. There's no way Mother would want me there. My own home will be gone. Someone will have stripped my bed, packed up my belongings, de-Osira'd the house to make room for the next librarian to move in before one day being Moved On. Even if I could make my way back, there's no home for me to return to. Right now, I have nowhere to go and no way to get there.

I'll find the children. I may not be able to make it back to Curdle Creek but maybe I can make my way to them somehow.

Rather than tell Constance she's right, I walk past the well as if I'd never thought about slipping over the side, jumping right back in. My shoe squishes as I walk. No matter how hard I squeeze my toes, I can't get all of the water out. I give up. I may as well be walking on lily pads. My toes slip against the sole, daring me not to fall. The *squish, squish, squash* sounds sort of funny; they giggle, and the sound helps to clear my head. No one was really going to kill me. They're my friends. They needed to teach me a lesson, that's all. And these girls aren't much older than my own children. Misunderstandings. My own children would have welcomed a stranger into Curdle Creek by calling the Council. The Council would have taken care of everything, even the Moving On.

There's no room for doubts or doubters in Curdle Creek. If I hadn't hidden away Daddy's stone, I would still have been in the well in the morning. They would have hauled me up, accepted my whimpering as apology, helped me out of the well. I would have missed everything. The Warding Off, morning and noon bells, the Creek running red with thanks. They would have told me about it. The way Mildred, Isiah and maybe even Daddy—the town and band not more than two left, right, lefts behind—ran straight into their traps of muddied leaves and shallow holes. How one of them might have lost themselves and smiled, nearly glad to see them. They'd have told me how true their aim was, how many hits had been given to whom and where. Some would have lied, claimed more knocks than was true, but it's all in good fun. The merciful aim for less than ten blows. They'd all brag about needing less, breaking records as well as bones.

* * *

I don't know where we're going but the girls seem to trust me to get us there. We walk down a mud road. It looks like any other road. Lots of trees, a few houses. Only empty. Thankfully, there's not one face, smiling or otherwise. We could be anywhere. The houses are scattered apart. They dot fields of corn and wheat, groves of berries and grapes. It seems like anything that can grow does grow. What would be winter harvest back home grows here right alongside summer grains and winter nuts. This place has a plentiful harvest. They must have luck and skilled farmers galore. We move slowly, the mud sucking the soles of our shoes, making puckering sounds with each step. Between that and the rustle of fabric sticking and unsticking to drying skin, we sound like some sort of macabre band parading through town.

We reach the end of the road. I don't know why but I thump the stop sign like I would back home before turning right, onto a wider, even muddier road. I can't help but jump when I hear the sound that makes. This place reminds me so much of home that it scares me. Thinking of home don't seem to calm me like it used to.

"You walk like you know where you're going," Constance says.

I picture Opal nodding her head along. "It's a stop sign just like any stop sign. Anywhere I've been," and it doesn't seem necessary to tell them I've only ever been in Curdle Creek, "a stop sign means you have choices. Turn one way, the other, or go back the way you came." I turn to look at the girls. "I would rather not go back to the pot, thank you."

"I don't believe this is your first time in Curdle Creek," Opal says.

"If I had been here before, would I bother coming back?" I put my hands on my hips, purse my lips. For a minute or two it blocks out the smell of fresh, baking manure. This whole place smells like one big pile of—

"You remind me of someone when you do that," Constance says. She looks me up and down. "I'm sure I know you."

There's something familiar about her too. I don't know what it is but I know not to trust her. "Fine, you two lead the way."

Constance smiles and shakes her head. If I could read her mind, I know she'd be calling me a fool. "We should get out of these wet clothes," she says. She walks ahead. "If anyone sees her," she says to Opal, "she'll be your cousin from out of town."

"My cousin who?"

They stop to look at me. How much do I want them to know? What do I really know about them? "Cheyenne," I whisper.

Constance shivers. It's not quite a lie. Mother used to say if I had been a little cuter when I was born, I would have been a Cheyenne. It was nothing personal, she said, just the name reminded her of someone and if I wasn't going to look like that, I shouldn't be named something I wouldn't grow into. Instead, she let Daddy name me.

"Fine, your cousin Cheyenne, which is really no sort of name for a woman like her. Who would believe that?"

"A woman like what? My name suits me just fine." My cheeks are burning.

Constance rolls her eyes.

"No one ever comes here," Opal says. "Unless they're running from their obligations back home."

"She look like she running to you?"

I pretend not to hear them bickering over where I'll sleep, how they can use whatever powers I have, what to do with me when my powers run dry. If they think I'm going to stay here long enough for them to figure out I don't have any powers to begin with, they can think again. They promise one another to keep me as a lie "for my own good" until after the Moving On. That suits me just fine. Who would believe I was delivered out of a well and didn't bring death with me? They wrap their pinky fingers, both dripping with spit, around the other's, stage-whisper "*Two by two until it's through*" and shake on it. I'm dragging my feet behind me to leave a trail in the mud even though I'm pretty sure I could make my way back to the well with my eyes closed. Maybe it's some sort of door, able to get me back to Curdle Creek. No, I don't want to go back to the well. I just need to get away from this place and find a bus stop or a train station or something. I'll have to find a way to get on. Can't afford to pay and can't afford to hope for kindness. Timers always said, *Ain't no kindness beyond Curdle Creek*. They sure were right.

Back home, I picture Mae delivering the news to Mother personally. She wouldn't send a Messenger with something like this. She wouldn't tell Mother they had set upon me, made to push me in the well, given me no choice but to jump in. She would say I had hidden in the bucket, lowered myself down, waited so I could miss the Warding Off. She would claim I had wanted Daddy's spirit tied to Curdle Creek and refused to Ward it Off when it was time. That I had left him to linger, to wander and haunt the town. If Mother called for the bucket to be pulled up, though, Mae would have to say I ran off. That I somehow pulled myself up when no one was looking and made my way out of town. If I made it back and got to Mother first, the only thing worse than telling Mother that I had left would be my beating them to it. The looks on their faces when Mother opened the door, nodded along to their stories, then invited them into the dining room, where I would be sitting, my back to the mirror, watching them come in. They would think I was a ghost at first. I would give almost anything to see their smug expressions slip, their flushed cheeks turn to ash, their fear.

Of course I didn't want Daddy to Move On, but I wouldn't have kept him there trapped in a box like some sort of pet to pull out and play with then tuck in at night. After all he's done for us, not letting him be free would be selfish and downright evil. Even before I was born, Daddy protected Curdle Creek when the people of Salt Harbor turned on us, decided if we wouldn't do business with them, we wouldn't do business at all. They stormed the town with torches and shotguns. Armed with bows and arrows, bullets and hatchets, Daddy and his posse of elders, bankers, lawyers and shopkeepers caught up with them before they crossed the Creek. Buried them right there in the water just like the ancestors before them would have done.

The small box houses give way to larger houses and now shops. There's the Sweet Shoppe and a picture house, a guest-house. We stop in front of Fleming's Keys and Keys Music Shoppe. There's ragtime music filtering through the door. It's lively, and before I know it I'm jiggling the doorknob and in the shop. The girls, mouths open, follow me inside. A boy of around sixteen springs up from the piano bench.

"Ma'am! I'm sorry. I wasn't expecting anyone. We're closed. I was just tuning the piano."

It's him. Fleming from back home. I'd recognize him any-where. He's younger, handsome, closer to happiness than I can remember. "That's all right, you play wonderfully."

"I don't play, ma'am, sorry. I just tune instruments. My brother's the drum major. He plays."

"Fleming, you're so modest," Constance says. She giggles for no reason at all. Strums her fingers on the skins of drums, fingers violin and guitar strings, taps the bells.

"Constance, please don't touch anything. You know you don't have a musical ear. You're liable to—"

Constance is out the door before he even finishes his sen-tence.

"You really ought to do something with your talent. Find yourself a big city, join a band. You know, before—"

"I'm too old?" Fleming closes the piano case, pushes in the bench.

"Before this place kills you," I say.

"Come on, Shyyy-Annnn!" Opal yells.

They are half a block away before I catch up to them. Curdle Creek looks just the way it does in 1960 only smaller, less crowded. It's after the Founding. I just hope it's before the first year of plenty. That year, a dozen names were called. After that, pecans the size of biscuits fell from the trees. They were everywhere, in everything. Pecans, walnuts, cabbages, everything grew. The only thing that didn't flourish were the fish. Turns out all that red isn't good for laying eggs.

Now, there are fewer shops and more crops. I don't know when this is but it's before the population booms, that's for sure. And they have the Moving On, of course they do. The records will be in the Town Hall. All the names of the Moved On, the directory of who lives where and does what. The old newspapers. The date.

Up ahead, the girls' voices turn to murmurs and then stop all together. Their silence feels good in my ears. Here, with the crickets and night birds singing, the swish and suck, the last thing I need is their spiteful words. I should run for help. If I turn off Main and onto one of the small streets, I'm sure to run into a neighbor, a farmer, a Deacon. Someone who can get me away from them or distract them long enough so I can slip away. Word is that anyplace other than Curdle Creek is dangerous, but surely Curdle Creek of the past is as safe a place to be as my own Curdle Creek. Or safer. Maybe being here won't be so bad. I can be a whole new me. Have another chance. It can start right now. If only I can slip away. I'll find myself a strong, loyal somebody. Someone who would make Mae jealous if she was here. Someone bold enough to say *I love you*, make promises, keep them. Everything on his face will be in just the right spot. He'll be handsome enough to make me smile but not so handsome he can't think of anything else. He'll be a strong ringer with steady hands, thick arms, muscled legs. His voice will be deep and kind, and when he tells people to leave me be, they'll do it not because they worry he'll put in a word and have them Moved On but because who wants to make someone so good feel so bad? His name will be Onzelow or Lucius, I don't care which since I'll call him Dear and he'll call me Lovely. I'll take him home with me and the whole town will be jealous, mad that we flaunt our love—Book XII be damned. They'll be too scared to do anything about it since Mother will have granted him protection and everyone knows the Head Charter Mother's protection is a promise as good as her word. But if he's got any sense, Dear will want to stay here in his own Curdle Creek with its old rules, ceremonies and traditions, raising babies who live long enough to die in peace and run around saying *I love you*. It'll be our first argument.

Opal's cold fingers wrap around my wrist. I jump. Her hands are thin like bones. She puts a finger to her mouth, nods her head at Constance curled around an iron gate, legs through the bottom, arms wrapped around the top. She's in a trance. Watching the shadows pass across her face, I know what she's staring at before I turn to look too. The glassblower. Before he Moved On, kids watched for hours as blobs turned into lions, strands turned into women, and bubbles turned into wishes. The glassblower's hut was special. Constance can't be all that bad if she likes magical things. Opal and I take places along the fence outside the shop. Shadows fill the air.

The blower and glass contort into magnificent shapes. They fight and dance, glide as one then the other takes the form of a bunny, a farmer, a steeple. It's magic. The blowing is my favorite part. It starts with a glob of dripping glass. Even from here, I can almost see the blower's breath leaving his body, bringing the glob to life. Minutes or hours later, deft hands shifting and stretching, and the body of a bullfrog springs from his hands puff-first. I can almost hear it croaking.

"Let's go closer," Constance whispers.

The way she says it, I'm sure it's not a good idea. We shouldn't be disturbing something so special. But, just like her, I'm peering through the window. It's open a bit so the smell of baking glass hits us first. The window is slick with heat. Inside, there are shelves and tables lined with half-formed figurines. Baby doll bodies without heads, flowers without petals, chests without hearts. It's a glass graveyard. I can't turn away. In one corner, a band leader, one arm raised, leads a band of bodiless marchers. In another, a mother pushes a little swing, a baby rattle where the baby would be. The glassblower works, his back to the window, his body aglow, across the room. If he knows we're there, he doesn't show it. Sparks dance from the fireplace and if I didn't know better I would think he was standing in the middle of it.

Constance leans forward. I don't know what we'll do if she falls. Before I know it, she's half in, half outside the house. Still the glassblower ignores us. Opal shakes her head no but has a hand on Constance's back either to push her in or pull her out. Trespassing. She leans even farther until her feet waggle in the air. I'm holding my breath. Opal isn't. I hear her wide-mouthed breathing from over here. I clamp my hand over her mouth. I don't care if Constance gets caught but if I'm caught with her, no one will help me. It will be her word against mine and I'm pretty sure she'd say I put her up to it. Whatever *it* is. Opal's hot breath burns against my palm. I give her my best *stop breathing so hard* look and her tongue darts along my skin. I jump, almost knocking Constance right in. Opal winks. Of course she's a hellion just like Constance. I'll have to keep my eye on her. I bite my lip, close my palm even tighter on her mouth and grab onto Constance with my other hand. Constance snares something from the table and starts wiggling backward. There's no way she can get out if we don't help her. Opal doesn't move. She's staring at me as if whatever happens next is on me. If Constance gets caught stealing, will Opal say she had nothing to do with it? She might stand up against the glassblower, maybe against the town if it came to that, but there's no way she'd stand up for me against Constance. If Constance said the word, Opal would kill me.

If Opal really is so wishy-washy as to go with the strongest tide, I sure don't want her on my side. I pull Constance up. Opal shrugs. Someone's watching.

His hands haven't stopped guiding the glass into curves and angles. He hasn't even turned to face us. Still, I know the glassblower knows we're there. It's in his tense body, his straight back and legs, straightened arms, tilted head. In the measured breaths plumping the blob a puff at a time. The whole moment feels like waiting for your name to be called even when you know it's not your turn and nothing but spite or bad luck could make the Caller see your name but you worry tense as a string just the same. I hold my breath. He seems to hold his. His hands still, hover. In front of him, the glass ball is a head, bigger than the blower's or anyone's I've ever seen. Then it's a face—my face. It's not just a reflection. He makes my lips, my nose, my cheeks, my forehead. It's me, smooth and glassy all over. It's fully formed in his hands, a see-through head with no body. I feel them then, his hands pinching my nose, prodding my lips, pulling my ears. The clear glass bruises beneath his fingers. There are patches of black and blue on the cheeks, red on the forehead. I can't stop watching.

Fingernails scratch my scalp. I have to leave.

As if right from the air, the glassblower pulls out a mallet. It's small, rubber tipped. Nothing special, not the way I thought I'd die. He's going to kill me. Maybe not me, but the me in his hands. The me he made perfectly without once looking at me. Now, the glass me's mouth gapes, her eyes widen. She's staring at me. She blinks.

I let go of Constance. She can dangle there waiting for that head to join a body but I won't be there to see it. I run. I hear the glass shatter and my own screams ringing in my ears.

The girls are right behind me. Constance doesn't stop giggling until we reach the Creek. She's giddy. "Did you see that?"

"Of course I saw it! What is he, some sort of wizard?"

"He's a glassblower," Opal says. She waves her hand in the air as if brushing away my words. "He blows glass. That's not magic. That's a job."

"Then how did he make it look like me?" My mouth is dry. I'm going to be sick.

Opal and Constance look at each other. Their giggles turn to outright laughter.

"Don't they have mirrors where you're from?" Constance asks.

"Of course they do. You can't tell me that girl didn't look like me."

"You think quite highly of yourself, don't you?" Opal shakes her head.

"It didn't look like you, silly. It looked like her," Constance says. "His daughter, Mercy."

"I guess you really aren't a witch." Opal manages to sound disappointed. "I can't imagine anyone being here for more than a minute and not seeing that girl's ghost."

The Original
Curdle Creek Sign

Being here is like walking through the archives. The mill,
school, and library are where they are in the old photos. The
Old Post Office is new and grand. There's one postbox, painted
yellow, around the side.

"Y'all get mail here?"

"Of course we do."

I imagine letters from places like New York City, LA,
Philadelphia, talking about life in big cities with big cars
and big problems. Letters filled with news about lynchings
and Jim Crow and towns burning. But also catalogues. Thick,
plump ones filled with pictures of things you don't really need
but which would make you the envy of the whole town if you
had them. Like iceboxes for indoors and lounge chairs for
outdoors.

"The Council reads all the mail coming into and going out

of Curdle Creek before the Post Office delivers it. That's just to make sure it's all right."

Temptation comes in the unlikeliest of forms. One of Mother Opal's sayings.

"Let's see if it's changed now you're here," Opal says.

She's already sprinting, and because she's a good twenty-five years younger than I am, she wins. I'm out of breath, puffing and holding on to the big, wooden sign that's smack-dab in the middle of a half-finished one-way street.

Welcome to Curdle Creek, Population 119.

"It must be stuck. It said that yesterday. With you here, it's 120."

There's no counter that I can see. No whirring to speak of that I can hear. "How does the sign change? What does it count?"

"Signs can't count, silly," Constance says. "The carpenter comes out to paint it once a month like the tides. He comes in, scrapes off the numbers that need replacing, sands it down, blows that away, traces the outline of the new number, then paints it in red. Seems fitting, don't it?"

Opal shakes her head. "That's a shame really. He seems nice enough. But it can't be helped."

"Opal, you wouldn't."

"His name is as good as called, you wait and see."

"We need a better system than grudges."

"It was good enough last year when that hairdresser put that hot press on your hair and it all fell out. Why isn't it good enough this year? Because it's Osiris's daddy?"

"You're just being petty, that's all. You know he won't marry me if his daddy's Moved On."

"When, Constance. *When* his daddy's Moved On." Opal folds her arms. "Maybe there's a way he can make it up to me." She smiles. There's no joy in it. No friendliness either.

The House at the Bottom of the Hill

We set off once we catch our breath, and part ways at the next stop sign. Constance leads the way from there. The road feels so familiar that she could be following me. I know where it bends and dips, curves and grooves. All these years and things haven't really changed as much as folks like to think they have. The dark blue houses with white trim and brown doors look like ones I've seen all my life. Back when they first settled Curdle Creek this would have been the workers' cove. A whole road made just for the people who kept the town running. The butchers and blacksmiths, shopkeepers and tailors. All of them living in one place so everyone knew just where to go when they needed them. If someone wanted to move house, they moved job to do it. So few people ever changed jobs that there was a day for it, part celebration, part not. Those moving to the left enjoyed fish fries and barbecues, moving wagons and a band. Those moving down to the right moved in cardboard boxes, on foot, and in a hurry. *Right by nine, left anytime.*

We turn up from the blue row onto a row of brick houses. Back home this would be where the doctors, lawyers and schoolteachers lived.

"Who lives in those houses?"

Constance shrugs her shoulders. "How would I know?"

"You don't know your neighbors?"

"These aren't my neighbors."

We pass the dimly lit lights, Constance humming, me keeping up and trying to stay out of the shadows.

"How come nobody's outside? I haven't seen but one friendly face since I been here."

Constance sucks her teeth like I'm interrupting her. "People stick to themselves here; they mind their own business. Besides, they can see you just fine from where they are." She nods toward one of the houses. Sure enough, the curtain twitches. "Why are your teeth chattering? You scared of something?"

"A little. I think the glassblower saw us."

"Who cares?" Rocks crunch beneath her feet.

"Won't there be trouble?"

"Who can he tell?" Constance skips ahead.

For a minute, it's too dark to see anything. I stand still. There's hot breath on my neck, my back, my cheeks. It's unsettling. Like when you come face-to-face with a soon-to-be-departed. It's the part you're never quite ready for, no matter how much you practice. If you aren't quick enough, you're in a sort of trance, felled by the hot, whispery breath of the Moved On. It hasn't happened to me. Anyone it's ever happened to can't sleep again. Before long, they see the dead everywhere. The kindest thing to do is to indulge them. Tell them yes, the clock does have a face. Yes, it's staring straight at you. Yes, the Caller said your name. Now, I'm surrounded by folks still hanging on to hope, love or fear, blowing out death to steal wisps of breath. I hold mine in.

We stop in front of a grand pink and white house. It's exactly the sort of place I'd expect her to live in. It's a lot like Mother Opal's.

"Is your mother a Charter Mother?"

"Is that some sort of group?" She hums and snaps her fingers. "My mother, in a band? She couldn't carry a tune if it came with a handle." Constance runs up the steps. "Come on, you're safer in there than you are out here."

Curdle Creek was founded in 1864. The Council was formed in 1865 and the Charter Mothers in 1915. I don't know how I got here but it's at least 1900. 1910, maybe. The wild times. Before some of the ordinances were decreed. I need to get to the Town Hall.

A curtain twitches in another window. If I wait out here long enough, someone will come outside. But then again, they already are. We aren't alone. Someone's following us. Has been not more than a few steps behind since we left the glassblower's hut. They're good—stopping when we stop, breathing when we breathe, blending into shadows when I peek over my shoulder—but I still feel them too close, taking up space. When we dropped her off, I had hoped whoever it was would follow Opal, but instead of chasing her down the dirt road they stuck with me and Constance. Anyone with any sense would have followed Opal instead. It's easier to catch one person than it is two. Opal only weighs but so much. Her bony legs don't look used to running. They could only carry her so far for so long. But even if they did, if they were as limber as worn rubber bands and able to get her to her doorstep, she's the type to look behind her when she gets a little way ahead but not quite far enough. She's the type to slow down and get caught. Constance is the type to save herself.

She hasn't mentioned it so maybe she doesn't feel it, doesn't care, or they're working together. I don't know, but I'm not safe out here. As soon as she turned her back, whoever, whatever it is came closer. Their too-close heat presses against mine. They match my breathing breath by breath. I don't know what they want. I never thought I'd see the day when I don't feel safe in Curdle Creek but I'm not safe here now. Whoever it is, is waiting on me to be alone. I don't care much who it is. I don't intend to stay here to find out what they want. If Constance goes in that door, they'll be right behind me. By the time she closes it, I'll be dead. I know it. I run up the steps behind her.

I've never seen so many lamps. Of course we have electricity, we aren't stuck in the 1860s, but Curdle Creek is a bit old-fashioned. Things like lights, phones and cars are limited, so we don't get distracted by wanting too much easy living. Here there's a lamp—sometimes two—in every room. Constance lights them as we walk through the sunporch, which is bright even though it must be past midnight. She keeps lighting them through the foyer, up the spiral staircase, through the long hall until we get to her room all the way up on the third floor. Here, she lights candles.

I don't know where to sit so I stand in the middle of the room, shadows dancing around me. They slip up and down the wall, dart across windows, slide under the bed. This must be where she keeps her victims. My fingers tingle. It's been hours since I've cracked them. I'd do anything for the sweet pop, the release.

Crack. It wasn't me. My fingers are still tense, pressed against my sides to settle them.

Constance is perched on the edge of a high double bed, staring at her fingers as though she could gobble them up like little pork knuckles. Instead of sucking on them as I half expect her to, she takes her time, popping each joint on each finger one by one, not even worried about who might hear her. Mother says cracking your knuckles is an invitation to the devil. The noise is his music and he just follows the beat to your soul. The sound is as sweet as splintering wood. My own fingers jump with each pop. I can't seem to stop them. Before I know it, my right hand caresses, slowly presses against a joint. It's not just air but pressure. My friends turning on me, Daddy, Mother, the well, the bones, here, all of it. I breathe ten pops later.

"That's a horrible habit," Constance says. She's grinning, so I don't bother to hide my hands like I would any other time.

She hops off her bed and stands in front of one of her many shelves. They're packed, things crammed over and into one another. She has more things than I could even want, let alone own. "They're presents for being an only child," she says when she catches me looking. She's searching for something and, whatever she's looking for, she's making a show of finding. She twirls and hums, lightly touching spools of this, snippets of that. She slides her fingers over bottles, taps the skin of stones with her short nails. She's a collector like me. I know where she's going before she gets there. The dolls.

It's a mini museum within a museum. Mother still collects pretty things. A corner full of pretty. The dolls, a quartet of porcelain faces on stiff necks, thin bodies slipped into ball gowns, gather on the ledge watching me. Their tiny parasols twirl in slender fingers bent back at peculiar angles. Their crisp starched hats sit over long pin curls. They lean against one another, a tangle of entwined arms, legs, curls, long-lashed and grinning like sisters.

Constance lifts them off the ledge, tosses them in the air. If they fall, they will crash to the floor and shatter, slivers of eyes, mouths, noses rolling under the bed. Maybe that will teach her to take care of things. They sail over her shoulder, and, God help me, I catch them. Constance or the dolls giggle. Slender doll fingers snatch the tiny hairs on my hands. Curls swirl around my fingers, bending them back. There's a hole in the wall behind the dolls' perch. If only I were closer, I could see inside. Their limbs untangle; an arm slithers up my wrist, an eyelash blinks along my thumb. I drop the jumble of dolls on Constance's bed. They bounce before settling with a thump that's louder than it should be. Constance turns to glare at me, though she should be blaming herself. The dolls stare ahead unblinking, still tangled, arms and legs not where they used to be but at least where they should be.

By the time I stop watching them, Constance is standing

in front of me, arms stretched out, a glass figurine in each hand. "Pick one," she says.

Maybe this is one of those tests like when a Charter Mother or Sister invites you in for a cup of tea which means talk without tea but since you don't know it, when she asks what you would like in your tea you say *Milk and two sugars, please?* And she nods like it's fine and goes in to the kitchen to make it. It's not the nod but the stomping of feet across wooden beams, the slamming of the back door, the squeak of the pump and the gush of the water, the grunts of the woman no longer used to hard work. By then of course it's too late to stop her, so you listen to the grunts, the squeaks, the rushes of air, your name said like a curse through the door that though slammed has popped back open as if on its own so that you can hear what an inconvenience you are. Because that's not enough, there's the closing of the door again, the slam or the lift, grunt and slam that keeps the sticking door closed this time. The heavy steps that let you know your host is back in the kitchen, followed by the rustling of pots and pans in the hunt for the teakettle that you're sure is on the stove where all Charter Mothers seem to keep them. The hunt is for you, so you listen to more grunting, banging and scraping. The time between the first slam and the *hallelujah* that lets you know the kettle has been found, scrubbed, rinsed and filled with water you better not waste, then set to boil depends on whose daughter you are. Thanks to Mother, I'm sure of a less-than-thirty-minute wait, but not much less. I've heard some people have to wait for an hour. I don't complain, as that only ever makes anything worse. After the show, when the tea is finally served it is lukewarm and most certainly not the way you asked for it. That's when you realize, if you didn't before, that tea doesn't mean tea in Curdle Creek.

There's a glass elephant in one hand and a glass lion in her other one. The elephant is a beautiful blue-gray. It has a long trunk that thins near the end, a mouth open mid-chew. Its thick legs are lined with creases and dimples that somehow hold up a see-through body. It's the ears that really do it though. They are wide open and large, bold in their hearing. Dangerously brazen. I want to touch their cool folds. Listen to glass secrets. Through its body, I see Constance's palm pressed firmly against it. Her fingers are tight around it. She isn't so much offering it as inviting me not to take it. The lion is in her other palm. It's no less beautiful. Its bright orange fire mane is captured in peaks around its round head. The pink tongue makes up for its not being the elephant. It is long and swirled, delicately wound. It has four strong-looking legs, a long tail with a glass plume at the tip.

"From the glassblower?"

"He makes the most beautiful things."

I take the lion by the middle, carefully put it in my palm. Its mane is cool against my fingertips. I rub the little body between my hands. It feels like a small living thing. It would look almost perfect in my treasure box.

In silence, we sit cross-legged on the floor, snapping off little legs, breaking off ears and tongues, cracking bodies in two. The mane feels as good as I thought it would. It snips off clear, a peak at a time. She's right. It does feel better than cracking bones. I finish before her. I don't mind. With my eyes closed I picture a cemetery, a scattering of skeletons at my feet. Last-chancers and come-afters—folks running from heat and torches, chased from homes in ripped nightclothes, mouths wide open still screaming, running to me. Instead of Warding them Off, waving my stick at them, chasing them back out of town because *we don't need no trouble here*, I throw down the stick, open my arms and welcome them. Don't know where I'd keep them, but I gather them, an arm here, a leg there, pluck them up like seeds. We'd walk till I find a place to plant them. If I don't court trouble, what right do I have to expect someone to look after my own? Because if they aren't dead, half-buried at the bottom of the well, then my own children are running around somewhere doing ancestors-know-what to ancestors-know-who. My children have always been somebody else's trouble.

Constance's hands move quick, quick, knitting and stitching things together. Head cocked, tip of her tongue poking against her cheek. Her fingers are a blur.

"Made you this." It's a necklace of arms and legs, torsos and mane, a trunk. I take it, slip it around my neck. "I'll tie it for you."

Her fingers are cold against my throat. It's the feeling, even before her too-close hands set on my warm skin. Mother. This little bit of a thing, this Constance is my Constance, or will be. I don't know how she did it, but I'm smack-dab in the past. I know I'm here to be with her.

Grandmother's

I'm sitting around the table with my grandparents and mother but I can't say that so I'm stuffing my mouth with food. Shame too. Neither one of them has ever been any use in the kitchen. They watch me cram what I think is corn bread into my mouth. It's so dry it's liable to splinter my insides if I can get it down.

Grandfather points his fork at me. "Where'd you say you were from?" He raises it to his lips, waiting on my answer before he eats.

I'm doing him a favor and taking as long as I can to respond. I have to. The corn bread has turned to corn mush in my mouth. I haven't said where I was from.

"She's from round yonder, that way." Constance doesn't even look up. She scoops swamp-colored beans onto a spoon. Defiant, they slide right off, plop back on the plate.

"And your folks? Where are they?"

Grandmother shoots him a look like hot fire. It's rude to ask people about their family. That's usually because of the

Moving On. Other places, I would imagine it's because of plague.

"My folks didn't make it here." I cover my mouth with my hand the way ladies do when they're overcome. I hope it looks like that now. As if the words are too heavy for my tongue to carry. The emotions too painful.

Hoping they can't see my mouth through the cloth, I spit the mush into the long, puffed-out sleeve of Cheyenne's meeting dress. Constance wasn't always an only child. Stuffed with everything she ever wanted and everything she couldn't have while they were alive, her room is more a museum of dead siblings than a shrine to her. Mother never mentioned a sister, two brothers. I guess that's why we don't talk about the twins either. Talking about the Moved On don't bring them back. With my clothes still drying and since I *can't go around meeting folks looking like a wet hog*, the dress of my dead aunt will have to do.

I wait on the mush to slide down my arm, rest in the nook of my elbow. It will probably settle there until I get up and then plop to the floor, a thick puddle of lies. Even worse, it'll leave a trail following me around the house like a witness. *Thank you for such a hearty dinner*, I'll say. I'll rise from the table, each word punctuated by stiff fabric. I won't scrape the chair across their wood floor—that would be rude. I'll lift the chair slightly, push it back, dress crackling like the pops from the wood-burning stove, lie about how good the food was and how full I am, lift and push in the chair and rustle out of the room leaving a trail of supper behind me. They'll call me a liar and toss me out in the dark with whatever is out there still waiting and not even my stick to fend it off. There's a fire going in the woodstove. It cracks and pops, sizzling every so often. The sweet smell of burning wood masks the stench of supper. My back's to the fire. I sit stiffly, feet planted on the floor, one arm by my side, the other on my lap until I pick up the fork. I'm quiet mostly.

"You're married, surely. How many children do you have?" There's a light in Grandmother's eyes. She smacks her lips, shiny with pork fat, when she speaks. I've seen that look before. Desperation. The time of the Moving On is close and even kind people do desperate things. And Grandmother has never been kind.

I'm probably sixty steps from the front door. Thirty from the side one. The side door will lead to the yard. The yard's cut off from the street, shut tight with an iron gate. If it's locked, depending on how high the fence back there is, I can run and jump over it. Just leap. My shoe is drying out in the umbrella stand, a glass-blown orb stretched thin with cracks. I'd hate to leave them behind. My dress is still upstairs drying on Constance's window ledge. I'm wearing a pair of her stockings. I won't have time to take them off. The mush hasn't even moved. It's stuck to the inside of my wrist, a rock-in-waiting. One rock wouldn't take them all out. They're all grinning, hopeful. I'll have to run in my stockinged feet.

"Yes, my husband has gone ahead, the children too," I say. "I'm just passing through before I catch up. We're heading north."

Grandfather spits out his food. It crackles on the table. "Up north! With those heathens? I don't suppose you heard what's going on up there?"

I think back to the history books. If Mother's about twenty, this is 1905, give or take. He could be talking about any number of wars, movements, violences.

"I trust my husband has found a suitable town with comfortable accommodation."

"Suitable and comfortable are fine for some folks but I prefer safe and prosperous myself. Don't you?"

I nod.

"You could write a letter to your folks. Send for them to join you here at Curdle Creek."

"There won't be room until after the Moving On," Constance says.

"Constance, dear, do shut up while grown folks are talking."

Constance's shoulders slump. The grandfather clock in the sitting room *tick, tick, tick*s in between words, slurps and silences. I can see why Mother left it packed in a crate, stuffed it with newspapers, silenced its tongue. It gongs for no reason at all. I drop my fork on the plate. Scramble to pick it up to have something to occupy my hands.

Grandmother nods. "Sit up straight dear, we have company." She purses her lips.

"There's nothing much up north." Grandfather points a biscuit at me while he talks. Chews with his mouth wide open. "You know they don't even have the old rituals anymore. It's like the Wild West there. Only wilder. No rules at all. It ain't safe. It wouldn't sit right with me to just send you out with no one looking after you. Wouldn't sit right with me at all."

"That's all right," Constance says. "You'll draw with us until then."

Oh, no, I won't. I open my mouth to set her straight, her and her nodding parents. I'd no sooner draw with them than I would nominate my own self. Not just a quarter of an hour ago, she said how each house gets the same amount of votes as they've got people. Three people, three votes. That sounds fair enough to me, if outdated. By accident, I swallow the lump beneath my tongue. It scratches my throat, scrubs my insides grain by grain, then lodges there. Would a pinch of lard have killed her? Probably. Grandmother has always been a stingy cook. She always did have little use for seasoning, creams, gravies—on her food or yours. Anything that might help something go down and stay there is not just an assault but a curse on her. If you can't eat her food the way she intended, you don't deserve to eat. And if you won't eat her food at all, well that's like asking her to tell the Caller to call your name twice. If that were possible.

"This house was built by free people," Grandfather says. "Every brick."

"All the houses were built by free people, Father. Everyone here was free long before the Emancipation."

"Built by escaped slaves, dear," Grandmother says. "Fugitives from the law."

"For good reason!"

"Of course, I'm just saying. They may not have things like that where she's from. You know—laws, rules, customs."

"We have customs, ma'am."

"How do you know? I thought you said you haven't been there yet."

They are always trying to trick me into saying something I don't mean. Even now, before I'm technically even born. I don't know how Mother stands it.

"The place she comes from has their own customs," says Constance. "They moving somewhere else, with more rules probably. Osiris says—"

"Not at my table! Don't you mention that boy's name at my table, not in my house! That Well Walking, moonshine-swigging—"

"He does not drink moonshine—"

"Then he is a Well Walker! I knew it! A good-for-nothing run-away-er. He'll leave at the first drop of trouble. He is not a true believer and you know what else he isn't?"

Constance is up from the table. Her chair scraping across the floor.

"Constance Greene, sit down until supper's finished."

It's a standoff, with Constance staring down at her parents and them staring up at her. The clock gongs again. Constance drags her chair back up to the table. Slips in and scooches it underneath the table.

"He's not marrying any daughter of mine. You can marry that boy you been sneaking down by the Creek with. Snow. He's a strong ringer. Comes from a good family. Get him to take you to a dance, reciting ordinances, or roller-skating. That way Osiris's name won't be called and you and Snow will be happy. You'd like that, wouldn't you?"

Mother nods her head yes.

I choke on something I had no business swallowing in the first place. Gristle. My eyes are watering. Grandmother's sitting across from me, rubbing her not-yet-wrinkled hands together, watching me about to choke like all that time saved from not churning butter has gone to good use. None of them moves to pat my back so maybe I'm not *dying* dying, but my throat's burning, my heart's racing, and I'm sweating up something fierce. I rub my throat to coax the lump down.

Grandfather's forehead wrinkles. His top lip twists in what I hope is an uncomfortable position. "Don't have much use for manners where you're from, do you?"

It's impolite not to appreciate at least the effort if not the taste of someone else's cooking. It's also impolite to serve someone close-to-but-not-quite food, but I couldn't tell him that even if I wanted to, what with this food playing hide-and-seek with the taste in my mouth. Maybe it was a blessing I didn't get to know him much before he Moved On. He's still sore about the water. There were four glasses of cloudy liquid on the table. I had meant to have a polite sip but the warmth of the glass, and the stubbornness of the drink, its slow, sluggish slide to the lip, turned my stomach. He offered to pump me a fresh glass for supper. I said, *Yes, I'd be mighty obliged, thank you. Why of course, Queen Sheba, I'll ring the butler to get that for you*, he said. Grandmother and Constance had laughed.

I should have known to apologize. Jumped up to set it right. That would have meant five minutes of apology, back straight, eyes to the ground, hands outstretched. If it was accepted,

I would still have to drink the sludge. Lord only knows what would have happened then. None of them had even touched theirs. It was just as likely to be the same stubborn drink filled to the top until one of them gave in. So, while an apology would have made my family proud, I couldn't bring myself to do it. He could have gone out to the pump and, cursing me, got me a fresh glass of water. I would have drunk it too. Taken long sips. The kind that makes folk want what you're having. Now, it's me against the glass, the glass against me. Though most likely it's that glass against him too.

Something skitters across the back of my neck. My skin prickles at the touch of eight little legs dancing across it. I look up. The house is clean otherwise, everything in its place as though they just moved in or are about to move out. Above my head, there are hundreds, maybe thousands of little spiders spinning, running, gliding, watching. There must be a million little eggs in the nest. It's pulsating. I try not to stare. Mother's always hated spiders, said they remind her of home. Constance sits across from me. I should have known, when she'd offered me her chair, that she would take the good one—or the better one. This would be where a little brother or sister sat meal after meal racing against spiders to finish before one glided down a strand for a visit. They can have my plate.

"I'm going to get us all some water." I brush the spider off, careful not to kill it. The kitchen looks like I'd have expected it to if I had thought about it. Grandmother always was a just-so woman. I grab a pitcher in need of a rinse and head out back.

It's there when I open the door. A spirit. Right here in

the open, not bothered by me being alive. Maybe it's because I don't have my stick. If I did, I'd have to Ward it Off. I'd be doing it a favor. This town ain't nowhere to be tied to forever.

The pump is just a few steps from the house. I take my time getting there. Even if the windows had been closed I would have heard them hot-whispering or felt them saying not-quite my name, Cheyenne, like a swear word. Grandmother had crossed herself when I first came down the stairs. She must have seen the dress first. When I asked, Constance had said there weren't any pictures of her sister but that I shouldn't think I looked like her because I didn't; that Cheyenne was everything beautiful and I was everything left. She'd sounded just like Mother then. I almost told her so. But I knew from the way she kept staring at me and, if not then, from the way Grandmother's breath caught in her throat, and Grand-father's "Oh, Lord!" his hand splayed over his heart, his body doubled over, his rasping and heaving half-forgotten prayers, that there was more than a passing resemblance. It couldn't have been five minutes. Him nearly kissing the floorboards beneath my feet, Grandmother watching him do it, Constance watching her watching him watching me.

"It ain't her," Grandmother had said finally. She clutched a Bible in one hand, just in case, and a diary in another. It was Cheyenne's. Filled with drawings and sketches, scratches of thoughts. "*When I die, there's nothing on God's green earth that will bring me back here*," she read. "See, she promised." She'd thumped the cloth cover, letting loose a small puff of dust.

"You ain't our Cheyenne," Grandfather had said, like he was setting me straight.

Still, it's the water that he can't forgive. "Isn't she high-and-mighty? Miss Your-water-ain't-good-enough-to-touch-my-mouth?" He never liked me. I don't know why he would start now.

"It would serve her right if her name gets called come Sunday." Grandmother's never cared too much for me either.

"Sunday can't come soon enough."

"It could just as easily be one of us," Constance says.

The room is silent except for the scraping of forks. I picture the plopping of food back on streaked plates. The nibbling of bone.

"I promise I won't put none of your names forward if our family's turn comes up," Grandfather says. This place sure is backward. If the family's name is called, the head of the household can choose one name. Grandfather would choose either Constance or Grandmother. He could choose his own but he's not the sort of man to do that. I know because he lived longer than he should have and even if our system is nothing like theirs, it's also something like it too.

"Please," Constance says, "don't."

"I said I won't, didn't I?"

"I mean promise. Please don't promise again."

"A man's only as good as his word." There's a lilt to Grandmother's voice that makes my heart drop.

"Did I promise last time? Give my word?"

I imagine Constance nodding. Grandmother's silent yes.

"Well, this time I mean it."

No one says a word.

"I can't believe I'm being doubted in my own house!" He slams the table.

Plates and silverware clatter. A glass or something must tip over. It would be a slow slosh anyway, no need to bother with it. Instead, there's the scrape of two chairs. Constance and Grandmother tripping over each other. Their words rush and tangle together. The apologies. Each one blames the other.

Grandfather doesn't accept the apology on the first round. He's probably leaning back, eyes closed, head shaking. Thumping his middle finger, the one with the nail thick and neatly curled under, on the table. Reminding her without needing to that the next Mrs. Greene will keep a better home with less effort than it takes Grandmother not to keep one at all. Grandmother must be wondering which one will replace her. There's always someone newly widowed in waiting. Just for spite it will likely be someone he knows she doesn't like. Surely it will be someone more fluent in spices. Someone better acquainted with kindness. Someone Constance will call Mother. Grandmother must know she would: not embracing her would lead to double graves, mother and daughter buried one Moving On after the other.

Constance knows what it's like to lose somebody. It would have happened at least three times. Mother Opal would have called it bad luck. Whatever happened to make Mother Opal wise and kind sure hasn't happened yet. If it had, she'd have told Mother to ring their bells off-key and out of rhythm for twenty minutes a day for thirty-two days to unsettle the bad luck and make room for good. They must have ganged up on my uncles and aunt, outnumbering, convincing, casting their names in the pot or box or some other backwater contraption. Stepping back to put someone else forward. Cowardly. It would take a whole lot of bell ringing to undo what they've done.

However things are done here, they launch in again.

"It's the girl, turning us against one another," Grandmother says.

I've brought something on them that hasn't been there before, she continues. Constance joins in. They blame me for five full minutes. What a waste of an apology.

Outside, I take my time at the pump. The metal is cool in my hand. I press it harder than I need to. Hard like it's Grandfather's neck. No, not quite. It's too thin. It's more like Grandmother's, curved, sturdy, just the right size to wrap my hands around. The spirit watches me. In the Curdle Creek I know, we all get our own chances. We don't turn against one another like heathens at a wake. I wouldn't be knocking on forty-six if we did. If these are the old ways Mother Opal kept talking about and Mother claimed not to remember, we are better off in Curdle Creek present than in Curdle Creek of the past.

I picture a ghost next to me at the pump, hands mimicking mine, pumping magicked-up water. "Shoo," I say. "Go back from whence you came." For all I know, though, she *is* right where she came from. I wait for a response. Nothing happens. The pump drips slow and stubborn.

I look back at the house. If somebody's watching, they'll see me talking to myself. They'll wonder if I've escaped. If my folks had locked me up somewhere, not to keep me safe but to keep themselves safe from me. A tower or something like a medieval princess. Or an asylum like a spinster aunt twice removed. They'll wonder if I can be trusted. I won't give them the chance. When I go back inside with a half-empty pitcher, their dead daughter's dress stained with wet grass, I'll cough deep and long, the call of the last-chancers come to Curdle Creek trying to outrun the influenza or something else their folks caught hold of. I'll cough and say it's nothing, that my folks have it, that everyone back home does. I won't say what it is. Won't need to. No matter when this is or where, death wasn't invented in Curdle Creek.

"Mercy Lumpkin, is that you?" I whisper. The leaves in the trees rustle and twist. There's a cool breeze. It's dark and damp. The perfect night for ghosts. "Mercy, if you hear me, look after my children, please. Just please do that for me."

I listen out for a response. Other than the stubborn drip of the pump, there is none. "And if you can, please get far away from this place."

If I take too long out here, they'll only come out to find me. They'll usher me in, pretend to help me with the water, apologize for anything I may have misheard or misunderstood while telling me it was all in my head anyway, that they are happy to have me. We'll sit around the table, Grandmother and Grandfather making small talk, Constance twiddling with her fork, stuffing food in her mouth to keep down the words. After dinner, they'll invite me to sit around the fireplace while they read from their family book, how so-and-so begat so-and-so and so-and-so begat so-and-so. There will probably be stories about long-dead great-relatives I've never heard anything good about. When they tire of telling me how good their family is or was, we'll all claim to be tired. I'll sleep in Constance's room, folded up in her too-small bed. They'll lock the door and even then I'll have to sleep with my eyes open. If I live through the night, I'll have to do the same thing for three days. Pretend to not want to leave while they pretend to want me to stay. Come Sunday, they'll try to coax me out of the door, lie about some family outing since now, they'll say, I'm just as good as family.

The house goes dark and I look up. Their shadows move across the window, the occasional flicker of candlelight turning them into characters in a silent picture show. Grandfather moves across the screen, a raised club in one hand. Grandmother follows with a cord of thick rope held high. Constance skips across next, carrying a large sack with two hands.

I make the sign of the bell, and run.

WELCOME TO

THE UNDERWORLD

Population 13,833,599+

Town Hall

The few people I see stare at me. It's unusual to see a woman running down the middle of the street after dark. I make myself slow down. Then, I greet the occasional passerby with a curt nod and a quick glance, just like any Curdle Creeker with a right to be here. I even stop by Fleming's. I rattle the doorknob. Knock on the door. He isn't in. The shop is shut for the night. The handmade sign is turned to *Closed, Come Back in the Morning*.

I need to see Daddy. I go by Carter's. It's not yet Carter's Everything Store. Since they don't sell food and drinks, they aren't open after suppertime according to the sign on the door. The only thing open is the *Curdle Creek Gazette*, out churning news till midnight because according to them, *The news doesn't sleep just because we do*. The mill is closed this time of night. The guesthouse is shuttered.

Daddy knows everybody and everybody knows Daddy. Where would he go to have a few minutes to not worry about rituals and ordinances, rules and systems? If it was me, I'd go to the sign. As soon as I think about it, I know where to find Daddy. Even though he isn't my daddy yet.

The streets are not paved here so I follow a rough mud path and the sound of running water down to the Creek. There's a sliver of a moon and no stars. The Creek is beautiful when you can hardly see it. It's easy to forget how many bodies are in there. I walk down to the edge. Breathe.

"Be careful, it's slippery down there."

The voice is kind, friendly.

"Thank you," I say.

"I don't believe we've met. I'm Osiris."

"It's nice to meet you. I've heard about you."

"That cannot be good."

Daddy has a lovely laugh. I can see why Mother's smitten. She's stingy with her laugh. Doesn't use it near often enough.

"What brings you to Curdle Creek?"

"I'm visiting. Just for the day. Heading out in the morning."

He looks me over. I picture what he sees. No shoes, stockinged feet, too-large, old-fashioned dress, hair in an absolute mess.

"Take my word for it: leave tonight. No telling what the morning will bring in a place like this."

"You ever think about leaving?"

"I got a girl here. I love her. Wouldn't leave her for anything in the world."

"Not even if you could live a longer life?"

"Not even for that."

The stench of burning wood fills the air.

"It's too early for the Moving On. I wonder what that's about." He points to the edge of the woods. All I see are bobbing, glowing lights.

"Lamps?"

"Torches. We used to use them in the old days, back before the new declarations, but, once the other towns started using them for riots, raiding, and stuff, we stopped. Tonight must be a special occasion."

I'm getting fidgety. My hands are starting to itch. I'm bouncing on the balls of my feet. The light is getting closer.

"Check the Creek!" Grandfather shouts.

"Looks like we got company," Daddy says. He takes a deep breath. "You'd do best to leave the way you came." He presses a warm stone into my hand. "Use this. You're going to need it."

He slips back along the bank. The trail of torches is not far behind; I say a quick prayer, take a deep breath, climb back up the slope, and run.

* * *

FILLED with newspapers, books, photographs, records, and more trinkets, gadgets and knickknacks than one person could ever catalogue, the Town Hall is plum in the middle of Main Street. It's a grand mausoleum of history, a forebear of justice. It's massive. And above it, winking and gleaming, near-twinkling in the sun so that you have to squint to see it, is the bell. It's gleaming and new, adorned with flowers and ribbons.

I've only ever been in the Town Hall on school trips and special occasions. Even as an adult, I've only gone inside when

I've been summoned. Witness a statement, verify a form, swear to a new ordinance. I've never just walked in without an appointment. Not that I'm counting but this might be the third rule I've broken. If there's a Hell, I'll go straight to it. Breaking rules is one of the surest ways to show you can't be trusted. If the ancestors, escaped slaves with nothing but a sense of what's right and a need not to be like the all-white districts on the outskirts of town, could see me now, they'd be appalled at my rule breaking.

"Forgive me, but I'm going in," I whisper.

There's a large, gaping keyhole above the front doorknob where the oversized key to the city that Mother Opal had specially made would fit. I don't have a key but I still have the pocketknife bound to my chest. I look around to make sure no one's looking. I peer through the glass like a tourist might, to be sure there's no one inside. It's empty. Not even a night watchman. Nobody steals anything in Curdle Creek. Just as we learned to in survival school, I pick the lock. *Twist, twist, jiggle, jiggle. Click.* I push the door open. I'm inside.

Moonlight streams through the windows. It bounces off the marble floors and tiled walls. There are gilded handrails and large chairs with lions carved on the armrests in the waiting room. All of the doors are closed. They aren't locked. I try them all. I find boxes filled with old almanacs, discarded rules, handwritten Life Books, thick, leather-bound Books of Sorrow. I could lose myself here. It's just like Mother Opal's basement only there's no room to walk in here.

I flip through the stacks full of newspapers. Just as the textbooks said, Curdle Creek was founded in 1864. There's a photo of Father Seamus looking sour and Mother Creek looking bitter. The papers go up to October 31, 1905. Today's date, I reckon. I don't have to read the paper to find out what happened. Today, there were nineteen names called. Biggest vote in Curdle Creek history. Even the Council was in cahoots with it. It's the last time they use the family nomination system. The last time the Council can override the vote. The last time the Warding Off was unregulated. That doesn't save the nineteen soon-to-be Moved On souls.

I make my way to the reception stand, though of course there's no one here to greet me.

There's an ink blotter, an hourglass, an empty sheet of paper, and a guest book labeled "Turner" in the center of the table. I sign it. Thick stacks of books cover the rest of it. I only mean to read the first page but each page has a little heading followed by key words and a detailed summary of a wrong committed and of the name of the accuser. Of course there are no good things to be found; it's the Book of Sorrows not the Book of Thanks. The conclusions are worse than the summaries, and the recommended punishment even worse than that. I turn to the back. Read the verdicts. My heart stops. Guilty, guilty, guilty, guilty, guilty, guilty. The punishment—death by any means necessary.

There's a *boom, boom, boom*, in my ears and the room spins. They've found me. Outside, Grandfather, and what sounds like the rest of the town, bang on the heavy doors, demanding to be let in. Torches light up the night. Someone throws a rock through a window. Glass shatters. I lean against the desk to steady myself. The first rock is followed by larger rocks.

Before long, there's glass and splintering wood everywhere. The splintering is followed by cracking, pushing and shoving. The mob is inside the building now. There's a sharp whistle. I know it when I hear it but I can't make myself move fast enough. The rock sails across the air just as I turn to face it. There's Mother, arm still crooked, aim just as steady as it will be decades later. Just before the rock hits, I'm reminded what else happened in 1905. It's the year of the Great Fire. The one that burns the Town Hall, and everything inside it, down to the ground.

The Courtroom

Death is not how I expected it to be. There's no ancestor waiting to list off all of my deeds, the people I've Warded Off, the debts I've paid to the town. No angel to greet me. No heavenly gates. It's just me, a courtroom, and the *boom, boom, boom* vibrating in my head. I'm dead and still the booming's getting louder. It's no longer just in my head, it's coming from all around me.

"Order, order, order! Court is in session," the bailiff says. "Ms. Turner, please approach the bench so we can proceed."

I've been widowed three years and still when I hear "Ms. Turner" I think of Mother. I'm not ready to have my deeds weighed, my actions questioned. It's too soon. I had so much life to give. I want to say no, I will not proceed. But I'm being pulled to the bench just the same.

There are dead roses everywhere. Laced over the archway, scattered down the aisles, flowing over the judge's bench. The petals are crisp to flaking. With each tap of the gavel, the judge sends another puff of dried flowers into the air in a halo of perfume. It smells like dust and twice-used breath. The air is warm, heavy with the closeness of bodies and decay. It tickles my nose, threatening to make me sneeze. I'm not doing it on purpose but if I sneeze again I'll be held in contempt. She glares at me, lips twisted in a permanent frown, leaning over like I'm too small and doing that on purpose too.

Her wig is powdered, the tips adorned with dried leaves and petals. Her Honor's cheeks and forehead are caked with foundation, dotted with rouge that's also dry. It takes a lot of effort to hide the fact that she's dead and just about everyone else in the courtroom is too.

"Conspiracy to commit murder, murder, actual bodily harm, destruction of property. How do you plead?" she asks after reading a long list of charges.

"I didn't murder anyone, Your Honor."

"I see. How would you describe the . . ." She flips through a file in front of her. "The Moving On?"

"It's not murder. It's population control. It's the law."

"I'm quite familiar with laws, Ms. Turner, and I think you'll find murder is not one of them."

"It's not murder, it's . . . The town nominates someone to be Moved On and whoever gets the most votes, or whose name gets called, gets Moved On. It's not murder, though. It's tradition."

She taps the gavel into her palm. "And you partake in this—tradition? Do you swear to tell the truth, Defendant Creek?"

"No, ma'am—" Before I can finish, the courtroom erupts into *Lord have mercies* and *lands alives.*

Her Honor springs to her feet, clacking the gavel against the bench hard enough to shatter it. Flowers scatter, raining down on my head, shoulders, hair. "Guilty! Guilty! Guilty!" she yells. Again she bangs the gavel against the oak bench.

Hands spring up from out of nowhere. I'm surrounded by bailiffs, witnesses, clerks, onlookers and reporters. The stenographer *click, clicks*, taking note of every grunt, gasp and pop. I can't stop myself from cracking my knuckles. The judge stares at me as if I'm cursing in court. "I'm a Turner, not a Creek!" I yell above the crowd.

The judge bangs again. "Order!"

Everyone is silent. Heads down, they march back to seats and posts. The women cool themselves with paper fans advertising sales of torches. The men lean forward, hats clutched between hands, mopping their faces and necks. Children, caught mid-whoop, scatter back to their families, wiggling like this is the best thing to happen since Christmas. Bailiffs tap batons against palms. Reporters scribble away.

"Your last name isn't Creek?" The judge adjusts her robes, straightens her wig, then flips through reams and reams of pages.

"No, it's Turner, I'm—"

She raises a finger, shushes me, points to a line. Without holding it up to let me see it, she asks, "Are you or are you not from Curdle Creek?"

"Yes, Your Honor—"

"Do you represent, in thoughts and deeds, Curdle Creek?"

"Yes, ma'am, but I have to. I don't have a choice."

"Are you a believer?" She taps the paper as if everything

she needs to know about me is right there, the sentence already dried.

I'm not one of the revered and sometimes ridiculed true believers. No one calls on me to interpret an ordinance, remember a rule. Am I a believer, or a do-as-I'm-told-er? I've always been true to Curdle Creek. Even though Mother would call me a fair-weather believer, I've been truer to Curdle Creek than the Creek's been to me.

The judge slams the file closed. "You are, indeed, the appointed one. Hereby known as the accused." She settles back in the chair, points the gavel at me. "Court is back in session. In the case of the People versus Creek, how do you plead?"

I was six for my first Moving On. Quick and mean, I got to the bridge the same time as the Moved On did. He was gasping and panting, clutching his chest. Begging. At the time, aiming straight for the spot between his eyes seemed the most merciful thing I could do. But I was six. There was nothing else I could do.

"Not guilty, Your Honor. I didn't do anything I wasn't told to do."

"Then how do you plead?"

"Your Honor, can I represent myself?" I step in front of the table to approach the bench.

"That won't be necessary," she says. "I have all the evidence I need."

A bell gongs, filling the courtroom with vibrations and echoes. "Guilty!" *Gong*. "Guilty!" *Gong*.

The benches clear. As if on cue, the crowd lines up in rows

down the aisles. They march in place, torches, already lit, in one hand; in the other they hold pitchforks. Even the children march, with child-sized pitchforks raised. The band strikes up a tune in time to the audience's chants of "Her time is up! Her time is up!" Reporters take notes, snap pictures with bright flashes that make me close my eyes with each click.

I'm surrounded by bailiffs. There's no way to make it past them all. Her Honor bangs the gavel. "Order in the court! There will be order in my courtroom!"

The band is the first to quiet. Then the children, men, women. The judge is still banging. The crowd has stopped chanting. They're still marching in place, the sound of their feet slapping against the marble floor as loud as drums. We must be right beneath the bell tower because the room's still shaking with the echoing. The judge rises. Except for me, doubled over, everyone silences mid-sound. Unfinished sentences cloud my head.

"How do you plead on the charge of chasing the dead?" Her Honor asks.

I would have Warded Romulus Off, the way I did Remus. Just fifteen, he had heard rumors that their names were going to be called. Schoolyard gossip, nothing to worry about, I told him. Kids don't get Moved On. Everyone warned him. I wouldn't listen. So when he snuck into my bedroom that night, asked me if I would be the one to Move him On, then promise to do the Warding Off myself, I said yes. It was after midnight. I was tired from a long day of setting up for the Moving On. When he needed me to say no, I said yes.

"Not guilty," I say.

"Let's begin. I'd like to draw the jury's attention to the screen."

Spread across the ceiling, a black-and-white film plays reel after reel of Mariah and Rumor playing house with stunned squirrels. A little arm, held stiff, slides into a suit clasped in the back, a paw or two out of reach. Another rodent is posed a bit too seductively, cheeks blushed, bodice half-on, half-off. My mouth goes dry. I'm watching the girls dress and pose the squirrels with rodent-sized props made just for the occasion. They shoot photos, change outfits, freshen makeup, and then lose interest. They're bored. I know what comes next. One pulls a stray cat from a box. They call it that even though it's more of a trap with a spring and a latch. Mariah invites the hostage cat for dinner. Both girls double over with laughter. The guests are already dressed to be eaten. The squirrels try to run with their eight little paws stuck in mismatched shoes—two of one kind on one set, two of another kind on the other—while two what could only be described as monsters laugh and whoop while playing makeshift drums made out of pots, pans and hollowed-out gourds. There's me in the corner, looking on, not even shocked. The cat corners the bodiced squirrel. It's caught one of the laces in its claw. *It's time for dinner!* I'm yelling, on the screen. I'm trying to distract the cat, to call the girls into the house, but right here, right now, the audience gasps and I see that it sounds as if I'm inviting the cat to do what it's about to do.

Before I can say that's not what I meant, the film goes black. Behind me, the reel spins and flaps in the projector.

"Now for Sister Pearl's testimony."

I look up and Sister Pearl is settling into the witness stand. We've never met, I'm sure of it. As soon as the questions start, another film starts to play. There's Sister Pearl running through the woods, a parade of torches and rifles not far behind. She's tired and scared, exhausted when she slides down a slope and lands in the Creek. By rights, we have to help her. It's in the Charter. Anyone who reaches the Creek is granted sanctuary until we figure out what to do with them. She's in the Creek splashing her way to our side of it. There's someone waving her over. Thank the ancestors! That's exactly right. Last-chancers don't lead angry mobs to Curdle Creek on purpose. Most of them don't even know the town exists. We're so deep in the woods that even candlelight doesn't make it through. What leads outsiders to Curdle Creek is fear.

She's making her way to the Good Samaritan. *Don't step there!* I shout it out but, just like in the cinema back home, she can't hear me, so she steps right into the deepest part of the Creek. By the time the swarm of white faces reaches the other side, she's drowning, skirts billowing. If they could see across the Creek, past the thick trees that guard it, they'd see a group of townsfolk, rifles aimed straight at their heads. They don't bother to look. They've seen what they came for. One of them unlatches a long, thick line of rope he seems to be carrying just for situations like this. He unwinds it. It's yards and yards long. The white men put down their own rifles, lay down their torches. They make a chain, each taking a slip of rope between rough hands until they reach the woman not-yet-drowned. She's struggling but it does her no good, she's rescued any-way. They pass her down the line, pawing her body, pinching and groping her back to safety. Once on dry land, they pump the Creek out of her. Sister Pearl can't be much older than me. Her eyes are swollen half-shut like she's already seen too much of this life.

The men gather around her, checking her pulse and heart-beat though there's not a doctor among them. Once they are satisfied that she's good and alive, they drag her back through the woods, a reverse march. A crowd of folks gather to watch as if making sure she's really gone. Sister Pearl's mouth is closed but I still hear her screaming.

I wasn't even born then. Each of those folks has long been Moved On. Not for that, though. Although I'm mouthing *That shouldn't have happened, that shouldn't have happened*, I know there is an ordinance that justifies exactly that thing. Helping Sister Pearl would have put the town in danger. It would have meant killing the white mob, burying them, risking sheriffs and National Guards poking around trying to find them. With the Salt Harbor reckoning etched in the town's mem-ory, it was too great a risk. If they hadn't killed them all, had instead scared them so that they knew not to bother her this night, the mob would come back. Maybe not sober, but they'd come back with more of them. Hate's like that. It grows and grows, just like what happened to the other all-Black town down the hill. There'd be no stopping them, until they'd done to us what they do to her.

On the screen, we watch the mob drag Sister Pearl back to a neighboring town. Their women and children have fed the fire with broken wooden furniture, doors, beams, books, photos, clothes, anything that can burn and some things that can't. Some have unrolled picnic blankets, checkered red, white and blue Fourth of July remnants. Bunting and ribbons stream from trees. There are baskets full of fat sausages, barbecue chicken, homemade potato salad and thick-slabbed sandwiches, as well as teacups and dainty napkins to keep fingers clean. A band plays a celebration song full of shrill notes and bass drum. Meanwhile, children tease and taunt Sister Pearl, who drifts in and out of consciousness, her body and mind wanting to be as far away from this scene as we do. There's a prayer, followed by hooting and hollering. Someone reads the charges: *Uppity, needs to learn her place*. Someone offers to teach her. They cheer. She's falling over so they lean her up, snatch pictures with her. Someone else slips the noose over her neck. The children are gathered around for photos with their old teacher. They are dry-eyed.

Sister Pearl is hauled up to the tree. Although she weighs almost nothing, six men have offered to do the job so six men get to do it. They string her up. Mercifully, she is dead before they let go of the rope. The screen goes black. The *flap, flap, flap* of the film fills the room.

"Any questions?" Her Honor asks.

If it happened today, right now, would I turn someone away, or would I put the town at risk to save them? "No questions, Your Honor."

I don't know who to apologize to. The court cannot forgive me for what I might have done to someone who won't grant me an audience. Even back home, she wouldn't be obliged to listen. Of course, back home, Sister Pearl wouldn't be around to decide to listen or not. If she had died in Curdle Creek, we'd have Warded Off her soul like she was one of our own. It'd be the least we could do.

*　*　*

THE trial lasts for weeks. Days stretch into nights. Once a trial starts, they say, there's no stopping it until the case is decided, the defendant sentenced. There are no breaks, no end to the witnesses willing to take the stand, and no chance I'll be found not guilty. We've spent so much time protecting Curdle Creek that we've become just as bad as anywhere else, according to them. And to hear them say it, which they do, it isn't just one of us to blame. It's all of us Creekers. The young ones are just as bad as the old ones. There's no one forcing us to stay. Never mind that there isn't anyplace else to go. No one place in the world where we're guaranteed to just live in brown skin, see with brown eyes. The evidence is overwhelming. Even poor Father Seamus and Mother Creek testify against me. Turns out the boys were right after all.

When it's quiet the crowd whispers *Guilty, guilty, guilty*. Which is even worse than their earlier, louder, bolder *Guilty! Guilty! Guilty!* chant that Her Honor said was out of order. If I sit still, it's a sign that I'm *remorseful, made immobile by the weight of sin*. If I lean forward, I'm *morbidly fascinated, enraptured by the promise of doing it again*. If I close my eyes, I'm *bored, and can't be bothered to even grant the witness/victim the proper respect*. The reporter from the *Curdle Creek Gazette* and the now defunct *Creek News* narrate their headlines so the court can hear them and the stenographer can record them.

There's a charge for unlawful imprisonment of Mother

Creek and Father Seamus. They have the distinction of being in the Curdle Creek history books twice: once for founding the town and the next for inspiring the ordinance against jealousy and coveting. Anyone with good sense knows to appreciate what you're given. Not that they deserved the town turning on them, running them down like that. Throwing them in the well.

The stenographer *tap, tap, taps*.

The jury stands. Of course there would be a jury somewhere but I'm surprised to see them up in a box as though they're in the good seats at the theater, or the bad seats at the church. They are high above us all, close enough to step into the evidence films if they wanted to. The jury is made up of all the witnesses and victims. It doesn't seem fair that they get to decide if I'm guilty or innocent and I can see, since they're mouthing *Guiltyyyyyy*, that they've already made up their minds anyway.

Her Honor bangs the gavel. The flowers have all withered so that even the dead ones are mostly dust now. I bury my nose in my sleeve and breathe in the scent of Cheyenne. My girls didn't deserve whatever happened to them. Neither did Little Moses.

"Your first witness?" Her Honor asks.

I don't know who I can call. I'd give anything to see my girls again. To hold my baby boy. But the thing is, if I'm guilty for what Curdle Creek did to them, I already know the verdict. I'm guilty. I should have protected them somehow. I can't take seeing them here. Admitting that they're gone. There is no one I can call. They'd all say I was overzealous about the Warding

Off, dutiful about the Moving On. An ordinance-loving, rule-fearing Curdle Creeker. A model citizen. I even have an award for that. For all the good it will do me.

"I don't have a witness, Your Honor."

"You really should be more prepared. I'll give you a moment to think about it."

The judge stares at me, waiting. Her makeup is cracking, her wig wilting, pushed back a bit too far. Her forehead is suddenly luminous. It's large and shiny while the rest of her seems to be aging in front of me. There's a whiff of decay. It's the sweet smell before the rotting. The trial must be coming to an end.

"I call to the stand . . . Mother Opal," I say. I don't know how things work here, but if they can call up spirits, so can I. I don't really expect her to come. If there's a Heaven like she preached about all Charter Mothers going to, Mother Opal is too far away to hear me. The waiting will do us all good. Well, all except for Her Honor. She doesn't look like she has much longer to be around.

There's a soft cough, a dry clearing of thick mucus.

Mother Opal's at my table waiting for me. The bailiff leads her to the stand. By the time she's settled in, her film's already playing. I can't watch it yet, though. It's so good to see her, even dead. She's wearing one of her favorite dress suits. It's You're Welcome red, a color she always said was *made to complement beautiful brown skin*. She's right. With the little bit of light streaming through the windows, Mother Opal looks like a beaming ray of thanks. Her skin is nearly glowing. Her favorite hat is pinned in her hair. There's nowhere else in the whole wide world that I would rather be than right here.

Mother Opal peers down, smiles at me. It's the first smile I've seen, the first real one, in ages, and it warms me through and through. If I've been hungry, her smile fills me up. Mother Opal will fix everything. She'll set this backward town full of dead people straight. But everyone here isn't dead. Outside the Town Hall, the town—or most of it—is alive. Mother's still there and so is Mother Opal, even if neither of them are mothers or Mothers yet. In here is before then but she's after. It seems like we're all stuck in time. Once what's settled is settled, we can catch up in private. I can ask her if I'm dead without being overheard by ghosts. I can hear them now, laughing at me. *Imagine not knowing what side of the grave you're on.* I'll offer condolences if she is too. Bake her a pie.

Before I can stop myself, I'm at the witness stand reaching over to touch her. If I'm honest, I mean to hug her. Traditions be damned, I'm going to wrap my arms around that old woman and not let go this time. I reach over, but the gavel's banging, the bell's ringing and ringing, and I look up and see my own face. In the film, I'm making my way to Mother Opal's to ask her to do one more thing for me. I'm running, carrying my burdens to her door. There's an ordinance against that but it doesn't seem to weigh me down. I'm breaking ordinances as if it's my birthright. Reckless in my haste, running up the steps, about to kick in the door, entering the back yard without appropriate blessings, entering the house without invitation. The reporters can hardly keep up. I'm slipping into the cellar. There are boxes askew, some with lids barely on. I don't notice. I just close the door behind me. I move through the darkness, so sure of my footing that I slide around bodies that I think are nothing more than wardrobes and chests. I'm slipping through the museum of boxes that I thankfully do not peek into as I've done hundreds of times before but I'm being watched and don't know it then. I'm surrounded by Mothers.

If I had turned on the light I would have caught them hunting through Mother Opal's things. Rifling through Father Opal's treasures, claiming to be searching for the box and taking anything that tickled their fancy while doing it. It's as if they're robbing the same grave twice. I don't turn on the lights because I don't want to scare Mother Opal but here it looks suspicious, that I could walk through them and not feel them waiting, wanting me to accept that *what's done is done* and agreeing without a word shared between them to teach it to me later.

As I'm sneaking up the stairs, the Mothers search every space within Reason. They've got mattresses ripped open, innards where the outards should be. Drawers hang open, closets are empty; papers, clothes, books, and most of Mother Opal's things are all packed up waiting to be Moved On. They haven't found the box, don't know what it looks like though it's brought out every Moving On day. They just want *the old fool* to tell them where the rites are so they can *put an end to this foolishness*. Only, even watching them from here I know the ending won't be a good one and that "foolishness" means Mother Opal. She seems to know it too because she doesn't talk. She doesn't plead for mercy or launch into apology, won't point out the box, wooden and plain, barely even hidden now, tucked away with the cutlery like everything else they labeled useless. She's *Opal, dear* now and Mother's mouth is telling her that she wishes it could be another way though her hands aren't saying the same thing because they're tapping on the stones brought out for this purpose. The Mothers have carefully spelled out her name so that *each stone finds its way home.* It's blasphemous, their talk of made-up games and traditions, and, even though the sky is telling them to stop, they're misreading the signs as proof that putting an end to the Moving On, to the Warding Off and to Mother Opal are the same thing.

There's me pressed into the little closet fretting about scaring her, realizing she isn't alone and wondering if I should walk away or enter. Watching me now, I see she would have heard any of the steps squeaking, me tiptoeing up the stairwell, and instead of worrying about an intruder she'd have been smart enough to be scared of the Sister she thought was on the other side of the door. There's the crack of Mother's hand on Mother Opal's cheek and Mother Opal's head spinning. There's me moments later, slipping down the stairs, past the Mothers, out of the door. Even if she'd heard the door closing, Mother Opal would have known nothing good would come of it. Just as if it was proper, the Sisters are bundling her up, tied and bound, tucking her into the carriage. They parade her through back streets where there's no band, no cheering and no witnesses.

They are gentle then, fingers swiftly untying her arms and

legs, massaging her wrists, undoing bruises they may have caused in haste. Knots unknotted, rope rolled up, they dump her, fully dressed, in the Creek. I know she can swim but she won't do it. She treads water, feet not touching the soft sand below, arms opening and closing, motioning welcome, surrender, welcome, surrender as if they don't know which tradition the situation calls for. The Mothers line up on the Curdle Creek side of the bank, coaxing her to make her way to the other side. They proclaim her banished, destined to never set foot in Curdle Creek again. She knows them better than that. She stays in the middle of the Creek, reddish water flowing around her like she's a pebble hardly worth mentioning. She watches the Mothers stationed along the edge. They work quickly, ripping pages—sometimes chapters at a time—out of bound books that haven't been opened in decades. Between them, they crack book spines wide open, use slender nails to undo stiches that up until now had been thick enough to keep the town together. They tear out ordinances, rules, oaths and amendments. They wrap the pages, threads still dangling, glue still sticking some together, around stones they've piled up in front of each of them. They rub their gift-wrapped rocks between their hands as if warming them. When they finish, they wait in silence.

Mother is the first to run out of patience. As their leader, she pulls a silver dinner bell from her pocket. It catches the moonlight, glimmers. The tinkle is soft, almost pleasant, as if it's calling friends to supper.

Even the left-handed ones raise their right arms. They aim. The Mothers wind up, right arms moving around and around and around, picking up speed with each whir. Mother tinkles the dollhouse-sized bell again. It shimmers, winks. The Mothers release at the same time. Some rocks land close to Mother Opal, some far away, some meet with skin, hitting the top of her head, her shoulders or chest. They've planned it so that none of them will know the rock that does it. I know and so does Mother Opal. Mother's rock sails through the air, hits Mother Opal in the temple. It's not the one that kills her, though. Each time they release, there's a bell, another series of throws. Mother manages to hit her every time. There I am standing in the middle of the street praying for divine intervention and there's Mother delivering it.

"Any questions?" Her Honor asks.

I'm on my feet in front of the stand. Mother Opal is wet, soaked through from the memory. She's shaking as if the sight of me in this nineteenth-century dress, high collared, high waisted, stiff as a boiled sweet, is just what she thought the devil would look like. I wouldn't have expected to live to see the day where Mother Opal would be afraid of me. I want to ask if she regrets the whole thing. If the Moving On, the Warding Off, and everything was really worth it. But the reel spins, the film wavers and falters, threatening to start up again, and I say no.

*   *   *

THE sentence is lighter than it should be. I should be dead. The court takes mercy on me though I do not deserve it. The judge clears out the courtroom after the sentencing. The victims, jury, stream of witnesses and reporters seem relieved to go wherever the dead go from here. The bailiffs, band and judge remain. Still, I feel like the Moving On. Alone, scared, upset. Not at all the sense of pride I thought I'd feel when I was a kid.

A well is constructed right there in the middle of the courtroom. Builders measure, dig and stick together slabs of stone with concrete mixed fresh for the purpose. Someone hauls the bell from a back chamber that I imagine exists—overflowing with bells of all sizes—for just this purpose. It's not much bigger than the hauler but it must be heavy. They drag it down the aisle slow. It scrapes across bare floor, screeching like a secondhand groom. It's bronze, dull and worn. The bell is about my height, about as wide as me and is eaten through by rust in so many places that you can see the clapper clear through the sides. What's left of it is etched in intricate symbols laid one on top of the other, running together like an argument.

Her Honor gestures to the well. I edge toward it expecting to see someone down there staring up at me. But there's no one there. And here I am just me, Osira. Not a mother, a Mother, barely even a daughter anymore. Nobody's wife, friend, neighbor. The judge said I'll be banished. I don't mean to but I'm crying. I can't seem to stop. Can't catch my breath. Can't stop thinking she's right, I don't have a home to go back to.

"Let me talk to her," Daddy says.

I spin around and there he is walking toward me. He's wearing his favorite outfit, shirt still tucked into plaid trousers, checkered suspenders bright against warm brown skin. My breath catches and I double over, unable to get it back. Mother would have never let him wear that outfit. That's how I know he's dead. I close my eyes and bury my head in his chest. He's warm all over. He holds me close, wraps his arms around me. All I can hear is Daddy telling me how much he loves me and how he wishes he'd told me all the time even if he had to break the rules to do it. I'm crying and moaning "I love you too, Daddy, I love you too."

He shushes me, hands rubbing my back. I don't want to see his film playing so I keep my eyes closed even when he pulls me back to see if I've grown since he's been away. Away. He doesn't call it dead or Moved On. "You haven't been away long," I say. I don't know how time works here and he doesn't either.

He tilts my head up. "Open your eyes," he says.

"Please, I don't want to see it." I'm begging. I'd drop to my knees to implore him properly if his grip wasn't so tight on my shoulders.

"I'm not testifying against you, it's not that," he says.

I look up and there's Daddy and me fishing in the Creek. We aren't catching anything even though he's got the bait and I'm in the water trying to coax fish out from beneath rocks. In the film, he's telling me there's something wrong with Curdle Creek, telling me to get away as soon as I can, to follow my brother and don't even write when I'm safe. Curdle Creek has a way of leading people back to it, he's saying. I'm not listening then because I've caught something and it's wiggling in my hands and I'm giggling at the slimy body trying to slip through my fingers. I'm about to toss it into the bucket when a larger fish starts circling my ankles, diving below the surface to nip my toes, gentle at first, bobbing up to look at me each time. The nips get harder the longer I hold the little fish in my hands, and it is getting slower too, not as flippy or flappy. Finally, I get the hint. I put the baby fish back in the water. The pair dash off out of grasp.

"I can't go back, can I?" I ask.

"Do you want to?"

I'm scared. Curdle Creek is all I know. "What will happen to the girls if I don't?"

"Same thing that'll happen to them if you do," he says. He sits on the edge of the well, swings his legs back and forth.

"Isn't that dangerous?"

He laughs. "I have other things to worry about here."

"What happens to you when I'm gone?"

"Don't be like your mother," he says, "the world is much bigger than you and me."

I sit beside him, letting my legs swing in time with his. "Are my children here with you?"

"No, they ain't here."

For a moment, I'm happy. Maybe that means they're in Heaven, surrounded by love and angels.

"The living don't end up in Heaven."

"They're alive?"

"They made it out of Curdle Creek alive. If they could do it, you can too."

"Can you help me find them?"

"I wish I could. Take this." He presses a stone in my hand. Now I have three. "I love you, don't ever forget that," Daddy says. His voice is so low that I have to lean forward to hear him, so gentle that I hardly feel his hand on my back pushing me in. There's the rush of the air as I fall, the cheers of the courtroom, the *boom, boom, boom* of the band and, of course, the ringing of the bell.

WELCOME TO

EVANSHIRE

Population 531

Estelle's

I was expecting to wake up dead or, more precisely, to open my eyes halfway, flutter them beneath long lashes made longer in the moment, moan a sweet, memorable tune, gasp, shudder and then die a beautiful death like the ladies do in the catch-a-beau magazines. Instead, I climb, alive, freezing cold, wet as an otter, with this dress sticking in the most unfortunate of places, and then tumble out of the mouth of the well with the sun in my eyes and the screams of schoolchildren piercing my ears.

There are children everywhere. A whole gaggle of them pointing, crying, squealing and screaming about how I'm *the witch in the well come to drag them to hell* just like the preacher said would happen. They are sure. They saw the tips of my blue fingers clutch the lip of the well, my dirty nails digging into stone, my muscled arms poking through ripped no-longer-puffed-up sleeves hauling the rest of my body, my hair coarse, matted to my head like a cap, and my feet shoeless, naked except for the mud sticking my toes together. They are so certain—would swear on the Bible if only someone would get them one—that my first words—even though they could hardly understand the way that I talk—were "Would you please shut up!" but of course nobody believes them.

The adults come running out of the church to see what the fuss is about and why the children aren't practicing hymns like they've been set to do and who is this brown-skinned woman on the playground and why is she soaking wet when the sun is hotter than it's been in days and oh my goodness, what have they done? The children try to explain but no one is interested. They are red-faced and upset and though they use words the wrong way around they speak the same way as the adults do, only the adults seem not to speak child and the children seem not to be able to speak adult. I translate as best as I can.

We are all speaking the same language, though theirs has a sort of melody, a lilt I've not heard before, so that when they say one thing, they seem to mean another. The men decide, with no help from me, that I've stowed away on one of their carts and traveled from the castle to their village because hadn't they warned the women that nothing good comes from beyond the village? I'm proof that only men should be allowed to travel and even then, only merchants and traders. They decide, again with no help from me, that whichever of them can prove I've stowed away with them can have me as a wife.

The women circle me, form a wall between the men and me. "That's not how things are done here, Samuel Klegg!" a woman interrupts.

Samuel squares up to her, hands balled into fists. "You would deny me?" he asks. His chest is puffed up, stressing the buttons of his shirt. It makes him look large before her.

"I would deny you again and again," she says.

A gentle breeze stirs, scattering leaves across the playground. In front of me the women are tense; behind me the men are too. "God Save the Queen!" someone shouts.

"God Save the Queen!" they all reply.

I've never seen a queen. There's not one in Curdle Creek. If there had been, Rumor, vain as she is, would be first in line to overthrow her. If she can save them, maybe this queen can save me too.

The crowd seems to breathe again, to settle down and remember that their children are still watching and that they are, if not on holy ground, near it.

"I'll go back the way I came," I say.

They all turn to face me. They speak at once. I'm not a burden and shouldn't talk such foolishness. I'm here to stay, sent by the heavens, a blessing. The preachers are called for. The Protestant one arrives first since we are, he reminds us, on church grounds and if there are any blessings to be had, he'll be the first to receive them. The other Protestant preacher comes next. His church was built second. Not as an afterthought, he says, but to assure redemption. It's a small town but there's more than enough sin to go around. They both laugh.

The churches are across the street from each other like arguing siblings. They are the same height, the same somber red brick. They share ground for carts, wagons, stables for horses. They share the same playground and sometimes the same congregation. They do not share a bell. The first church has an old bell, borrowed from Lancaster Castle and not yet returned. It's silver, thick and tall, snug in the steeple that is two hundred steps above the chapel. The second church has a larger steeple but a smaller, bronze bell. The old church sends a boy to ring my welcome. The second one, being more progressive, sets a maiden to the task. Once settled in, the boy rings a loud, raucous melody. The girl, not too far behind, rings back an equally offensive bell reply. They do this for hours.

They are still ring-replying when the rain comes. Instead of going into the church to stay dry and get warm, the congregations decide this is a sign that I must be cleansed first. The rain's doing a good job of washing away the mud and I wish that was the dirt they're talking about. The choirs are gathered. They sing praises for the glorious rain falling in plenty on the town of Evanshire, for the bountiful harvest, for heavenly mercy, and for me. They open their mouths wide in praise, swallowing rainwater a capella. It's a feel-good song; it makes them feel good about anything they've done before now and anything they might do after. I'm humming along when they drag out the tub. It's little more than a bathtub really but both preachers bless it as though both it and the water the deacons have pumped from the well are holy. I've already been baptized so I'm thinking, *Fine, dunk my head under water, say the blessings, do the symbol, let me up so I can see what sort of place this is and how long I want to be here.* By now the dress is starting to itch all over, and I'd like to get out of it. The women are all dressed in smart frocks, the men in overalls, the children in school uniforms. Only the choir in their thick, brightly colored robes, drenched and flinging water each time they swing their arms in hallelujah, are as overdressed as me.

I'm lifted, hands placed modestly if not too tightly around my waist, while the preachers take turns praying over me. I'm not really moving and can't weigh but so much, but the man holding me buckles under the weight of the blessings and another takes me in his arms. I'm passed around the men, getting closer and closer to the tub before one of them just dumps me in, preachers mid-prayer. The job done, they rush to bless me in the name of the Father, the Son and the Holy Ghost and I'm christened Estelle, which they say sounds close enough to Osira but holier. My soul cleansed, the choir breaks out in song as the congregations, their children behind them, run to seek shelter in the churches from whence they came.

I don't know which to go into so I let the music guide me to the canal. I'm sitting beneath the bridge, the occasional *drip, drip* keeping me company, scooched back to feel the cool stone against my skin. The rain's coming down harder. By morning the canal will be flooded. *May your banks over-floweth.* For a place that don't seem to have no Moving On to speak of, the people seem quite normal so far. They aren't running around at war, setting fire to folks, swearing or anything the Books warn places like this are like.

There's too much damp to sleep and the smells of thick air, wet grass and fresh dung won't let me settle here for long. The people have been kind so far, but there's no sense in planning on staying. I need to find the children. I'll get to the main road, head to the castle, take a peek, and—*plunk*. A stone plops near my feet. It's followed by another one, and another one. A shiver runs through me. My heart beats loud enough to march to. My body tenses. I am ready to run or dive into the water thick with soot and waste. I look up and there right in front of me, a hand full of stones, is Romulus, my dear sweet brother Romulus.

I'm up before I think about it, reaching for his elbows to greet him. It's been so long. He shoves the stones in his pocket, gives me a two-arm-wraparound hug.

"Is this allowed here?" I ask. Just because nobody mentioned rules, doesn't mean this place doesn't have any.

"Don't be silly," he says. "Curdle Creek is so backward. I can't believe you're here!"

"I'm so happy to see you," I say. That I'm happy to see him *alive* goes without saying. I'm breaking an ordinance and it feels good to do it. Nothing good comes from declaring feelings like this. "How long have you been here? How did you even get here?" I'm asking all my questions at once in case, just like home, you have to get them all out at the same time and let the listener choose what to tell and what to keep for later.

Romulus looks down into the murky canal water. "I couldn't stay there after what they did to Remus."

"I know. I'm sorry I didn't do nothing to help," I whisper. I drop to my knees.

"Get up!" he hisses. "We don't do that here." He winks. "You can apologize later."

"How did you know I was here?" we ask at the same time.

He sounds just like Mother. Just like her, he's vain enough to believe I set off to find him on purpose. He's just the type to think I had followed some sort of trail to end up here. He might have been wondering if the town had forgotten all about him—or worried that they hadn't. He surely would have known I'd have had to give up on my dreams of being a Charter Mother. That there would be a price for him slipping out of town and that, as the oldest one left, I'd be the one to pay it.

"Is Remus here too?" I say, without much hope. I picture him with a scar the size and shape of the rock I hit him with.

"He didn't make it," Romulus says. He turns toward the water. "Just couldn't do it. I came alone."

Of course not. It must have killed him to have been Moved On by his own sister. The wailing starts from deep inside. It's a rumble that rattles me. I'm trembling. It comes out like a siren, a loud *wrahhhh!*—and then there's silence as Romulus clamps his fingers over my mouth. His fingers vibrate against my lips until the wail quiets.

"It wasn't you that done it. Curdle Creek killed my brother."

* * *

CHURCH is over by the time we head back. The congregations are gone. We walk by the well. I don't mention how I got here. Romulus doesn't ask. He doesn't say a thing about how he got here either. I don't ask. Neither of us talks about the well or the stones hidden inside my dress.

For the whole summer, while everyone is pairing up, I'm set to work helping Romulus at the shop. He inherited it like a welcome gift from the previous owner though they'd never met. That's what Romulus likes about this place. Anyone can step right into a waiting spot.

I don't plan to be here for long. I'm not one of them and I don't plan on staying here long enough to become one of them either. I keep this to myself. I don't want to ruin it for Romulus and besides, *no one appreciates a moping Margaret*, according to Margaret, Romulus's inherited wife. Margaret's always smiling. Even if there was no reason on God's green earth and no one left alive to see it, she'd be smiling and grinning in that unsettling *I've got a secret* way that makes people want to cross the street when they see her. Margaret is my best friend, according to her.

I tighten the lids and line the jars up on the shelf by order of people's favorites the way I've been told to do a hundred times and only do when she's around. More people like peach so they're in the front next to the apples, a village favorite, and in front of cherries, bilberries and rhubarb. With them all the way in the dark, they'll be first to spoil. It's just wasteful. "What difference does it make when no one's going to want them anyway?" Romulus says. Only, I'm not to call him Romulus either. He's Clement here. A new name, new wife, new job. He spends all day acting like it suits him just fine.

"I'm not being picky," Margaret says between mouthfuls of cherry pie. "It's just always been done this way." With the fork catching the sunlight just so, it looks as if there's dried blood in the corners of her mouth. Her plate's streaked with leftover cherries. Now she's dipping her fingernail in the juice, stripping the nail clean with her tongue.

Margaret sort of came with the shop. She's been married to a line of grocers for as long as she can remember. What luck! She gets the first pick of any fabric, gadget, spice, sweet or stationery item that the shop stocks. It's the least the village can do, given that she's so unlucky in love. Five husbands at forty-five. Margaret's a bit of a legend.

"All anyone's talking about is pairing up," I say. I shuffle jars around, hoping she'll pick up the conversation. I clink them together, retwist already tight lids, read and reread labels. She eats, sucking the fork after each mouthful. "I'm the only one who doesn't seem to have a match. Is that normal?" I ask finally. It's just before the after-school rush, before we're flooded with children hyped-up on the promise of penny candies, boiled sweets and "fresh-baked" chunked apple pie. The pies are made a batch at a time, weeks in advance. Half lies are good for business.

Margaret taps the fork against the side of her head as though it's helping her think. "Have you been lighting the candles, Estelle?" I nod yes although I don't know what candles she's talking about and I know if I ask her she'll unfold that damned card, take a pencil from the jar, lick the tip, and make another strike like she does each time I *forget my place*. I don't know how many I have now or how many it takes. It'll be in the Book of Estelle, of course it will. "Then you'll still be mourning your Sampson, the love of your life. Won't you?"

She scrapes the crumbs off the plate, lays the fork across it and covers them both with a cloth. The tip of the fork peeks out from beneath it, looking like Estelle in the coffin. Estelle died just before I got to town so I live in her place and work in the shop three days a week like she did. Thanks to her, I got a job and the regulars got fifty percent off fish-and-chips as long as they brought in the "You Can't Take It with You" flyer with Estelle's face taking up half a page and her coffin taking up the other half.

"You're lucky you don't need to worry about pairing up," Margaret says. She shakes her head while she talks so that the words coming out of her mouth disagree with her. "You'll always have Sampson in your heart."

Sampson has been dead for five years now. Estelle is a per-petual widow. Margaret uncovers the fork, wipes the counter with the already stained cloth, leaving smears of fruit behind. "You were so lucky to have a love like Sampson's. At least you don't have to settle. There's nothing worse than a long pairing with an old fool." Margaret giggles. She's only like this when Romulus isn't around. He'll be busy chopping candies in half to cheat the children, too preoccupied to *fill his head with gos-sip* when he can *fill his pockets with coins*. "It'll work out for you. Just like it did for me and my Clems."

"More pie?" It's still warm. I wave the dish close to her nose to be sure she can smell the cinnamon and cherries. Even though she has another slice right in front of her, Margaret licks the plate like I knew she would. "How'd you get paired?"

I mean with my brother but, since Estelle didn't have one, I don't either, so I can't say what I mean.

"At the funeral, silly. But, of course, you weren't there."

Estelle was busy dying so her page for this day is blank. Margaret's up now, swishing back and forth pretending her shop apron is a fancy ball gown.

"When I woke up that morning, I didn't expect to be burying my best friend and taking on a new husband." She's twirling around, humming and kick, ball, changing while she dances across the store so I'm not sure I heard her right. She cuts herself off for the jazz hand routine that I'm meant to do since Estelle has *a good sense of humor*. "One minute I'm mourning my friend and the next I'm stepping into the season as the new Mr. and Mrs. Clementine of Clementine's and Clementine's Shoppe Extraordinaire. Talk about luck." She stops dancing, contorting her body into an awkward position before crossing her hands over her chest as though she's in a coffin. "Death is such a blessing."

The pie dish slips from my hand, and the china breaks and shatters. Cherries splatter all over my apron, my feet. They stain the hardwood floor. I don't even notice I'm bleeding until Margaret hands me the dirty rag to clean myself up.

* * *

IT'S not that she's bragging, Margaret explains the next morning at the church fence, it's just I'm such a beautiful widow and I'm lucky I don't have to worry about finding love since I already had my fill of it. I should be thankful not to have to endure the pairing. An unpaired woman doesn't stand a chance, she says. She stares at the well for a moment. "Sorry, Estelle," she says. "I don't know what's come over me." She points to my pocket, clears her throat, then clears it again.

"It's fine, really. Maybe you're sickly. Fever will do that, don't you think? Mess with the mind?"

I really don't want to do this. She frowns, pursing her lips as though I'm letting her down. I reach in the skirt pocket, fish out a pencil, then the engraved notebook. I flip to a blank page and, pressing hard on the paper, I scribble the date, Margaret's name, and the misdemeanor, just like Estelle did the day before she died.

We part at the playground. Margaret heads to the old church. I go to the new one. I don't get to choose. Estelle's run the Sunday school for decades so it falls to me to do it now. We're in the Second Protestant Holier Trinity Children's Center sucking on sweets I stole from the shop. The children are gathered around me, sitting cross-legged on the floor taking turns reading from *The Goode Book for Goode Children*. One book for their everything. We're looking for a story to act out. Last week was "To Be Seen and Not Heard" and I'm not sure there's one in here that can top it. But if we finish too early, it's a *sign of the wicked* and I'd hate for the children to be punished for that again.

"This place is just like the one in the story you told us," Elias says. He's pointing at a page covered in bright red and orange squiggled lines.

I flip through stories of obedient children triumphing over disobedient adults and obedient children triumphing over disobedient children. A few pages later and I'm staring at Curdle Creek. At least, the way I told it to them. This place is called Hellshire. There's a picture of a little town in the middle of a glen, right next to a bright-red flowing river and a well brimming with water. The whole place—the houses, school, even the bell-less church—are on fire while the townsfolk run around trying to put it out with empty buckets. We vote and agree to do this story. Since he found it, Elias is the lead. The children say I'm playing favorites and it isn't fair but I give them all good parts and tell them we'll all do the singing since there's always singing and we don't always do it. They pipe down and the play is cast.

He may be my inherited grandson but Elias makes a brilliant Town Father.

"As my first order of business," Father Elias says, "I banish all rules!" His voice booms and he keeps his hands in his pockets to show he can't be trusted. No one sees his hands until later, after he's learned his lesson.

The adults, played by a chorus of children, sing a joyous tune about life without rules and laws, no governance to weigh them down. I clap my hands to help them keep time. There's nothing worse than a bunch of off-key children singing high-pitched praise songs in a low key and no rhythm. Tobias, my other inherited grandchild, rushes in to tell the townspeople, who are all mid-sin, that there's a fire at the edge of town. There's a search song which ends with a beautiful solo about how far away the fire is and letting it burn itself out. The next song is fast and calls for a wide range of voices so the children all have a part in the singing. While one group chants about having no burdens, another sings warnings. The fire, played by the youngest in the class, gleefully sings and hums its way burning down the town and everyone in its path while the people sing round-robin style that *the shire, the shire, the shire is on fire*. The wail of the consumed is so touching it makes us all weep.

*   *   *

AFTER church, I put two pies in the oven, then go and make the rounds to the neighbors. Estelle was the town nurse too. It takes hours to doctor them all. Partly because there are so many ailments, partly because Estelle takes the long way everywhere, and mostly because I never could stand the sight of blood. Because she walked with a cane, I do too, but because they're all watching I need to take as long as she did to reach the sick and shut-in.

I'm ushered into each house without needing to knock, offered a cup of cooling tea, and handed the patient's card. I read Estelle's meticulous notes and reread the diagnosis and treatment. Oil feet, a dose of castor oil. Pluck hairs, a dose of castor oil. Pop boils, a dose of castor oil. With the help of castor oil for them and a nip of gin for me, I pull teeth, set bones and cure fevers. I've never seen so much blood, pus and fluids. I check off the box "doctor the ill" on Estelle's list. By the time I get back in, it's cloudy and there's a pile of washing at the door. It's filled with the town's dirty linen. Once a week, Estelle takes in the wash. Estelle's diary is filled with pages and pages of chores, favors Estelle does to repay the town's generosity.

My arms are filled with thanks—a basket full of dried meats Estelle doesn't eat, vegetables she doesn't like, herbs she's allergic to, and hard-crusted breads she's paid with instead of coins because *she loves what she does and wouldn't think of taking a coin for it*—so, I push the basket of dirty clothes to the side. I doze off, and wake up to the sound of screaming. My inherited daughter has let herself in, started the wash, taken the pies out of the oven, put a steaming plate onto the table, and checked chores off my list. She's my age, kneeling in front of me, shaking my shoulder softly and yelling, "Mum! Mum! Are you dead again?" Her voice cracks when she says it, like a person can die more than once and I'm living proof.

"I'm fine, sweet potato," I say. I pepper sentences with food the way the Estelle character card calls for. After what feels like an overabundance of *honeys* and *sweeties*, Delilah helps me up so we can eat together as usual. She's made my favorite, which must be mushed peas, mushed fish and mushed rice. It's a slab of gray on the plate. Her plate is filled with roast beef and gravy, mashed potatoes and green beans.

"I hope you don't mind," she says. She waves at her plate. "I just popped round to have supper with my favorite mum."

Delilah calls me that all the time. She says she feels closer to me than she has in years, that we talk more and I listen more too. She hasn't noticed it before now but maybe we've both changed.

I don't look anything like Estelle. For one, I'm a good thirty years younger. I'm also Black, and the last one and the one before that weren't. I imagine death changes people. Maybe burying Estelle made Delilah see how much she'd miss her and now's her third chance to be the good firstborn. She's nothing like my own free-spirited children but Delilah grows on me just the same.

"May I?" I ask.

I don't really wait for her answer. Estelle doesn't eat meat. *Can't stomach the thought of animal flesh across her lips* according to the card. The roast's so tender that I cut it with the fork. I scoop potatoes and beans up with the meat and slide it all into my mouth. I *mmmmmm* for a good minute just to see her eyes well up. She wraps her arms around herself and rocks side to side so much I'm worried she'll fall out of the chair.

"You're a wonderful cook," I say.

My child cries like it's the first compliment she's ever been given and it's just like Little Moses crying after one of his pet rabbits got eaten by a fox. I give her an entire pie to take home for my inherited grandchildren and the inherited son-in-law whose name I pretend to forget. I'm not trying to out-Estelle her but Estelle really could have taken a bit of time getting to know her own children. I'd give anything to be with mine. Delilah leaves, promising to come back earlier next week after church, and, although I really do like her, I hope not to be here long enough to make this a habit.

* * *

THE church bells ring for twenty-five minutes. The Holy Cacophony. I can almost see the bell ringers sweat soaked and red-faced trying to out-holy one another. It'll be seven o'clock. Most of the town will be settling in, children finishing homework, parents arguing, making up, loving, depending on their schedules and their cards. Estelle's schedule is filled with tallies, chores, reminders and meetings so I've been up since dawn. From the supper bell until now, I've dusted walls, plumped furniture, beaten rugs and washed windows. I'm sweating from scrubbing the cobblestone path in the garden. Every so often I dip the wire brush into the soapy water, clink the wood against the tin to hear the soft *clang, clang, clang.*

Estelle rings the Monday morning bell. I'm practicing so the head ringer doesn't give me another mark.

Although I've read the book and know what to expect, the high-pitched voice stops me mid-scrub. I let the brush drop from my hand. I jump up and, though I nearly slip on the wet stones, I'm at the gate to play the part of dutiful daughter-in-law.

"My Sampson would be alive if it weren't for you!" my mother-in-law yells. Her voice is filled with tears, anger and hate.

Sampson was her one allotted birth. She had petitioned the town for years and only now that she's close to a hundred do they seem close to yielding. Estelle voted against it just last winter. Sampson really is all Mother Sampson has.

She stares at the gate as if she hasn't seen one before and is surprised to find herself on the other side of it. Estelle never latched the gate like I do.

"Do come inside for some tea."

There's no rule against it but Estelle never invited her inside either. I swoop my arms around her, rest her body against mine, and practically drag Mother Sampson inside, though I'm sure she doesn't want to be in there any more than I want her to be. The candelabras are already in place so as soon as I shut the door I set about lighting them. I've added rose petals and vanilla pods to the wax. They smell good enough to drink. The room is warm from the fire, the candles and my mother-in-law's glare but I change into the heavy mourning dress, though it drags when I walk and is two sizes too big like the rest of

Estelle's clothes. I fetch the tea on my way to the sitting room, place it before her chair, and then sit on the floor.

"I loved Sampson more than anything," I begin. The more I recite Estelle's memories, the closer to the truth it sounds. They really loved each other. That's why there's still meat in the icebox, his clothes are laid out, and I suffer visitations from his family. We're all propped up by his ghost.

With my eyes closed like this, my fingers wrapped around his book, I can almost feel Sampson with us right now. His presence is warm, like sitting too close to the fireplace. It's a comfort I haven't known. Like, I can be myself, Osira not Estelle, and still be loved by Sampson whose name really was Sampson. He adored his mother, cherished Estelle. There was nothing he wouldn't do for either of them even if he hadn't written his own book, created his own card, been one of the original settlers. Sampson wanted so much for them to be a family that I want that too. I feel his words flowing through my body, touching my heart the way they did when I ripped open his book the first time. I had half expected it to burst into flames as the pastor had declared in his sermon "Thou Shalt Not." Or to disappear like the people in the children's play *Read Today, Dead Tomorrow*.

Sampson's book is filled with drafts of rules sometimes written on the spot, in the middle of so-and-so doing such and such. He was spontaneous, my Sampson. Declaring and decreeing and overriding declarations and decrees sometimes on the same page. His book has been bound and unbound many times, new pages added to make room for new rules.

It's a wonder that the leather binding doesn't burst or that the other Originals didn't turn against him before now. Estelle loved him too; she wrote it daily, a schoolgirl writing lines, one hundred of them each night, until *I will be a loving wife, I will be a loving wife, I will be a loving wife*, became *I am a loving wife, I am a loving wife, I am a loving wife*.

Poor Estelle takes on the town's burdens without thanks. If she minds keeping their secrets, she doesn't speak about it. Unless that's what killed her. It's hard to tell who to trust in this place. Thankfully I have Romulus. When he's him and I'm just me, we can talk like when we were kids. Better than when we were kids.

"I can't believe Daddy ran off too. What's going to happen to the girls?"

"Maybe they'll leave one day too. I hope they do."

"Do you mean that?" he asks.

"I'd hate for Mother to keep paying and repaying old debts but if they don't leave that place they'll end up killing each other."

We can be deep in a field, surrounded by sheep and trees and *Estelle? Estelle is that you?* Someone always needs something. The whole town's watching me. Always interrupting.

While I'm sitting here rocking and moaning, pressing the book—thick double stiches facing outward—against my breast, Mother Sampson reminds me how much Sampson gave up to be with me, how the only way to repay him is to be alone forever. That my reward will be to join Sampson in Heaven soon enough.

No one really took the time to get to know Estelle. Instead of a Mae or Jeremiah to confide in, she had Margaret. Sometimes, Margaret wishes Clem was dead too. If not dead, quiet, at least for a little while. She didn't mean it really, she said. Still, that confession cost Margaret five marks. Estelle recorded it word for word in the section marked Testimony, a section so full I know not to trust even the pastors.

Even here I'll be a widow until the day I die, and something about the glimmer in her eyes when she said "soon enough" lets me know that Mother Sampson doesn't intend to make her son wait long for him and Estelle to be reunited. I'm crying real tears now. Curdle Creek, Evanshire—there's no place in the whole wide world where I'm safe.

Mother Sampson sees herself out. As soon as she leaves, I cook his favorite dinner the way Estelle used to do each night, crack open a bottle of wine that I drink but do not like and make a plan to leave this place and find my children before it's too late.

Second Protestant Church

I have never been one for surprises. When we were kids, Remus hid a honey cake in my dollhouse. It wasn't on purpose. He'd snuck a piece of the delicious honey-soaked cake before supper and needed to get rid of it before Mother found out. The only thing he could think of was to put it in my dollhouse and leave it out back on the porch. It wasn't his fault that the bees claimed it. He had no way of knowing I would carry the wooden dollhouse to school later that week. Shake it up and down, up and down, as I skipped to school. I opened the house during show-and-tell.

"See the pretty furniture my daddy made?" I said.

Daddy had carved each piece of furniture, painted the house inside and out to look just like our real house. Mirrors and all. There I was, holding up a tiny couch with dark red cushions filled with bees. Angry, they streamed out of the dollhouse and stung the nearest flower they could find. Me. I wouldn't have known it was Remus's fault if he hadn't come crying to me, apologizing for it. I warned him I'd get him back. I warned him.

* * *

THE bells ring and the whole town files in for Sunday service. It's midmorning but there's no sun to speak of and the air is thick with the promise of rain. I'm wedged in between Delilah and Elias, with his brother and father close to the aisle. We're in the family box. The boys sit on phone books, their little legs swinging, backs straight, faces streaked with tears as the pastor preaches about damnation and love, damnation and duty, damnation and damnation. I don't have a favorite and even if I did, I wouldn't wish nothing bad on the other one. I would take them with me when I go only I know that would crush poor Delilah, who only ever had good luck and now has Margaret whispering in her ear about how even though he's been gone five years, Estelle doesn't seem to be mourning her father.

"Mum, are you all right?" Delilah pats my hand, gives me a handkerchief to wipe my own wet face. She's as tender as Jasmine would be at a time like this.

I squeeze Delilah's hand tight, hoping she reads it as *Get away from this place* and hoping her squeeze back means *I promise to.* The pastors take turns talking about the importance of good deeds. To hear them tell it, folks should be grateful for kindness, grateful for one another and grateful to be here in Evanshire instead of anywhere else in the world. Folks should count their blessings, and by folks, they say, they mean—and they point here—me. I'm nodding along like everyone else until the choir, pastors, Sunday schoolchildren, Mother Sampson, Delilah and even Elias turn to stare at me.

I'm suddenly hot, skin scalding, scalp tingling, fingers cracking in a way Estelle would never do although, from the sounds of it, pre-rescued Estelle just might have. Delilah's hand feels like an iron pressed against my back. My grandsons slip off with the rest of the children to perform the first part of the two-part *Turn Not Your Back on Home*, a play about an old woman plotting to run away from Evanshire. My heart's beating so loud that I'm pretty sure everyone can hear it. In the play, the children ask if anyone has a confession. I might be imagining it but the child cast as "the woman" looks a lot like Estelle and I'm pretty sure she's wearing a dress that up until this morning was out hanging on my line.

It's not possible. Unless they've slipped into my house and overheard me praying to the ancestors, rifled through my papers and read them, they can't know I'm planning on leaving. I know it but my hands are still shaking. The junior choir's singing the finale. It's a capella. In round-robin they chant about *lights, lights, and torches in the night*, while Elias and Tobias have their first duet in falsetto. My little angels sing beautifully about fallen apples overflowing with rotten seeds. It's like they're singing just for me, which is only fitting since the lead female, now revealed as Little Estelle, opens her mouth to confess just as the curtain closes.

They get two standing ovations and, even though I don't

really want to, I'm on my feet clapping and whistling like everyone else. When the collection plate comes around, once to build a wall to surround Evanshire and once for the Christingle, I leave two coins in each plate, twice as much as Estelle would have done, to show there's no hard feelings. Delilah is sorry but although she's been for supper every night for more nights than I could have imagined, tonight she has to be with Mother Sampson and won't I join them?

Everyone stops. Children rushing from the stage down to their waiting parents stop mid-stride. Parents are mid-congratulations, words plastered on tongues. Pastors are mid-blessing, caught between giving and taking. Even the coins seem to stop clinking. The windows are open so the birds are still singing except for the whorish seagulls who scream throughout the service and scream even louder now as if I'm the best sort of fish. One that's done the work for them and caught my own self. Everyone's waiting. I gather my stole, the flowers and the beautiful program, check it again and note that Part II is at dusk. I kiss Delilah on the cheek. "I'll be there as soon as I pick up a fresh pie," I say. "It's going to be a long night." My mouth's so dry that the words almost get stuck in it.

Margaret offers to get it for me, take it to Mother Sampson's this afternoon so it's ready for us. My heart stops, but I thank her and tell her I have to bake it first and ask if she wouldn't mind also hanging out the wash I've left in a pile so I wouldn't be late for church and if she wouldn't mind that, while she's hanging out the wash, please and thank you, fetch the casserole from the sideboard since bringing supper is the least I can do and if she doesn't mind that too, thank you very much, visiting the sick and shut-in since I have a leeching scheduled that I'm not sure can wait much longer. Margaret doesn't mind doing it, of course, but wouldn't feel comfortable with the sick visits and actually she has remembered some chores of her own so she'll just meet me at Mother Sampson's after the play if that's all right? Of course it is.

* * *

AT home, I strip out of Estelle's clothes immediately. They're too heavy, too bulky to be good for anything other than bedding, so I fold up a sweater to use as a sack. I put on a dress I sewed myself with pockets in places pockets aren't meant to be. I hide the stones in the pockets and stuff the sack full of beans, canned fruits, thick-crusted sandwiches with thin streaks of jam, and trinkets I've taken from neighbors I've nursed. They won't be missed. It's almost dark. I light the candles, place them in each window. I'm wrapping a fruitcake in wax paper when there's a knock at the door.

My legs tremble. Another knock. Inside, the house creaks and settles. It must be windy out there. I'm shivering. I haven't lit the fire though I've brought in fresh logs, rotten all of them, to sit in the woodstove. At the sign—a sharp rap, followed by two short ones—I open the door. Romulus is there, his wooden stick raised, all set to knock again.

"Got everything, Osira?" he asks. It feels so good to hear him call my name that I almost cry out. "We have to hurry."

We're going to find the children, I can feel it. I stumble a little. He steadies me, hushes me. He's already down the front porch ready to slip into the night. I don't even know where we're going. It doesn't really matter, he's my brother, and there's nowhere I wouldn't follow him. Sooner or later we'll find our way home, or run out of wells to fall into. I say a silent goodbye to Evanshire. This place is full of secrets.

Other than the lights from the house casting shadows across the windows, the leaves and our feet, the only other thing moving is the thin line of light from the torches headed toward the Town Hall. I imagine this is the gathering—the part where someone—more than likely Margaret, one of the pastors or Mother Sampson—reads out all of the strikes against the accused and someone else determines the amount of the debt and the terms of repayment. The whole town will be there. To hear the children tell it, it all ends with pitchforks and torches just as I'd expect from a place with no Moving On. Judgment is quick. The bells ring. It's the start of the procession. Both congregations, led by the pastors and the children, make their way toward us.

"Ready," I say. We'll take our chances at the next town. Unless plague or word about how Romulus and I got here reaches there before we do, the well won't be sealed yet. The song is louder. The rhythm is moving, fast-paced, something to run by. It beats so loud it almost sounds like singing. I look up to see if Romulus can hear it too. The look on his face, his lips parted, eyes half-closed, arm outstretched reaching for me, show me he does. The singing is the choir. Even from here, I hear their a capella hymns, voices lifted high in praise, almost like angels leading wolves to slaughter lambs. I close the door, turn the key in the lock, and slide it under the welcome mat for the next Estelle.

The Hill

We slip into the trees, letting our feet lead the way. Of course, we're lost. Estelle's visits never take her out of town and Clem *hasn't gone to market in years, why would he need to now?* the Council declared. They denied Romulus's monthly petitions to sell wares at the castle even if it meant more money to take care of the children he and Margaret wouldn't be permitted to have. All he's ever wanted was a family.

We run along the tree lines. No matter how far we go, the torchlight isn't far behind. We slip on pebbles, slide on leaves and scramble down banks. The procession marches on. Snatches of song reach us every so often, making them sound closer then farther away. The wind plays tricks like the moon does. Sometimes it feels like they're in front of us, leading us toward them.

"Just keep running!" Romulus says. His breath comes out ragged like a squeeze-box. "I'm slowing you down."

I'm faster than he is. Always have been. I can run ahead,

scout the way to be sure we aren't running straight into the arms of another town with more sin than it can carry on its own. As soon as I find the well, I can come back for him. *Leave him, leave him*, a little voice in my head says. I try to ignore it. *Find the well, jump in to test it, then come back and get him*, it continues. I stop. Make the sign of the bell right then and there. Romulus is bent over, breathing from his mouth. The voice isn't even mine. It's Mother's. She'd leave him behind even if there was another way. You can take the woman out of Curdle Creek but you can't take Curdle Creek out of the woman.

Romulus's hand is sweaty but I grab hold anyway. We run. Although they aren't walking fast, jogging or running behind us, the music is even closer now, the *boom, boom, boom* beating in time to my breathing, the rhythm in time to our footsteps. As soon as it ends, there's a sharp trill, a drum roll, followed by a chorus of chants, then song. If nothing else, the mob is in tune. I don't know the song they're playing but its familiar chords tell me that the band will march all night if they have to. In an uplifting baritone with jazz undertones, the soloist's smooth voice croons that we can run to the next well and the one after that, because they've already sent word. The wells are nailed shut all over England. The choir repeats the chorus, *From sea to sea and knoll to knoll, not one well will save your soul.*

Romulus presses a pebble into my hand. Another Well Walker stone.

"Keep it, I already have one."

"You're a Well Walker too?"

I say a quick prayer that we'll find a well and that it will work some magic of its very own. A pebble thumps against my back. It's followed by another one and another one and soon we are running even faster, sprinting, legs cramping, sides sore. Romulus huffs and wheezes beside me. *Please, Lord, give me the strength to not leave him,* I pray as his legs slow and his arms seem to sag. If he says it again—"Go on without me"—I will hate to do it, will hesitate slightly, and I will leave him behind. I'm sure of it.

At the top of the hill, just at the slope, there's a well, a tiny almost child-sized one. *I hate hills, I hate hills, I hate hills,* I think as I puff my way up it. I nearly drag Romulus gasping for air along with me. We're in rhythm, his haggard *tssszz* matching my whistled *whizzzz.* Near the top, there's a welcome wagon of bricks. They are scattered around the mouth like tombstones. Someone must have tried to blow it up. All that water, wasted. Leaves and grass crunch behind us, rocks and sticks, words hurl around us. It's not much more than a hole with some water in it. It will have to do. There's a hand on my shoulder, another near my calf. I kick, lunge forward, and jump.

ACKNOWLEDGMENTS

My world is made fuller because of stories. They center and ground me. As a reader, they take me into places and spaces I might never visit. They introduce me to characters and people I might not otherwise meet. Stories connect me to pasts, presents and futures in ways that allow me to feel, imagine and reflect. My life is made richer because of stories and the people who read, share, write, encourage, remember and live them.

My first storyteller was my mother. Thanks to you and your pursuit of your own dreams and Lorraine, my beautiful, talented, rock star of a sister, I know that boundaries are imaginary. You were my first readers and listeners too. Growing up, I told and retold long, winding stories that I loved falling into. Thank you both for listening and encouraging and for cheering, imagining and reimagining with me then and for cheering, imagining and reimagining with me now.

Much of writing is solitary but so much of *Curdle Creek* is made possible because of the support of others. Amira, Marat and Noah, thank you all for listening to my stories and for supporting my pursuit of my passion for them, for waking me up so I could write in the early hours of the morning and for believing in what I do and why I do it. You all empower me to imagine and inspire me to hope for a brighter tomorrow. You all lead me home.

Thank you to my niece and nephews and to my father for your joy. And special thanks to my family, extended and otherwise, blood and not, living and deceased. I write because of you. I was often surprised while writing *Curdle Creek*. Characters were doing unexpected things in unexpected ways. There seemed to be no end to the harms they were willing to inflict on other characters. No end to the things they were willing to do to survive. My dear friends kept me grounded during the writing. While I was writing about characters capable of hurting one another, I was nourished by friendships that have survived years, life and miles. Wanda Hawkins, Candace Hantouche, Peace Toleito and Naomi Kruger, I appreciate your friendship, support, advice and laughter.

Thank you to friend and fellow writer Peter Kalu for inviting me to write a piece for *Shots in the Dark*, a crime fiction anthology published by Commonword. That's when I first met Osira (then named Riley), her best friend Mae and the eerie town of Curdle Creek. And thank you for the invitation to be in the next anthology. That commission gave me the opportunity to revisit the town and to dig a bit deeper into their story. Writer Conor O'Callaghan, years ago you recommended I write a book set both in the US and the UK. I was then, and still am now, thinking about home and where it is. Your advice led me to explore home on both sides of the pond.

While individuals provided support, so did the wider writing community. I was able to use part of my time as a British Library Eccles Centre Fellow to research the Tulsa Race Massacre and the Red Summer of 1919. Some of these horrific events are imagined in *Curdle Creek*. Thanks to funding from Sheffield Hallam University I was able to attend the Kimbilio Fellowship. The fellowship felt like a returning. Being back in the United States for a short time allowed me to remember the kindness of strangers and how good people can be even during times of political uncertainty.

Thank you to New Writing North for your continued support and to writing groups that kept me company through the editing process. My 5:55 a.m. writing group, thanks for saying yes! to early morning writing and joining me in starting my days doing something that I love. I've been editing while joining writing sessions hosted by Torch Literary Arts, the London Writers Salon, and Sisters in Crime. Thank you all for the space and community you create.

Where would Osira be without my wonderful agent? A special thanks to Elise Dillsworth for supporting this book in all of its forms. Your editorial eye is appreciated as is your patience and support for my writing. I appreciate your encouragement to follow my creativity and curiosity wherever it leads. *Curdle Creek* is in good hands and, again, you've found the perfect publishers to bring it to readers. Thank you to Sharmaine Lovegrove. I appreciate your enthusiasm for *Curdle Creek*, Osira, Mother and the residents that make Curdle Creek their home. Thank you for the space to tell this story in its many twists and turns. Thank you to Michelle

Brower of Trellis Literary Management for your keen editorial insight.

I've also been fortunate to have wonderful editors who could recognize what I was trying to do in *Curdle Creek* as a draft and whose feedback strengthened the story. Hannah Chukwu and Retha Powers: your belief, enthusiasm and expertise have been everything. Thanks for believing in Osira, *Curdle Creek* and in me. It was also a special treat to work with Linda McQueen on copy edits. Your attention to detail is superb and I appreciate your insights. I'm extremely fortunate to have an amazing team of copy editors, assistant editors, publicists, marketers and more supporting *Curdle Creek*.

Thank you to the many writers who have shaped me and to the many libraries that have fed my imagination.

Finally, thank you to you. I appreciate your being on this journey with me. I'm looking forward to where it takes us.